Paris Mafia Princess

A chick lit of finding love, a beautiful wedding and a secret baby...

By Nerissa Marie

Title Imprint Chick Lit an imprint of The Quantum Centre, Australia.
Published by Happiness Bliss Press an imprint of The Quantum Centre, Australia

ISBN: 978-0-9874341-3-5

Most Happiness Bliss Press books are available at special quantity discounts for bulk purchase for sales promotions, premiums, fund-raising, and educational needs. For details contact books@happinessbliss.com

National Library of Australia Cataloguing-in-Publication entry
Creator: Marie, Nerissa, author.
Title: Paris Mafia Princess - A Chick Lit of Finding Love, a Beautiful Wedding and a Secret Baby (Romantic Comedy, Chick Lit, Rom Com, Romance Books, Romance Novel, Inspirational, France, Chick-Lit, Rom-Com) / Nerissa Marie.
ISBN: 9780987434135 (paperback)
Subjects: Australian fiction.
Dewey Number: A823.4

FIRST EDITION

To Darling Mark

With All My Heart

A Star So Bright

Whose Guidance Helped This Book

Discover the Light

Across Universes and Galaxies

I Love You

I came from nothing,

I came with nothing,

I leave with nothing,

And yet, love, has given me everything

- Hugo De La Laville

One's own reality, which shines within everyone as the Heart,

is itself the ocean of unalloyed bliss.

- Sri Ramana Maharshi

CONTENTS

CHAPTER ONE

MONSIEUR IS SINGLE

"You're a delicious specimen, Hugo. I can't see a reason why any woman wouldn't want to marry you. Shack up, pop out a couple of cherubs, and start a family."

Hugo grunted, his warm breath tickling whiskers that had grown on his upper lip over the last three days. "After everything that's happened with Arabella, I doubt the existence of true love."

Clemency came to sit on the Italian white leather sofa that Hugo rested against from his vantage point on the floor. Wearing a prim, knee length, pastel green Chanel dress, yellow Hermes silk scarf, and white diamond studs, Clemency blended with ease into the luxury of her surroundings. Both woman and couch were groomed to perfection.

"You make everything sound so simple."

"Love is supposed to be simple. Mon Dieu! You smell like man. Like beast. One heartbreak and you've become immune to showering. Hugo, what am I going to do with you? We're supposed to be arriving at Poppy and Yves-Jacques' for dinner, and you look like you're recovering from a week of partying at Pacha, Ibiza."

"Grrr, if only," Hugo said before taking a gulp from the Vodka bottle resting on the antique mahogany coffee table that lay strewn with photos of him and Arabella - kissing, being goofy, eating spaghetti, dancing, holidaying in St. Tropez, and looking a lot happier than he felt right now.

"I meant beast as a metaphor, darling, not in a literal form." A blonde curl fell loose from Clemency's bun, tickling her plump, blood red lips.

"Grrrrrrrrrrr!" Hugo pulled his face into a lopsided grin as he drunkenly rose from the floor. Stumbling over a discarded Mövenpick ice cream container, he arched his hands back creating claws.

Clemency stifled a laugh. She didn't have time for games anymore, Hugo thought - not like when they were kids. With a depressing thump, Hugo was hit with the realisation that both he and Clemency had lost their childlike innocence to the thump, thump, thump of progress.

Paris had drained them of joy, of fun, of their fire. Their careers had become the ignition, and they'd taken off with rocket fuel. The only problem was, it left them cold and stripped them bare. If money and status didn't bring happiness, then what the hell did?

"I get it, you're the Stinky Man Beast. Go take a shower, darling, before you go feral."

"Raaaa," Hugo screamed like a child. He scooped Clemency off the couch and holding her lithe form in his strong arms, began to swing her in circles, twisting faster and faster the way his dad held him, when he was a young boy, before he'd died.

"Put me down, Hugo!" Clemency squealed.

"Do you dare question the Man Beast?"

Clemency squirmed like a worm. Hugo didn't stop spinning. He spun faster and faster until Clemency let go, flung her hands back, and began to laugh. Hugo hadn't heard that laugh in years, the one that tinkered like a cherubic fairy, playing with a pipe organ. It flooded through his body, boosting his serotonin levels, and fuelling him with a happiness that he'd been numb to for so long. Her blonde hair fell loose from its tight bun and swished through the air. The fragrance of rose filled the room.

When the world stopped spinning - window, Banksy art, kitchen, lampshade, books - Hugo dived for the white sofa and found his body cushioned by Clemency's, slipping like water underneath his. Bodies pressed together, Hugo felt the curve of Clemency's breasts, firm and pert; she'd had implants last year. They felt incredible pressed to his chest, and her warm body shaking with laughter lay underneath his.

He looked into her blue eyes, flecked with chestnut drops. Light freckles shone through the makeup on her porcelain skin. Hugo could see the little girl he'd grown up with; images of mud fights, hide and seek games, and walks through the forest in Normandy flashed through his brain - summers spent in St. Barth's, back to school shopping trips at Harrods, London, and warm milk staining their top lips before bed.

Blinded by the beauty of the woman lying beneath him, her lips beckoned. The scent of Clemency, wild flowers, roses, and ash; made him at ease, and more nervous than ever before. Hugo brushed back the blonde curls that had fallen loose over her face.

"You look like one of those Botticelli chicks."

"Do you think so?"

"I know so." Hugo ran his thumb across her chin. He bent down and felt his lips brush Clemency's. It felt like an electric shock. He bounced back; whiplash caught his neck as he bounded up from the couch. "I'm so sorry, Clem. I shouldn't have done that." He brought both hands to his face and pulled them down, stretching his skin. "I'm so hollow; I'm drunk. I'm a mess. Have I broken the friend barrier?"

"Broken?"

"Well, you know, you and I are not like that. I don't want to lose my best friend over a kiss. You're not going to go all weird on me, are you? Arabella's left me. I couldn't bear to lose you too, Clemency. It'd break me."

"I'm not going anywhere. I'm an expert on broken hearts." Her voiced softened, and she searched Hugo's eyes as though looking for a piece of his sanity. He hated that look - the one where you know someone so well, you could tell what was going through their mind. How much of a complete mess he'd made of his entire life!

"I thought I'd lost you for a moment. You're the best, Clemency. You're my best friend in the world. Have I told you that before?"

"Okay, you need a bath." Clemency switched into her ordered, high maintenance self. This time, there was no hint of the child within shining through. "We can't miss dinner."

"Will you chat with me in the bath? Otherwise, I'm taking Mr. Vodka here. We've become close."

"As long as you're covered in suds. I've seen enough of your wild side for one day."

"I promise to behave."

Slabs of marble lined the walls and floor of Hugo's bathroom. A white spa bath sat in the corner, and a jar of rose scented bath salts rested on the marble lip. A giant chandelier that Arabella and Hugo had found at the Porte de Vanves flea market cast shadows over Hugo's face as he studied his chiselled features in the gilt-framed mirror.

His skin had an olive tanned glow, and gentle crease marks softened the edges of his sea green eyes, running in concentration lines across his forehead. Thick lashes clumped together above and below offsetting his eyes.

He didn't look bad for thirty-five, his body still toned from his morning runs. He could feel the skin sticking to his muscles, powerful and sharp. At six foot seven, he knew he was handsome, not in the conventional way, but good looking enough for women to take interest. Then why didn't they stay? He asked himself the dreaded question. Maybe they didn't like him. Perhaps, he wasn't enough.

"Considering chopping it off?" Clemency purred, breaking Hugo from his slump.

Hugo looked down at his black silk boxers. "Excuse me?"

"Not that, silly. Your hair! I didn't think of it earlier. Perhaps, it was too unconventional for Arabella, too bohemian. You look like a scruffy writer."

"I am a scruffy writer. Besides, Arabella loved my hair." Hugo ran his fingers through the black-brown, loosely curled hair swinging about his shoulders.

"Does her new lover have long hair?"

"No." Hugo had no reason to feel defensive, but it felt like Clemency wanted to pick on his already bruised heart, make him squirm. "He's balding, has a shaved head."

"So she left you for a balding, chubby, middle-aged director. Hmmm."

"Drop it, Clemency. Frederick isn't middle-aged, he's thirty-six. He's not fat either. He's lean, verging on skinny. His family's been in the business for generations, and he's Jewish. And he has two pet beagles, Bluebell and Agynus. I Googled him."

Clemency walked across to the tub, turned on the hot tap, sifted through Hugo's cupboards, and poured a bucket load of organic bubble bath into the roaring stream of water now filling the spa. She pulled off her Louboutins and perched herself on the edge, feet dangling into the warm stream of water.

"As my oldest friend, I need you to be honest with me, Clemency." Raising a thin brow, Clemency scooped up a handful of bubbles and blew them across the room. "Do you think I'm handsome?"

"I think you're delicious."

"I need you to be serious."

"I am. You define rugged charm - nice eyes, a good body, irresistible. Are you asking me to go to bed with you?" She asked, her voice light and teasing.

"You know I'm not. But I need to know; if you didn't know me, would you go to bed with me, or date me?"

Clemency paused. "Perhaps. But I have a terrible track record when it comes to men. I can't help myself. Even you know that. Give me a damsel, or should I say mansel, in-distress, and I go weak at the knees. And if you're looking for self-pity over your withering good looks, you can forget it. You know you're handsome, charming even. In our twenties, you ran all over town, sleeping with any girl that battered her lashes at you."

Hugo looked at himself in the bathroom mirror. The bachelor that delighted in sleeping with an entourage of women had disappeared. He felt used and swallowed up as though his previous conquests now counted for nothing.

* * *

"Darlings, we're here! What is that vile smell?" Clemency pulled her shoulders inward and sniffed the air like a Sphynx cat. She loosened the scarf around her neck. "It smells like... mould." Her lips puckered in distaste.

Hugo laughed, "I think it's dinner."

"I heard that," Poppy said, emerging from the kitchen with a pink silk apron tied around her waist. Her short honey-blonde curls danced about her dainty forehead. Her hands gripped a kitchen knife, covered in blood red tomato juice.

"I meant you too. Mon Dieu! What are we eating tonight? Or should I say who? What have you done with Yves-Jacques?"

A wicked smile flashed across Poppy's lips. "The question is what haven't I done with Yves-Jacques?"

"I knew Australians were primitive, but I didn't think that spread as far as consuming their mates," Clemency purred.

Hugo raised his brow, sensing the subtle undercurrent of female competitiveness.

"Aussies aren't primitive."

"Do you think that is the wisest thing to say to a woman wielding a knife?" Hugo asked, turning towards to Clemency.

"I like to live on the edge. Where is Yves-Jacques? Fancy him not opening the front door for his beloved sister."

"I'm here," came a muffled voice from the kitchen.

"What have you done with him, tied him up? He sounds strained. Yves-Jacques, darling. I'm coming." Clemency stalked past Poppy.

Hugo was left, unsure of whether to keep looking at the scuff marks on his brown leather shoes. Poppy looked ready to cry - either that or gouge his eyes out.

"He's probably opening a bottle of port," Poppy said to Hugo.

He stepped forward and kissed her on both cheeks. "You'll have to ignore Clemency. Being mean to you is part of her game."

"I don't want to play games. I want to marry her brother, not murder him, for goodness sakes."

"Well you could always murder Clemency."

A smile flickered on the edge of Poppy's lips. "Thank goodness you're always so sweet, Hugo. I never know how to handle aggressive people."

"I always find the best thing is to ignore them. I fear Clemency believes you've stolen her brother. Tell yourself, *I love and approve of myself,* and forget the rest."

"Out loud?"

"No, in your head. I do it all the time."

"Really?"

"Sure, it's effective."

"Okay, I'll try it," Poppy grinned. "Life's much easier when you're around, Hugo. I don't know what Arabella was thinking."

Arabella - the name stung like a bullet.

"Too soon?" Poppy asked.

"I'm trying to let the pain go. I wish *she* loved and approved of me. The wound is fresh. I feel like I'll never love again."

"Come on; I have a plan."

* * *

Dinner, in Hugo's opinion, was heaven - savoury crepes, topped with wild mushrooms, marjoram, and fresh cracked pepper. It was a shame he'd lost his appetite.

"The meal is fabulous," Yves-Jacques said. He leant over and kissed Poppy on the cheek. "My wonderful fiancée, we'll make a true Parisian of you yet." Poppy's cheeks flushed with pride at her culinary creation.

"I think she's already more French than you," Clemency said. "It's the la qualité des aliments, that counts."

"What's that?" Poppy asked.

Clemency, compliments aside, went back to her meal, ignoring Poppy's question.

"She's talking about the quality of the food, darling. I think it may be the first compliment Clemency's ever offered you."

"Thanks, merci beaucoup." Poppy said, a slightly bemused expression slipping across her face.

Clemency shrugged her shoulders, not looking at Poppy. The tension felt crisp, like cool morning air.

"Hugo, did you hear what I just said?"

"What?"

Hugo had been daydreaming. Who cared about compliments and family disruption when the woman you loved had left you for another man? Who cared about food when your heart had been split into a thousand pieces? No one - that's who.

"I asked how your new book is coming along?"

"Oh that," Hugo shrugged.

"What's it about?" Poppy asked.

"It was about love, finding it. I think I might write about unrequited love now; maybe the lead character could reach some tragic fate, like death from a broken heart." In truth, he hadn't even lifted his pen. What could he offer the world when his whole being felt hollow? All he had was an empty shell, lying amongst the sand on a deserted island. He'd been carved out, stripped bare, and his soul stolen by the night. Hollowness surrounded him.

"Like Romeo and Juliet," Poppy said. "My favourite. I love Leo!"

"Who's Leo?" Clemency purred.

"Leonardo DiCaprio, only the hottest Romeo ever. He's been

immortalised on screen to make every woman's heart flutter."

"I thought my brother was supposed to do that? Are you saying that he's not enough for you?"

"No, I, it's just a girlish fantasy." The candle flickered its warm light, causing dips and hollows in their faces. Clemency's looked sharp and angler, like a wicked witch, thought Poppy.

"Romeo and Juliet is a terrible love story," Yves-Jacques said. "We read it and begin to believe love is about pain, family feuds, and death. Love, amour, is unconditional, it comes from the heart centre. It's forgiveness; it's wanting to live forever; it's acceptance."

"Ahh, I love how Frenchmen always speak their feelings," Poppy crooned. "You're making me melt."

Poppy and Yves-Jacques kissed. Clemency rolled her eyes and kicked Yves-Jacques under the table. "Uggh, you two are making me feel ill. Can't you show some respect? Think of poor Hugo; the love of his life has just left him for another man, his writing has gone to shit, he hasn't eaten a meal in days, and his house is a mess - all because of love."

"I can't help it. I am a passionate man, and when I see something I like, I want to touch it, kiss it, and caress it," Yves-Jacques retorted.

"Enough," Clemency said.

"I think I need to go to the bathroom," Hugo said. The wine had begun to make him feel giddy.

"See what you've done?" Clemency hissed, as Hugo made a hasty escape.

"What we've done? You're the one who mentioned Arabella. You stabbed a knife in his already wounded heart."

"So, would you prefer me to ignore our depressed friend? I thought you said you were in touch with your inner feelings?"

CHAPTER TWO

ARRANGED BISOUS - KISSES

"Guys, calm down, I think I have an idea," Poppy said, a mischievous grin playing at the corners of her lips.

"What could you possibly have to say? You hardly know Hugo. You've only met him three times. I've only known you for three weeks, and you're marrying my brother."

"Be nice." Yves-Jacques said, his voice in a low growl warning his sister.

"Well, it's true," Clemency stuck her nose in the air, her lips pursed tight.

"I love Yves-Jacques; therefore, I love Hugo. I want him to be happy. When Hugo is happy, Yves-Jacques is happy. That's important to me. It wasn't as though Yves-Jacques and I planned on falling in love."

"Ughh one trip to Australia, and your world turns upside down. This wedding is a monstrueux mistake."

"You have no right to judge who I marry or when I marry, Clemency," Yves-Jacques snapped.

Poppy interrupted, diverging the conversation away from her

upcoming nuptials. "I was going to suggest that Hugo needs a distraction - a female distraction."

"Disastrous," Clemency snapped. "Hugo has terrible taste in women."

"That's why," Poppy said, ignoring the malice in Clemency's voice, "I thought we should pick the women."

"Like in an arranged marriage?" Yves-Jacques said.

"Yes, and on dating websites, like Emma did in Jane Austen's, *Persuasion*, or like The Bachelor on telly. Many people find true love with a bit of guidance. Hugo doesn't need to get married, but his heart needs to heal. Everyone needs a fairy godmother. Think about it; who knows you better than your best friends?"

"The best way to get over somebody is to get under somebody," Yves-Jacques said.

Both women scrunched up their noses. "That's not exactly what I meant."

"Men," Clemency said. "It's a good idea. I like it."

"Really?" Poppy said unable to hide the surprise in her voice.

"Great! My two favourite ladies are getting along."

"I didn't say we would become friends," Clemency's voice was back to ice. Poppy felt her hopes at forming a friendship begin to melt.

"So we make a bet," Yves-Jacques said, running his hands through his straight light brown hair, hazel eyes sparkling in the candlelight. The top buttons on his pink shirt had come loose, exposing his cotton white chest hairs. He leaned forward like a poker player, eyeing his sister, no sudden movements.

"A bet? How childish," Clemency purred, tilting her head backwards.

"Only childish if you are afraid to lose?" Yves-Jacques had his sister where he wanted her.

"Name your stakes."

"Oh, this is very Mafioso," Poppy said, ignoring the tension.

"If I choose the winning woman, you will be nice to Poppy - forever."

"You can't make someone like me," Poppy said shocked that Yves-Jacques would even think of using her as gambling stakes. She felt like bait, the worm on the edge of the line, luring dangerous predators towards her.

"Deal," Clemency said. "And if I choose the winning woman, Hugo's forever, I never have to be cordial to Poppy ever again. Plus, I get the villa in Cannes, the one Uncle Oliver left you in his will."

"Fine, I don't use it anyway," Yves-Jacques lied. "As long as you step up to your part of the bargain, you can have the crumbling villa."

"I don't have to come to these stupid bonding dinners. I don't have to buy her a gift at Christmas; birthdays are forgotten. And when I want to see you, Yves-Jacques, you will come without her. I don't have to say *Bonjour* when Poppy answers the phone. I can just hang up."

"Okay, I get it," Poppy said, feeling like she'd just been slapped in the face. What had she done to deserve such negativity and such loathing? She'd left her life behind in Australia, her clothing boutique, her friends, her family. "It'll be like I never existed," she whispered.

"Exactly," Clemency replied.

"Deal," Yves-Jacques said, and brother and sister shook hands.

"And if I win," Yves-Jacques and Clemency stared at one another as Poppy spoke. If I win, Clemency agrees to come to dinner with me - to give me one chance. I'm not asking you to like me." Poppy looked at Clemency.

"Make it lunch, and we have a deal."

"Okay," Poppy shrugged, a shy grin tugging at the corners of her lips. She had a chance to make things right. She might not know why Clemency hated her so much, but Poppy was an optimistic woman who liked to look on the bright side of life. She wouldn't have come to Paris if she didn't believe in true love. She had faith.

"Hugo is taking a long time in the bathroom," Yves-Jacques said.

"I'll check on him; after all I am the one who knows him best." Clemency got up, her heels teetering over the wooden floorboards.

"I can't believe you just did that," Poppy said turning to Yves-Jacques once she was certain Clemency was out of earshot.

"What?"

"Played me like a prize in a game of cards. It's disgusting."

"I thought it would make you happy to form a bond with Clemency."

"You can't force someone to like me. Besides, what if you lose?"

"Don't worry, darling, I've got this. I know Hugo better than anyone. We'll let Clemency try to like you, and she'll come around. I promise; who wouldn't adore you? She'll learn to love you."

Hearing the tap of Clemency's heels, Poppy pursed her lips and didn't say another word.

Clemency's face was flushed. "He's not in there."

"I'll check the kitchen," Yves-Jacques said.

"I'll check the coat stand," Poppy said.

They gathered back in the dining room seconds later.

"No sign of him," Yves-Jacques said.

"He's gone."

"What?" Yves-Jacques and Clemency both turned to stare at Poppy.

"His coat isn't hanging in the corridor."

"And so, my angel wins round one," Yves-Jacques slipped his arm around Poppy's waist, kissing her hair.

"Mon Dieu!" Clemency said.

"Where are you going?" Yves-Jacques asked as she turned and picked up her bag.

"To find Hugo."

"But we haven't had dessert," Poppy said, thinking of her soufflés

"Au revoir," Clemency said walking towards the front door.

Yves-Jacques turned to Poppy with one brow raised, his eyes burning bright with fiery determination. "The competition has begun."

CHAPTER THREE

DREAMS

"Charles, can't you come with me? At least for one week?"

"Sweetheart, you know I'd love to come and visit your mother in England, but I don't have the time. We're closing the deal with The Dragon Property Group in three weeks." Charles Rupert shrugged his shoulders. His custom grey suit cut in around his waist, highlighting the delicate rim of fat that had begun to form after months of stress-induced eating.

"Can you come in three weeks then? We could travel though the English countryside. We'll drive to Brighton to visit Mum, and then we could take a weekend in Glastonbury. I know you'll love it there. The village is full of quirky shops. We'll have the best time. We can even take the train from London to Paris. I'd love to attend cooking classes together in Paris." We. We. We, thought Sophia, liking the sound of it.

"You know I can't leave New York, not while the firm needs me."

"But this isn't just a holiday, Charles. It's about spending time with family. And while we're on the subject, your mother called. You haven't visited her in weeks. She's getting old, Charles; she won't be around forever, and sporadic visits from her daughter-in-law doesn't compare to ones from her only son," Sophia pressed. It broke her heart to tell her mother-in-law that her son was *busy* every time they met for afternoon tea.

"I guess we could take a weekend break and go to the Hamptons house to visit mother."

"When have you ever visited the house in the Hamptons, Charles? The only people to step foot in the place are Ollie and I." That wasn't entirely true. She and Ollie, her best friend in the entire world, had managed to hold some impressive A-list parties over the summer, some of which Charles had attended. Mostly, the house was as lonely as it was big. "When we got married, I saw us building a life together, having a family - summers in the Hamptons, children, creating a home, a marriage, building a lifetime of memories, not just the Charles Rupert, Architectural Firm."

"You knew who I was when you married me, Sophia." Charles's steady brown eyes, the same cool, calm, brown eyes Sophia had fallen in love with no fewer than seven years ago, studied her. They were the same eyes she'd promised to love and obey for a lifetime. Sophia huffed at the thought of a *lifetime*. She was lucky to him with see his eyes closed, as Charles slept next to her in the morning, breathing softly, smelling of the delicious musk of man that cannot be bottled.

Sophia bit her full bottom lip. She raised her head, black eyes burning, her loose tousled auburn mane flew down her back, and her curls caressed her ample bust. "Before we married, you promised me one thing - time, time to build a life. Now Mum and Dad have moved to Brighton. I feel like I have nothing left.

I don't even have a husband."

"Sophia, now you're being unreasonable. You have loads of friends. All you ever talk about is Ollie. If he weren't gay, I'd be worried the two of you were having an affair." Sophia bit her tongue; Ollie and Charles had always disliked each other. Charles's jealousy was palpable. He didn't want to spend time with her, but that didn't mean he wanted anyone else to either. "Don't you want me to be successful? Most women would kill for your life. All you ever do is complain. But I haven't heard one word of complaint about your new Hermes Birkin, or the shoes, or the clothes. You love to shop, but you don't want to support the man bringing you all those things."

The hairs on Sophia's back arched. "You think that I all I care about is clothes and shopping? Well, that's not true. One of these days I'll prove it to you."

Charles bent his head to the side. His face handsome face broke into a gorgeous smile.

"What?"

"You're just so cute when you're mad."

Sophia felt her blood begin to boil. "I promised myself I wouldn't say anything." She whispered to herself.

"Say what? Darling, what are you mumbling about? You're so funny, so melodramatic."

"You think I'm funny?" Cocking her head to one side, Sophia glared at Charles like an angry bull.

"I think that you're confusing. Is it that time of the month, darling? Your hormones seem off balance. You should start taking dong quai. My secretary says the stuff is incredible."

Right, that did it. "All I ever asked for was your love, Charles. It's all I've ever needed."

Something changed in Charles's expression. He took on the innocent look of a wounded kitten. His blue eyes opened wide, blinking like a deer caught in headlights. Did he know Sophia knew? Did he suspect what she was about to say? She hadn't said anything. She'd tried to act normal around him for the last three weeks, playing it cool until the time came when they could talk about it like adults. She hadn't even told Ollie...

"I found a bra, after the Texas trip." Sophia bit her inner lip to stop from crying, to stop herself from screaming.

"What nonsense!" He cocked his head to the side and laughed. "It amazes me how you always manifest farfetched lies to get my attention! It's childish."

"The A-cup bra was in your Louis Vuitton suitcase, the suitcase I bought you for our third wedding anniversary."

"Such a silly gift," Charles grumbled.

"You're away so much, it seemed practical."

"It was most likely your bra, darling. You're being over dramatic."

"I'm a Double D. There's a big difference. How would you like it if you found a tiny pair of men's underwear in my suitcase?"

"I'd think they were mine. Probably just shrunk in the dryer."

"You're going to deny that something happened between you and this invisible woman? With very visible panty hose?"

"For heaven's sake, Sophia! If you ever suspect a man of not being as perfect as your Mr. Darcy, you start crying like a banshee. I'm not perfect. I know that. I've been distracted."

"Distracted? Is that what they are calling it these days? For the record, you're nothing like Mr. Darcy. You're just like Wickham."

"Who on earth is Wickham?"

"Maybe if you took the time to read some Jane Austen, you'd know."

Sophia escaped, slamming the front door behind her. She couldn't stand another moment in that apartment. The air was stifling, hot and sticky with the sap from poisonous words.

"Sophia, be reasonable. Come back; let's talk like adults. What do you want from me?" Charles screamed at the back of the oak door.

"I want you to want me, to love me. I want a family," Sophia whispered, back pressed against the entrance to their Fifth Avenue apartment filled to the brim with life's luxuries - Louis Vuitton suitcases, cashmere throws, Royal Dolton glassware - all the stuff that was supposed to make a person happy. She knew it was a futile wish. Charles and Sophia's sex life had whittled down to a stream, so low you couldn't drink from it. She could hardly blame him for cheating. She'd promised herself she wouldn't say anything, that she'd brush it off. Why did she always open her big mouth?

Educated at Dartmouth and surrounded by the elite of American society, Sophia should've had an easy life. "Simple as a walk in the park," her mother had always said. "Ladies marry; they do not fawn over dreams."

Sophia had no desire to displease either of her parents, grateful for the magical life she led - a world of privilege, etiquette, glamour, expectation, and comfort. After receiving the statutory English degree that would hang in her closet as a rank of achievement for her entire life, she had spent her days planning charity benefits and her nights attending them, clawing her way through the mass of wannabe socialites and successful bankers.

The door handle began to twist. Sophia dashed for the stairs. There was no way Charles would suspect she'd take the stairs. But today wasn't like any other day. Avoiding the comfort of the lift, she pushed open the emergency exit door.

Sophia's auburn curls bounced in front of her eyes as she jogged down the stairs. Her breasts jiggled like jelly on a plate. Her black Herve Leger dress clung to her curvaceous hips and her illustrious beauty shone bright. Fine bones defined her features; she was one of those women whom being a little roly-poly suited. What she did not suit was running downstairs in six inch Louboutins.

She heard the ding of the lifts, Charles bidding a polite welcome to the elderly Smiths on floor six. He'd catch her if she didn't move faster.

Slipping off her shoes to reveal a neat row of Chanel's bel argus midnight blue painted toe nails, she thrust the shoes under her arm and bolted. Her chest closed in like a collapsing stack of cards, making each breath create a sharp stabbing pain. It was so deep she couldn't focus on how ridiculous she felt trying to escape her husband.

There was, of course, nothing wrong with Charles. He was polite, sweet, endearing, a workaholic, and boring. Those were definitely not deal breakers. She pushed down her darkest thoughts into the deepest cavernous depths of her mind, because even though she loved Charles, deep down she knew she wasn't *in* love with him.

The light at the end of the tunnel gleamed as Sophia saw the staircase exit. She headed for the heavy door and pushed it open. The lift doors chimed; she'd run too slowly. Charles was bound to catch her. Looking from left to right like a mouse looking for a way out, she panicked, turning back to the stairs. No, she couldn't go back up; she'd die before taking another step. She needed time to think.

She thrust her back against the concrete wall. Something moved behind her shoulder blades. Something round and uncomfortable pressed back towards the wall against her weight. In horror, Sophia turned to see what she'd leant against. She'd been so distracted to escape Charles and catch her breath that she hadn't noticed the fire alarm.

Quickly, she tried to pull it back from the wall. Sirens sounded. She covered her ears. It was so loud! Sprinklers from the ceilings turned on, and coated in a layer of liquid she made her way into the lustrous lobby. The world slowed down; time stopped. Sophia strolled through the grand exit, sirens sounding in the distance, humming like strums of a string quartet.

Sophia turned to the elevator, as it chimed and opened to reveal Mrs. Smith clasping onto Charles's solid form. Her frail body was drenched to the bone. What had she done? Mr. Smith looking paper thin and drenched, clung to the right of Charles. The sun rose over the horizon sending shafts of golden light through the lobby, and it was at that point that Sophia realized just how messed up she was.

"I love you," Charles mouthed, his saturated tailor-made suit clung to his lean body with perfect symmetry.

Like a stampede of elephants leaving destruction in its path, Sophia could not stop. Waterfalls of broken promises and unshed tears crashed down above Sophia's head. The fire brigade arrived, and Sophia slipped outside.

"Mademoiselle, are you heading uptown?" Hugo stared, delighted by the woman in front of him. She was spectacular, dripping wet, oozing elegance that a billion Benjamin Franklins couldn't buy. Sopping wet and looking absolutely mad, she was a refreshing change from the barcodes surging past them on the street. Sophia ignored the man before her, continuing to hail a cab. "There's no way anyone will stop for you this time of day. Tell me where you're going, and I'd be happy to offer you a lift."

Broken from her spell, Sophia turned to the Frenchman dressed in cream pants and a white lined shirt. Chestnut curls floated softly around his face, falling loose below his ears.

"You're delicious," she spluttered.

"Why, thank you. I've never met a cannibal before. But as they say, expect the unexpected in New York."

Sophia blinked, her thick black lashes coated in great gallops of mascara opened wide to reveal the most beautiful brown eyes Hugo had ever laid eyes upon.

"Did I say that out loud? I'm having the strangest day."

"You did! Or maybe I can read minds and I didn't even know it." Sophia laughed. "Where did you say you were going?"

"I didn't," Sophia said.

"Can I take you there?"

Sophia turned back to the luxury of her Fifth Avenue apartment, the luxury of her life. She needed an adventure more than Alice and her trip to wonderful Wonderland. She had the cake; she'd eaten it. More than anything, Sophia needed a slice of crazy.

"I couldn't think of anything better."

He smiled, soft and reassuring. He was devastatingly handsome. Flying down the stairs, Sophia hadn't known what to expect. She felt suffocated. Charles had said he'd always been faithful. He'd never been a liar, and by all accounts, Sophia was prepared to believe that he was telling the truth.

Yet, here he was, Prince Charming. What self-respecting woman would walk out on a man like Charles Rupert and her *perfect life?* It was like a scene from all the romance movies she spent hours watching, and here was Hugh Grant.

"Where are we going?"

The gentleman turned to Sophia. She winced at his physical beauty, the soft lull of French tickling the undertones of his English. She was a married woman. Jumping in a car with another man was uncharted territory - uncharted and dangerous.

"Take me to Lexington Avenue, please."

"Anywhere," he said.

Sophia jumped inside the car before she had time to glance back at the apartment. Would Charles forgive her?

As her rump landed on the plush leather seat, her phone gave a shrill ring. Glancing at the handsome stranger swooping in beside her, she pulled it from the pocket of her dress.

"Sophia, it's me, sweetheart," Ollie's voice glided through the phone like a chirpy bird.

"I'm surprised you're up. It's nine thirty in the morning. Isn't this hour uncivilised for you?"

"Darling, I haven't come down from last night. You wouldn't believe who I met."

"Who?"

"The man of my dreams. His name is Wally Waldo."

"Wally Waldo?"

"I know, but it's easy to get past the name if you see the state of his abs. He is a slice of heaven."

"That's great, Ollie. I'm so happy for you. I'm a little busy at the moment, sweetie; would you mind if I called you back?"

"Mind? Of course, I'd mind! The Sophia I know is never busy, especially when it comes to gossiping about the love life of her very best friend."

"Yes, well, I'm sort of in a meeting." Sophia tried not to look at the adorable, strange man sitting beside her.

"It's the next right," the stranger called to the driver.

"With whom?" Ollie asked.

"No one you know."

"You didn't! Oh la la. I've been telling you for so long to let go of that fancy-pants Charles and have a little fun. Enjoy the sex life you deserve."

"Ollie, I said I'm in a *brunch* meeting."

"How endearing. You make it sound so formal. I'm getting turned on just thinking about it. What's he look like? Just give me a clue?"

"Ollie!" He knew her far too well. Was she that easy to read? How would she explain to Charles? She couldn't and wouldn't. Just like Charles couldn't explain the dreaded A-cup bra. Sophia wanted to tell her best friend to not to talk so loud, but that would have made the embarrassing nature of their conversation even more obvious.

"Ciao, bella, have fun, darling. Go with the flow. I want to hear all about him ASAP. After you're done, come to my place. We'll feast on details."

"Ollie! I'm not..." Ugh, it was hopeless. "I'll call you later."

"Toodaloo."

The phone rung dry. Sophia turned to the strange man. "Sorry about that."

"No worries." Green eyes swallowed Sophia's pride. She felt her body shake into a bundle of bubbling nerves. "Where are we going for brunch?"

"Brunch?" Sophia mumbled.

"Well, you did say you were in a meeting. And if one thing is certain, I'm famished." Hugo's gaze lingered over the voluptuous beauty sitting before him. She was perfect - everything he could possibly want. She was the antidote to Arabella's venomous love wounds. She was dripping water all over the Mercedes' cream leather seats, but what did it matter? She was divine, wholesome, radiating life. And, she was just what the doctor ordered.

Clemency would be proud. She wasn't another waif that would need to cling to his arm so she didn't break in the breeze. This beauty was real; he had to have her.

"I don't even know your name."

"Hugo."

"Hugo?" The name tasted salty and sweet, seasoned with a hint of danger. "Like Hugo Boss?" Sophia giggled; she felt giddy. She was flirting with a stranger. This wasn't like her. She was being irrational. Maybe Charles was right. Maybe she was having a bad case of PMS. No woman liked to admit it - especially to a man. Come to think of it, when had she last got her period?

When was the last time a man had invited her to brunch? Charles never did; he was always busy with his company or having sex with mysterious women... Sophia buried the thought; Charles wasn't like that. There had to be a reason for the whole bra incident. Didn't there?

Hugo raised a bushy, dark brow. He grinned; it transformed his face from a brooding masculine, mysterious man, to an impish naughty child. Sophia licked the corner of her lips - drool all clear.

"I'm Hugo De La Laville."

"Wow, that's a name to make even the real Hugo Boss jealous. So are you from some French aristocratic family?" Sophia joked. Her flirtatious humour was escaping her lips without warning. Just because she'd found a bra in Charles's suitcase and suspected he'd been cheating didn't mean she had the right to pick up gorgeous Frenchmen wandering the streets of New York. Did it?

Delete. Forget the whole bra incident. Sophia wished she could erase it from her mind. Maybe with a little bit of fun she could. Sophia braved another glance at Hugo; his cheeks glowed a lovely shade of pink. "I meant that as a joke."

"I know, I do come from a long lineage though, and sometimes I find it embarrassing to talk about... My family owns property in England and France, but I am a writer. It's all I've ever wanted to do with my life. I'm here on a book tour. And you are?"

"A writer? That sounds interesting. Well, I'm Sophia Rupert, and I don't have any aristocratic connections."

"Sophia? What a beautiful name! So, will you join me for brunch? You seem to hesitate."

"Well, it's just that." Sophia's fingers traced the line indented into her finger where she wore her wedding rings. They weren't there; she'd left her rings on the bathroom bench. She never went out without them, but after their dreadful argument she'd forgotten to put them back on.

"Do you have a husband?"

He's so French, Sophia thought, and gorgeous. "No." The lie escaped her lips before she could stop it. "It's just that, I don't usually attend lunch dates with strangers." She could hear Ollie cheering her on, the horny devil on her shoulder.

"Well, I'm hardly a stranger. After all, how many strangers have you met that know your first name and you theirs?" Hugo hadn't meant to blurt out about his family heritage. Yet, Sophia hadn't even flinched. She seemed more interested in his writing than his inheritance. He reassured himself that it was good to be open and honest.

Sophia thought of Charles; would he worry about her? He was always distracted. Even though they shared a bed, the time they spent together was with shut eyes, clamped closed so not even a breath of conversation would sweep between the sheets. Even their love life was mechanical, not wholesome or engaging. Their love had died, the romance buried.

Smiling at Hugo, Sophia said, "Brunch sounds fabulous."

Perhaps, a brunch with a handsome, exotic stranger was all she needed. A brunch date didn't count as cheating. It would be some harmless flirting and getting to know someone new; it was dangerous, but not immoral. She would break no wedding vows. The French were famous for taking lovers - no not lovers - Hugo was a friend, Sophia chided, as she felt her heart skip a beat. She laid down the ground rules in her mind, no kissing, no touching, but flirting was allowed! It would be a pleasurable business meeting indeed.

"Let's take a detour at Saks and get you something less wet. Then cupcakes for brunch it is."

"How did you know?" Sophia asked.

"Bedraggled and wet. I can think of no other store as fabulous as Sprinkles Cupcakes on Lexington Avenue. I have a feeling we're going to get along fabulously."

* * *

Three hours later, Sophia sat on the chesterfield in Ollie's all pink apartment.

"Darling, spill," Ollie pleaded, pouring himself champagne.

Sophia blew gently on her hot chocolate made with chili, a slab of dark chocolate, and organic full cream milk. It was hot chocolate to sooth her soul. Sophia's needed soothing to the highest degree. The events of the day whirled through her mind like a violent hurricane. The argument, getting wet in the apartment sprinklers, meeting Hugo, coffee, cupcakes, and the offer...

Sophia gulped a mouthful of hot chocolate, sweet and spicy; she felt herself beginning to relax.

"I'm dying here," Ollie said. He was wearing white jeans, a fluorescent yellow silk Versace button shirt and three coats of spray tan. He leaned forward on the edge of his chair. "Darling, I know you were up to no good. Now spill."

"Well, I wouldn't say I was up to no good."

"Hush, darling; the crimson flushing your cheeks, the swagger in your step as you walked through my front door. If you weren't married, I'd say you're in love."

"Ollie! Of course, I'm not in love with someone, other than Charles," Sophia amended, brushing a fine thread of her auburn hair behind her pixie-like ears.

"So who were you talking to when I wanted to tell you about *my* sordid affairs? I demand to know why you were too busy to speak to me."

"Ollie, why do you always expect the worst?"

"Darling, I never expect the worst. I just know with you to expect the unexpected. Besides, you've been nesting with Charles for what, seven years now? It's about time you did something exciting."

Sophia felt her spine bristle, preparing to defend herself. "It's been difficult."

"Difficult? The man's so busy he confuses you with his doormat."

Sophia laughed. As rude as Ollie could be, he always put a smile on her face.

"We're going to Paris together," Sophia said. Her face flushed pink as she remembered the proposal.

Ollie slapped his knee. "I told you. Make him sweat, and he'll become putty in your hands. You've finally broken Charles from his shell. All he needed was to pick up the scent of competition." Ollie sniffed the air like a dog. "You've snapped him into line. You deserve a romantic escape. I'm so proud of you, honey. The first thing every woman should learn is 1. How to manipulate your man. I've been thinking of writing a dating book; what do you think?" Sophia opened her mouth, but Ollie didn't wait for an answer, "I mean, the dribble they teach in school these days."

"I'm not going with Charles."

"Excuse me?"

"I'm going with Hugo. Well, not *with* Hugo. I'm going to visit him there. He invited me, and I said yes! We have sooo much in common. He loves food; I love food. He loves books; I love books. I told him about my dream to study cookery in France. And then he invited me!"

"My, my," Ollie shook his head, "and when did we meet this man?"

"Today. I thought this was what you wanted for me?" Why did

Sophia always blurt things out before considering how the other person might react?

"I want you to be happy. I mean, how much do you really know about this man? As dull as Charles is, he does love you. You can't abandon the man. An affair is like diving into a pool at dawn; it shakes you up, breaks you out of your shell. You don't stay in the water forever. You could drown, it's cold. You get out, towel off, and wait for another day when you need another swim."

"Ollie, Hugo and I aren't having an affair. I mean he *is* gorgeous. He has these eyes; they change from grey to green to amber in different lights," Sophia sighed.

Ollie clapped his hands together. "Darling, you're drowning. Drowning!"

"I'm not! I'm floating!"

"Oh dear, dear me. Details. I need details."

CHAPTER FOUR

PAST DARLINGS

Clemency looked at Hugo across the top of her steaming mug of coffee. "I've done something terrible, darling." She purred with the innocence of Lewis Carroll's Cheshire cat.

"That can only mean one thing." Hugo raised a brow. "Trouble."

"Before I tell you what it is, you have to promise me you won't get mad."

"How could I ever be mad with you? Even if you ate the last of my cupcakes from Sprinkles in New York," Clemency blushed. "You did! Didn't you? I had a feeling; at one point I suspected the maid."

"The temptation was too great."

Her full lips pouted, and Hugo knew most men sitting in his position would be smitten with the divine creature before him. Her curves would make Gisele Bündchen envious - a bottom the size of two ripe melons and eyes as blue as the ocean - and would catch most men off guard. A modern Aphrodite; they'd stammer, splutter, and be captured by Clemency's spell within seconds. Not Hugo. He loved Clemency through and through. But after years of crawling around his mother's living room in nappies, mud fights, getting high together as teenagers, an awkward first kiss never to be spoken of again, nights cooking scrambled eggs, and discussing dating disasters and successes, to him, Clemency was Clemency. She was fun, lovable, beautiful, and as clear a pane of glass.

"Spill."

"What? Did something dribble from the edge of my cocktail glass?" Clemency asked, batting lashes and flashing her perfect white teeth as she licked her plump pink, collagen injected lips. They'd been as thin as whiskers until she was nineteen and received the first instalment from her trust fund. Her platinum blonde curls licked the edges of her face as she raised her margarita to her lips and took another innocent gulp.

"You can't flirt with me and think I'll spin around your little finger like all the other men you date."

"All the other men? Are you implying that I'm slutty?" Clemency purred, a sultry smile caressing the edge of her lips.

"No. I'm implying that you are stunning. I'm saying that most men go weak at the knees when you bat but one eyelash their way. I, however, know you far too well to fall under your spell. Spill the beans on the *terrible* thing you've done, so you don't have to explain to me later why you didn't just eat my cupcake."

Clemency breathed in the chilly French air whilst flaring her dainty nostrils. "Hugo, darling, why would I confess? You haven't promised with all your heart not to get mad."

"Cross my heart, hope to die..."

"Okay, so I'll spill." Clemency flicked her fingers in exasperation. Her five-carat tanzanite ring spun in a swirl of ocean blue. "I've found the most talented, gorgeous, funny, lovable, single woman for you."

"That's not so terrible." Hugo breathed a sigh of relief. He'd been expecting something insane like the time Clemency raided his closet, giving all his tailored Valentino suits to the homeless, which was rather thoughtful for Clemency, replacing them with white linen shirts and Barbados shorts, all because he refused to go to the Bahamas with her over the Christmas season. Instead, he'd edited his debut novel and spent time with his grandfather. He'd frozen in his Parisian apartment the entire winter.

"She's a style editor at Luxe Interiors Magazine. She's fashionable and fun."

"How did you come to meet such a woman?"

"I have a social life, darling. I'm not like you - head in a book, busy writing all day. This woman is funny, charming, and is already halfway to begging for your hand in marriage."

"Halfway to begging my hand in marriage?"

Clemency sighed, "I may have sent several anonymous love letters, roses, and a big box of chocolates to her from an anonymous admirer... You!"

"You what?" Hugo dropped back into his chair with a hard thud. "I'm smothering her, and we haven't even met. She's going to think I'm a total creep."

"Don't worry; women love to be worshipped. That's why we invented Valentine's Day."

"Women didn't invent Valentine's Day," Hugo shook his head, a soft grin made his cheeks dimple. "That was Saint Valentine."

"It's beside the point."

"And your point is?"

"You have a date with the soon to be Mrs. De La Laville."

"I do? Oh, Clemency, why can't you focus on your own love life rather than interfering with mine."

"I am focused on my love life, darling. In fact, I have a date tomorrow with an Austrian banker. You know that men and I mesh like fine wine and cheese. I'm never in short supply. But without a bit of prodding, you'll likely end up a bachelor for the rest of your days."

"Fine, you'll have to give me more details on this mystery woman. I need time to prepare; and I'm sorry to burst your romantic bubble, but I think I've already met someone."

"Did Yves-Jacques introduce you?"

"Yves-Jacques? Why would I take romantic advice from him? I mean, Poppy is adorable, but we know of his past relationship disasters. It's Poppy that's been helping me out with this new lady. I've been so busy, and she's helped to book a hotel for her and bought us tickets to the Eiffel tower. Organising dates before she gets here; she's an American. I can't thank her enough. I really think Yves-Jacques has got it right this time. You shouldn't be so hard on Poppy; she's quite something."

"Maybe I underestimated Poppy," Clemency said more to herself than Hugo.

Hugo nodded his head. "She's lovely. She's even going to pick

Sophia up at the airport, as I'll be in London organizing some properties for the first days of her stay with Yves-Jacques."

"So, tell me all about this lucky lady."

"Her name's Sophia Rupert. She's a New Yorker, and she's coming to spend a month in Paris to see the sights and learn how to cook. You should see her; she's beautiful, in a wholesome real way. She's funny and smart. You are going to love her."

"She sounds fascinating. I'd love to hear all about her, but right now we have to be at the library, Bibliothèque Nationale de France, in five minutes or you'll be late," Clemency said, twirling a piece of platinum blonde hair around her pinky before stopping to chew on the end.

"What?" Hugo said, his heart skipping a beat.

"Your date with my mystery woman. I wish you'd bothered to shave; we'll have to make do." Clemency leaned forward and brushed Hugo's hair out of his eyes, her hands running through his soft hair. "You'll know she's the one the moment you set eyes on her. Come along, it's just round the corner."

"Have we met before?" Hugo ran his hands through his dark hair. He felt so visible, as though all the women in the library – of all places – would be summing up whether he was a worthy mate, his flaws, his looks.

Clemency shrugged. Dressed in a white lace vintage Valentino dress and a black broad brim, floppy felt hat, she looked stunning. All this *the one* hunting would be so much easier if he could have just fallen in love with Clemency, his best friend. He knew her ins and outs, the way she smelt of lavender after every shower, the way her face flushed pink when she was embarrassed, her determination to have everything her way. She was like the perfect sister.

They'd known each other for so long that Clemency didn't pretend to be anything other than herself around him, and he was nothing more than Hugo, her Camembert loving companion. This, Hugo realised, was the precise reason they had never fallen in love. They were too similar, like golden retrievers sitting in front of a fire. Years of unabashed openness had destroyed any chance of fatal attraction.

"You have to give me a clue. Something, anything! So I'm not walking around blind."

"You won't be blind. The moment you lay eyes on her, you'll know. She'll sweep you off your feet. You'll know you've arrived at the gates of heaven."

"So I should be looking for someone angelic. There's a good chance she'll be wearing a white cornette and habit. Do you think I'm that much of a sinner that I need a nun to guard my every move for the rest of my mortal life?"

Clemency snorted. "Oh, I know you're bad, and you have a wild imagination. She's just a girl, and you're just a boy, looking to find love. Passionate, irrevocable, unconditional love. When your eyes meet, you'll know how right I am. Who else knows you like I do?"

The answer was as clear as the sunlight streaming on the row of standard pink roses beside them. No one.

"Fine, let's make a move. I'm curious. You're going to wait for me?"

"Sweetheart," Clemency batted her long black lashes, her eyes flashing brilliant blue. "I've got more important things to do than spend all-day cleaning up your disastrous love life."

"Such as?"

"A lunch date with Valentino."

"Can't the shops wait? I'll need your support when I escape the library."

"Valentino is a human being, darling, and he's waiting for me right now at his apartment. I'm late." She kissed Hugo on both cheeks before shoving him in the chest. "Now go. Call me tonight."

In a swish of white, black, and floral perfume, mingled with scents of lavender and honey, Clemency was gone. Left at the front of the Bibliothèque nationale de France, Hugo felt small beside the great building, pillars looming over him. Hugo shook himself. What was so frightening? Books? If he wasn't careful, he'd soon become the world's biggest introvert. It was time to move forward.

The library smelt of ash and musty books. Hugo could remember the last time he'd been here. He'd escaped to the library with his *long term,* in teenage years, girlfriend. Fleur. Beautiful, funny, chubby, eccentric Fleur.

He had never known why he'd been drawn to Fleur, he just was. She wasn't the brightest girl, the prettiest or the most charismatic girl in his summer writing class. She was a quiet bookworm, who made him laugh, and had the biggest, widest, eyes he'd ever seen. Her black hair was so long she could sit on it. For hours they would escape into this old, dramatic haven, and make out behind rows of books until the library closed, or the cranky old librarian would kick them out.

Thinking of it made him blush. She'd been the girl who had stolen his virginity. Relishing in the power she held over him. Until, Fleur had found him kissing Clemency, at a party during the summer. One kiss, one breakup, one major disaster.

Since then, he'd never stepped foot in the Bibliothèque nationale de France. A major crush, for a writer. The library had been his safe haven. A place full of mystery and joy, transformed into a thousand shattered memories.

Why had Clemency, sent him here? She knew how much he'd mourned the loss of this space. Was she trying to torture him? Like Charles Dickens, dangling old Ebenezer Scrooge, from a piece of thread. Maybe she wanted him to repent his sins. Maybe she still felt guilty.

Books rose like great towers on all sides of Hugo. He looked up, tempted to pull at random, one of the leather bound volumes from the shelves and begin to read. Apart from memories of Fleur, it wasn't so bad here. Libraries had always been a refuge for Hugo, like churches for Catholics. A second home, where he felt at ease.

Hugo began to tear his focus from the books surrounding him. Tempting as their pages were, Hugo was here, to mingle. With women. Real women. Not the ones safely enclosed between soft pages. The ones who didn't let you down, but married you, and showed you the meaning of true love.

A group of nuns sat around a desk. Had one of them just winked? He began to walk toward the nuns, but the one whose soft brown eyes had caught his, looked away. No, thought Hugo, this must be a coincidence. A crazy coincidence. The women looked like props from a play.

The middle-aged librarian looked up at him, from behind a giant oak desk. Her hair, a mixture of black and grey, twirled in a chignon at the nap of her neck. She wore a charcoal suit, and rings glittered across her fingers. A wedding ring. Too bad, he thought. What guy didn't indulge in the librarian fantasy on occasion?

* * *

Fleur ran her thumb along a line of books in the Bibliothèque nationale de France. She loved the smell of old books. Their musty scent, reminded her of childhood. Hours spent with her nose buried between pages. Simone de Beauvoir, Austen, Dickens, Victor Hugo, Gustave Flaubert, some of her favourite authors. All whom shared their imaginative worlds with her, digging deep between the lines, veins of the books caressed her heart, creating friendships that would last a lifetime.

She wasn't here to dawdle with her old friends today. Even though the tall, high vaulted ceilings with their domed windows made her feel more at home than in her own apartment. Light spilled on the shelves. She was here on business, the business of researching designer homes. Timeless style.

Hugo stopped short, he blinked, and stared some more. It was like seeing a ghost. Strange. Exhilarating. He was the ghost, his heart no longer pounding in his chest, paralysed. Fleur.

How had Clemency, pulled this one off? The last time he'd been in Fleur's presence; she'd slapped him in an open bar and thrown her glass of champagne, including the flute at him. She'd been wearing glasses, a fringe too long for her pretty brows dangling across her forehead, covering the rim of her glasses, covering her wide eyes. She'd been cute in the reserved, good girl, dorky manner that he'd always loved about her.

But now, Fleur's hair had been cut into a choppy bob, bringing out the sharp angular features of her face, high cheekbones, pointy nose, sharp jaw and perfect pout. Her body had lost all of its puppy fat, and was now so tiny, she'd make a supermodel envious of her minuet waist.

Fleur, absorbed in what she was doing, climbed a ladder in a sharp red halter dress cut just below the knees. Her movements were graceful, controlled, and sexy. She was wearing something Hugo had never seen her in before; confidence.

Clemency, had said he'd know with whom she'd set him up with. He knew Clemency was right, a dose of Fleur, was exactly what he needed. Before Arabella, she was only girl he'd ever given his total heart to. Caught in the throes of teenage love. They could pick up where they'd left off. His life would take flight.

His writing would improve. He could visit the library again. He could make new memories. He wondered what Clemency must have said to make Fleur agree to meet him? She could've explained that nothing ever happened between them, that the whole kissing incident was a huge misunderstanding. Time must have dampened Fleur's fury. Or chocolates and roses and whatever else Clemency sent her way. Hugo knew from experience, Clemency could be very persuasive when she wanted to.

Hugo took a deep breath and began to approach his long lost love, the one who'd slipped through his fingers only to blossom from a simple daisy into a breathtaking red rose. His chest tightened and his heart began to pound once more, so loud, he was sure he'd be kicked out of the library. It sounded as though deafening drums were exploding from his chest.

"Fleur," he said in his most relaxed, charming voice. She didn't swivel from her position on the wooden rungs. She took another step up the ladder. "Fleur!" He tried, louder, more insistent. He wanted, needed, to get this woman's attention.

This time she turned in midstep; seeing Hugo, she lifted her hands from the ladder in surprise. Her mouth opened in a Betty Boop expression of shock; hands covered her lips. Fleur's gold Jimmy Choo caught on the back of the ladder. The motion of her hands pulling backwards, and her high-heel whacking the rung, caught her off guard.

Fleur screamed; Hugo ran forwards as she fell. Hugo got there just in time. Arms outstretched, he caught Fleur like a Barbie doll being thrust at him from a distance. Although slight, the force of her fall caught Hugo off guard and they both crashed to the floor.

The group of nuns looked towards the entwined pair and made shushing noises. Hugo looked into Fleur's eyes and beamed. It wasn't the Prince Charming entrance he'd been hoping for. He wished he were a character in a romantic movie. He'd have caught Fleur and glided her to an upright position. He began to laugh at the complete disaster of the affair.

"What the hell do you think you're doing?" Fleur demanded.

"Ssshh," Hugo replied. His dark chestnut locks had fallen loose around his eyes. He swept his hair back and arched a fluffy, wide brow. "I mean we're not in Church, but," he jerked his head towards the nuns, who were now staring at the pair.

"You belong in hell. He's over here," she called unabashed to the nuns. "I've found the devil himself. Call the hunt off." The nuns looked down at their books and papers, Fleur grit her teeth. "I could do with some holy water right now."

"I thought you'd be happy to see me? Clemency said…"

"Clemency said?"

What had Clemency said? 'I've found you the perfect woman' - and - 'he'd know' when he saw her. She hadn't said that she'd spoken to the woman. Only that she'd found her. And from the daggers Fleur was shooting, she knew nothing of their supposed date. "I'm going to kill her."

"Kill who? I always knew you were psychotic, but a murderer? The last time I saw Clemency, she had her tongue stuck halfway down your throat."

Feeling like a downtrodden teenager, Hugo pushed his thumbs deep into his brown corduroys. Standing up, Fleur towered over him. She was as scary as a supermodel, Hugo thought. Hugo scrambled up, meeting her gaze.

"Fleur, this wasn't supposed to be an ambush. Clemency and I - nothing ever happened between us besides that kiss. We're friends, that's it. Best friends. She set up this date, told me, when I saw the woman I was meant to be with I'd just know. And when I saw you, my heart stopped and then it sped up so fast, I felt like I was on a roller coaster. I'm sorry. I didn't mean to interfere in your life. I can see that you haven't forgiven me and I don't blame you. But for the record," Fleur's big brown eyes never left his gaze, "I've never stopped loving you. What happened with Clemency was a mistake. When you left me, my heart shattered into a million pieces. I never recovered."

He huffed out the remaining air from his lungs and retreated as fast as possible, past the nuns, past the librarian, past a bunch of hippy teenagers sitting at the front of the library, into fresh air, into a downpour of rain. The grey skies had cracked and within moments, he was drenched.

His heart had blossomed like he never thought it would again at the sight of Fleur. It was like the moment she'd dumped him all those years ago. Fleur had bloomed into a beautiful rose, only to stab his heart with sharp thorns.

"Hugo." He turned. Fleur was cutting through the rain, her feet gliding over the cobblestone road in nine inch heels like she was walking on air, the mark of a true Parisian. "You didn't wait for my reply." Her face had softened; she wasn't shooting him daggers anymore, just studying his features in the rain.

"What?" Hugo replied, his dry lips becoming wet and cold with the rhythmic beat of ice pinpricks kissing them softly.

They were so close that Hugo felt the heat from Fleur's, tiny body. He wanted to drape his arms over her shoulders and pull the lovable, beautiful woman towards him. But he didn't dare, afraid that if he did, she'd pull away. Instead, he took her left hand up to his lips and blew upon it. She looked cold; her hair was drenched and she was shaking.

She went on. "I presume the flowers and chocolates and love letters I've received over the past week are from Clemency?"

"How did you guess?"

"You mentioned her in the library and everything I've received smells of lavender."

"I'm sorry for everything that happened between us. What I did to you, it was wrong. I was young and foolish."

"Would you like to have coffee?" Fleur asked.

"You'd give me another chance?"

Fleur nodded. "It was easier for me to react with anger at seeing you. What happened between us in the past, well, it was a long time ago. We can at least try to be friends."

"Does that mean you accept my apology?"

Fleur's red dress crept up her thighs. She's so beautiful, Hugo thought, like a butterfly escaped from its cocoon.

"Oui." She bit her lip.

"In that case, I'd love a coffee more than anything."

Chapter Five

FLIGHTY BUTTERFLY

Three weeks later…

"You had sex with who?" Mia gasped, her eyes opening so wide Tabby was sure one eyeball was bound to fall loose and roll over the floor towards her toes.

"You heard me the first time. Married men are always so grateful."

"You're crazy, insane."

"I'm a woman with needs. A woman who likes to play." Tabby licked her lips, enjoying the horrified expression on her best friend's face.

"When his wife finds out, she'll kill you."

"She won't find out. Ever." Tabby, the picture of innocence, shook her loose white blonde hair.

"Why did you do it? You could have any guy. Look at you: eyes the colour of the Tahitian sea, lips that would make Angelina Jolie squirm with envy."

Tabby shrugged. "I didn't realise Francis was married, not until I saw his wife leaving his bookshop with their two teenage children."

"Oh, Tabby, that's awful."

"I was shocked at first; just another man who's managed to break my heart. The sick thing is, we haven't been able to get out of the habit of sleeping together. He's a disgusting little fellow in the bedroom. You know I adore vile men."

"No one adores vile men. They love to hate them. That's all. And last you told me, you'd sworn off men forever."

Tabby shrugged again. It was the easiest answer for any number of Mia's difficult questions. It was simpler for Tabby to feel like the victim than to change the path of her destiny and claim her power.

Mia knew how when Tabby's mum had fallen 'in love' with Ravii, she'd let their whole family unit crumble. And if the family hadn't crumbled, Zen wouldn't have either. He'd still be laughing. He'd still be breathing. They'd drink mountains of milo and dream about travelling to India and never coming home. But of course, you couldn't go on an adventure with a ghost.

"You're disgusting," Mia said, snapping Tabby out of her reverie.

Tabby stepped forward and brushed a lock of Mia's short black hair behind her ear. Mia's ears pointed upwards in two sharp triangles and reminded Tabby of an elf.

"Everybody loves disgusting women," Tabby replied.

Before Mia could stop her, Tabby pressed her lips to Mia's.

They tasted like salty crackers, and cherry lip gloss. They tasted beyond disgusting; they tasted delicious.

Mia pushed Tabby away. "I'm not getting drawn into your games. You know I'm engaged."

"You're boring," Tabby said before flopping down on the beaten up sofa, slinging her legs over the cracked leather cushions.

"I'm not boring. I'm stable."

"How come you'll kiss Richard and not me? Do you think I'm fat?"

"I think that you have emotional issues. I'm not attracted to the anorexic chic look, either. I think it's gross. You need to start eating."

"I eat."

Mia raised a brow. Her short brown hair, undercut at the sides, fell into her eyes. "How's the café?"

"I quit."

"You quit? Why?"

"Because I don't want to be like everyone else, getting up nine to five, working like a slave to the corporate system. I want something different. Haven't you ever heard the saying – 'Love what you do and your life will be a permanent orgasm.'?"

"No."

"That's because I made it up. I've decided to make my own rules. Screw the system."

"Good for you. Have you been selling any more pieces of your jewellery?"

"I haven't been artistically inspired. It's like there's this dark cloud hanging over me. Something's blocking my creativity. It's so frustrating."

Mia raised her hands to her eyes and pulled them down over her face. "Do you need money? Tabby, I want you to be a success. You have to tell me what you need and I'll do my best to help."

"I don't need money." Tabby cracked her neck. "Francis has got loads. He's paying me to keep our little secret and not tell his doting wife."

"Oh Tabby. How could you?"

"I don't need a lecture on morals either, just a place to sleep for a couple of nights. I promise I won't get in the way. I've stopped drinking too, so you have nothing to worry about. You won't even notice I'm here."

Mia looked around her small Battersea apartment, crowded with books and antique furniture she'd collected with Richard at markets. Her collection of teapots smiled at her from their place on the mantel. Already with Tabby laying feet facing upright on the couch, the place felt somehow smaller.

"You can stay. As long as you promise to keep out of Richard's way."

"Why? I thought he loved me? I think he's always had a little crush on me. Maybe we should test him out? See how loyal our Richard really is."

"Richard's not like that; he wouldn't cheat on me. He just doesn't approve of you."

"That's because he's mean and narcissistic."

"Tabby!"

"It's true."

"Don't let him hear you say that. The traits we dislike in others are often pieces of ourselves we'd rather not look at."

"That's so not true. Would you call me selfish?"

"Yes."

"Mean?"

"Sometimes."

"A cow?"

At this, Mia laughed. "It's a bit hard to call a vegetarian a cow."

"And your point is?"

"You haven't even given Richard a chance to get to know you. The real you."

"I think he's jealous of me, of us. He knows you'll never love him the way you love me."

"I've given you a place to stay. Can't you just give me some gratitude without the attitude?"

"Thank you," Tabby said, pulling her white blonde hair into a bun at the top of her head. She blew Mia a kiss whilst wondering how long it would take to destroy her best friend's relationship.

"Why don't I make you a cup of tea? You can turn the telly on."

"Every time I turn it on, I'm becoming more of a commercial drone. Seriously, if you go for a walk around Battersea this time of night, every obedient citizen will have his eyes glued to the telly. It's like a virtual prison and it gives me the creeps."

"Well, there's a copy of Jane Austen's, *Emma* on the coffee table. Why don't you read that?"

"I'd love to, but I have to get ready for my date."

"You're going out?"

"Well, you just said to stay out of Richard's way. He won't even know I'm here. I'll come back when he's tucked up in bed, snoring like a baby. You don't even have to tell him I'm staying."

"Do you think it's the best idea for you to go out right now?"

"Why ever not?"

"Well, you don't seem stable exactly."

Tabby turned away from Mia. At twenty eight, she felt like the Earth had never seen such a failure as herself. She wished it would open its mouth and swallow her whole, pull her into the hot molten lava in its core and devour her essence.

"All I'm saying is maybe you should take it easy for a couple of nights, instead of getting involved with some random guy."

"He's not random. Mum set us up."

Mia rolled her eyes. "Fine, take the spare keys." She passed Tabby a key ring with a funny looking teddy from France attached to the side.

"Thanks."

The spare room, dressed in peeling floral wallpaper, stacks of books, and old newspapers, was smaller than Tabby had remembered. Books on baseball, old sneakers, cricket bats - it was all very macho. The room smelt stale and musty, like Richard;

it made Tabby squirm. How was she supposed to get comfortable with her friend's fiancé lounging about?

Tabby pulled her black fishnet stockings up over the fine blonde hair on her unshaven skinny legs. Her favourite torn denim shorts slipped over the top. A black crinkled, Metallica T-shirt completed her outfit.

With ice white porcelain skin, so fine you could see the pale blue veins underneath, no moles or scars littering her perfect skin, Tabby looked like an albino Barbie. The darker scars lay beneath the surface, buried where no one could see them, stabbing at Tabby's heart.

Looking at herself in the mirror, Tabby felt disconnected from her body. The devil in disguise. Her eyes, the colour of snowflakes reflecting on a blue sky, stared back, cold as ice, tempting her to lift a razor to her wrist. The only thing bringing comfort was knowledge that this room, this life, was an illusion. She could escape reality. If she wanted it bad enough, she could escape into a black coffin, soar above the sky with other lost souls, with her brother, Zen.

"So you're going then?" Mia's head poked its way round her bedroom door. Tabby nodded, pinching the sides of her denim shorts in the mirror. "Let me do your eye makeup, a lick of violet, hint of silver shimmer in the corners, and under your bottom lashes will make them pop."

Tabby grinned "Only if you promise to go heavy on the black liner."

"Of course." When Mia had finished with Tabby, she spun Tabby to the mirror to reveal her makeover. "Now, you're what

I call one hot vixen. Your mystery man won't be able to resist."

"You are so talented." Tabby's eyes had transformed; the cold rocks that had stared back half an hour ago were now glowing with warmth. The pale ice blue contrasted with the black, silver, violet, and gentle nudes. Tabby felt a boost of confidence.

"Gloss. Take this." Mia passed Tabby a clear tube of clear Lancôme lip gloss.

"It's your favourite."

"You've got the lips for high impact gloss," Mia appraised Tabby. "So, where are you going?"

"Some place called Montfronts."

"Wearing that?"

Tabby groaned. Her friend was beginning to sound like her mother. "Damn straight."

"Isn't it supposed to be kind of, posh?"

"If he can't handle me, then he doesn't deserve me."

"I think you should change."

"I'm leaving, now." Tabby grabbed her favourite beaten up tan leather bag and headed for the front door, averting herself from any more of Mia's waspish blows.

"Have fun," Mia said meekly.

"Don't worry," Tabby said, a wicked grin licking her plump lips. "I always do." Her white blonde hair flew down her back as she made her way out the front door.

Tabby paused at the entrance to Montfronts. This was her

favourite part of London. Refined houses in neat lines, the streets smelt of old money worn by new bodies. A white Ferrari zoomed past; the kid driving looked barely eighteen. Neighbours were heiresses or young business tycoons, a couple of wealthy imports.

She belonged here, along the rows of white houses. She'd make it - make it on her own. It didn't matter how she got to the top as long as she made it.

"Focus on the positive," she whispered to the wind. "This is the life for me," she repeated the mantra, willing it into existence, imagining posh restaurants, the clothes she'd wear, the champagne she'd drink, and the friends she'd make. A life full of luxury.

Her Mum had done it. Ravii had given her Mum a life worth craving - organic food, glam holidays, a clean home.

"This is the life for me."

Tabby almost walked past the man waiting for her at the front of Montfronts. A chic French restaurant, tucked away in Chelsea's back streets, it had always held a lure for Tabby. Candles littered the tables. Men sat in circles, wearing grey and white custom suits. Women drank from deep champagne flutes, strawberries swirling amidst bubbles sparkling like diamonds.

"Hugo," Tabby said.

"That's my name," he eyed her outfit with his soft, whisky coloured eyes. He didn't lift a brow, or turn her away.

"I'm Tabby." She held out her hand and her mandala tattoo on her left wrist glittered under the fading light, Zen's name in the centre.

Hugo took in the creature before him. She was his opposite. It was a joke; he'd kill Yves-Jacques the moment he got off the plane in Paris. He should have known better than to let his best friend – a caged playboy – pick a girl that was suitable dating material.

Tabby cocked her white eyebrows, assessing him, assessing the damage she could cause, he thought bitterly. He looked like a fool dressed in his Christian Dior cream suit, his soft pink shirt with the white orchid in the pocket, standing next to this vixen. They looked like a poodle and rottweiler sniffing each other in the street - Hugo being the poodle.

Tabby picked the flower from Hugo's pocket and tucked it behind her ear. "Does it suit me?"

"Not in the slightest." Hugo couldn't help but laugh. "Shall we eat?"

"Thought you'd never ask. I'm starving."

They made their way through the diners. Women in cashmere suits, ostrich Birkins resting on the floor, enormous diamond earrings sparkling like shards of light hitting the ocean at dawn dragging their ears down towards the floor. Tabby began to marinate in the misery of her own life. These people looked so perfect. So together.

"Are you okay?" Hugo asked as a waiter in white linens showed them to their table, an intimate spot in the back corner. A Baroque-style bookshelf loomed above them.

"Why wouldn't I be?" Tabby asked. She felt like a spud in a bed full of strawberries.

"No reason." This one's going to be a tough nut to crack,

Hugo thought, looking into Tabby's ice blue eyes. They were cold and unresponsive.

Tabby didn't feel comfortable. She knew she was underdressed and undervalued in this restaurant.

"So what do you do?" Hugo asked.

"Nothing," Tabby purred, batting the thick clumps of mascara clinging her eyelashes together in heavy sweeps. Bits of black fell loose, enhancing the dark rings underneath her eyes.

"What about you?"

"I'm a writer. I'm here promoting my new book."

"Oh, Mum said you were a property developer."

"That's the family business. I do intend to check in on a couple of investment properties that our company is looking at acquiring whilst I'm in London though. My friend, Yves-Jacques, manages the portfolio."

"Cool. Mum said you live in Paris?"

"I do. My Dad was English. He wanted his son to have a British education, so I was shipped off to Eaton. After he died of a heart attack, I had no real ties in London. My Mum was a French model. She's nomadic; I have no idea where she is at the moment, probably in a yacht off Monaco. She always spoke to my father and me in French. It's probably the reason they divorced - neither could understand the other. I moved back to Paris to be with my Granddad. He's elderly, and when I was living in London, I worried about him. I have an apartment in Knightsbridge that I stay in when I come to town."

She looks a mixture of ethereal and modern, Hugo thought. A

fairy from Lord of the Rings meets punk rock.

It was obvious why Yves-Jacques had set Hugo up with Tabby. From her white blonde hair, the charisma of careless beauty, she had no sense of elegance, no sense of fashion - but she did have something. That much was clear from the discerning glances men shot her, unabashed. She hypnotized them with the swivel of her toned bottom and the curves caressing her rough clothing. Tabby was the girl every man wanted to take home – just not to their mother.

Hugo wasn't drooling at the lips, not in the way most guys looked at her. She glanced around. A balding old geezer winked at Tabby from behind his menu. His wife stared also, no drool forming at the edges of her lips. Fire bullets did shoot from her eyes, though. Tabby fluffed her hair and the woman turned away.

"This place is so boring," Tabby said. "Maybe we should go somewhere more private?"

It dawned on Hugo; this was the reason Yves-Jacques had set him up with this girl. She was easy. What had he said to him before he'd left for London - it's easier to get over someone by getting under someone? "I'm actually quite hungry."

"You're judging me. I knew you were a snob from the moment we met."

"I don't judge," Hugo said with marked seriousness. "I observe; I don't judge."

"And what do you observe?"

"When I look at you?"

"Yes."

"A woman who's tougher on the outside than she is inside."

"Blunt. Predictable, though."

"So, you're saying I'm wrong?"

"No. I'm saying you peeled the skin from the fruit, but you didn't dig your teeth in."

"Can you take it?" Hugo asked, and Tabby noticed the way his eyes slanted at the edges when he smiled.

"You tell me."

"Okay then, pass me your hand."

"Why?"

"I need a physical connection, so I can feel you, not just see you."

"Are you sure this isn't just an excuse to hold my hand, Mr. Hugo?"

Hugo smiled. "Might be."

Tabby placed her fine China white hand on the table. Light blue veins skimmed just under the surface of her skin. She ran her tongue behind the back of her teeth, suppressing a grimace. Maybe this date hadn't been such a good idea.

Taking Tabby's hand in the palm of his own, Tabby felt the heat between their two bodies collide. "Hit me."

"I'm concentrating," Hugo said. "You need to relax." Hugo's brow furrowed together; it creased in the centre, a sharp lightning bolt wrinkle shot upwards between his brows. "Your path has been difficult, not without danger." Tabby raised a brow. "You've broken more hearts than you can count. The man in your future is tall, dark, and handsome."

"Do you have his name and address?"

"I can't tell you specifics," Hugo leaned forward, eyes twinkling under the chandeliers. "But he may well be in this restaurant. A foreigner, stopping over in London for business." Tabby rolled her eyes. "You're creative, artistic." Well that's true, thought Tabby. "You've lost something, or someone special, in the last year."

Tabby recoiled, snapping back her hand as the waitress placed a bowl of mushroom cream fettuccine in front of Tabby. Veal, on a bed of mashed potatoes and parsley for Hugo.

"Will that be all?" She asked Hugo.

Answering with a curt, "Yes, looks great," Hugo didn't take his eyes from Tabby. "Did I say something to offend you?"

"Not at all." Tabby did not want to broach the subject of Zen. "Do you always have that effect on women? - the waitress."

Hugo flushed. "The opposite, actually."

"Who was she?"

"Excuse me?"

"The woman that broke your heart. That is who you're referring to, I presume?"

"I thought I was the one giving the palm reading?"

Tabby swirled the fettuccine onto her fork, slipping a bite into her mouth. Cream and sage tickled her taste buds. This stuff was good, real good. Tabby shrugged.

Hugo sighed. "Her name's Arabella Sparks, she's a French

actress." He took a gulp of red wine and proceeded with his story.

"She did a runner," Tabby concluded.

"You are psychic. How can you tell?"

"It's written all over your face - heartbreak, betrayal, jealousy." Tabby took another bite of dinner.

"No?" Hugo ran his hand down his face, hoping to erase his emotions.

Tabby grinned. "Stop fretting. You don't have the word *dumped* tattooed across your forehead. It's the sadness in your eyes that gives it away. I've broken a few hearts in my time and all men, no matter how big, small, tall, strong or rich, get the same look. 'Am I not good enough?' Mingled with jealousy a tad of guilt and repressed anger, a love bullet scar. It's nothing to be ashamed of."

"So some of my reading was right?" Hugo asked, trying to deflect the subject away from himself.

"It was; besides the part about my *soul mate* sitting in this restaurant. But I'll give you props for trying."

"I'll drink to that," Hugo said, the hurt in his eyes flashing to a cheeky enticing laughter. The chandelier's crystals reflected into the depths of his eyes and they sparkled.

"Who taught you to read palms?" Tabby asked, curious to know how Hugo had been so accurate.

"I learnt a few odds and ends about the art from my Grandfather." Hugo blushed. "It sounds odd but he says, 'it runs in the blood.' The real key is to look at someone and observe. You can tell a lot about someone from looking into their eyes, and searching for their soul. So what sort of art are you into?"

"You tell me."

"I'm not that good at palm reading. If I were I could have predicted Arabella leaving, right?"

"I guess so. I make jewellery. When I get enough money together I'm going to open my own store, maybe in Notting Hill. I've seen this empty shop there and it would be the perfect location." Tabby stopped herself. She never shared dreams with strangers.

"I'd love to see some of your designs."

Tabby held out her fine bone wrists covered in bangles and rocks, crystals jutting out of silver knuckle rings.

"Which ones are yours?"

"All of them."

"Truly?"

"Of course."

"Tabby, I had no idea. They're beautiful."

Tabby blushed. She always felt embarrassed when someone complimented her on one of her creations, like she wasn't worthy. Biting her lips, Tabby slid her hands off the table.

"How'd you learn to make jewellery?"

"My granddad," Tabby shrugged. "See, you're not the only one with interesting relatives. Granddad was into classic designs, had a shop and everything in Cornwall before he retired to the back shed. That's where I learned."

Leaving the restaurant feeling like a content stuffed hen, Tabby glanced down at her watch: ten p.m. The night was young.

"Where to now?" Tabby asked Hugo.

Hugo swallowed. "Look, Tabby, I've had a fabulous evening but…" Here we go, thought Tabby. It's so obvious that he is not into me. "I've got to make some business calls."

Tabby forced a smile that hurt her cheekbones. "Thanks for dinner, Hugo."

Stepping so close, Tabby was sheltered from the icy wind whipping around them on the street. She felt the warmth of Hugo's breath on her cheek. He smelt like red wine – quite a lot of red wine – sandalwood aftershave and a hint of lemon. Hugo pecked Tabby on the cheek and she felt her body recoil.

"I'll call you," Hugo said, holding up his phone.

"Sure you will," Tabby replied as she edged her way down the street. His friend had set up the date through conspiring with her mum, who obviously wanted Tabby, to meet a rich, gorgeous and successful man. She knew, deep down, that she was no match for Hugo De La Laville.

* * *

Hugo watched Tabby's lithe form slip though his fingers and into the moons shadows. She was, by far, the most intriguing woman he'd ever laid eyes on. There was something about her, some etheric otherworldly charm that mesmerized him. She didn't belong on Earth; she'd do much better in a fairy tale, Hugo thought.

Despite her doll like perfection, and irresistible pout, the killer was her personality. Tabby was cold. Even when he'd held her small palm in his own large hand, he'd felt it. His granddad had always told him, 'Looks fade, but a good woman will warm your heart.' For Hugo at least there would always be Clemency.

There was a sadness hanging over Tabby's head. She was so desperate to prove herself, and yet she appeared to have nothing. To want for nothing. To have shut herself off from the joy of living. She may not have been the woman for Hugo, but he knew one thing. He wanted to help his new friend. Hugo pulled his mobile from his pocket.

"How was it? Was she everything you expected? I want all the gory details," Yves-Jacques gushed like a schoolboy into the receiver. "I'll pop into the bathroom so Poppy doesn't overhear us." A door slammed. Hugo heard a faint tinkering and then the other end of the line crackled back into life. "I told you she was stunning."

"Yves-Jacques, listen, that's not why I'm calling."

"It isn't? Was she a no show? I'm sorry, I thought I had this one in the bag. Her mum was keen to arrange the date at least."

"Yves-Jacques, relax. I'm not calling to tell you about my date; well I am in a way. Everything went well brilliant. I have a business proposition."

"Business proposition?"

"Tabby - she makes jewellery. It's unique, different. If we invest, say, one hundred thousand in a collection by her we could sell it to all of the major department stores in Paris, then Europe. It's hand crafted art, nothing bulk made in China. It's made from crystals - gems and silver so the price tag would be relatively inexpensive. What do you say?"

"You're out of your bloody mind, Hugo. I manage your property development company, not your love life. I set you up on a date with the most delicious woman on the face of the Earth, besides Poppy, and you want to make her your next business project? Did you forget that you're a writer - not a venture capitalist? You were meant to sleep together, get over Arabella, and on with your life. She's an easy lay. Not a project."

"Tabby is smart, pulled together, and she's got guts. She's really talented. Besides, I thought you wanted me to meet someone new. I thought everyone did. Wasn't that the point of this whole date?"

"I want you to get over Arabella. Everyone else wants you to meet someone new. Trust me. Once you're in a relationship, you'll regret those missed opportunities."

"Yves-Jacques," Hugo heard Poppy's voice, gentle and sweet.

"I'm on the toilet and on a business meeting. I can't talk to you now," Yves-Jacques snapped.

"I can't believe she's agreed to marry you."

"And I can't believe you want to do business with a nobody."

Hugo felt his nostrils flaring; they always did when he was mad.

"Put Poppy on the phone."

"Why?"

"She's my friend and I need to tell her something."

"About?"

"A holiday I had with one of my best mates in Ibiza."

"That was before," Yves-Jacques whispered.

"Well, then you won't mind if I tell her all the details."

"You wouldn't."

"Yes, I would."

"Look, I'll consider giving Tabby a chance. On one condition."

"What's that?"

"Call her and take the time to get to know her better socially before you take her in, like some stray cat."

"Okay, it's a deal."

Hugo was - however much he wanted to deny it - very pleased at the idea of spending some more time with this tabby cat.

CHAPTER SIX

BUDS BLOSSOMING

"*D*arling, how are you? I haven't seen you in ages. Not since before you left me - for London. Before, dare I say it? Fleur. You promised you'd call! How was the London leg of your book tour?"

Hugo's apartment still looked like the home of a loveless bachelor. Sure, it was clean - his housemaid kept it spotless. But the lilies on the white cabinet that matched the white walls that matched the barren coffee table that matched the couch all looked so unloved.

"I'm sorry. I meant to. The book tour was a success, according to my agent. I felt like a fraud discussing love in Paris when my love life is so non-existent. All I could think about was Arabella, what she's been doing, how she is."

"And Fleur?"

"It's just, well, you know how much I hate people meddling with my relationships. It's putting sticky fingers where they don't belong. I was so mad at you."

"Oh dear," Clemency said with the regal air of someone not

bothered by her naughtiness at all. "Have you forgiven me now?"

"Yes. Of course - you know how much I adore you."

"Good. Then you can tell me about your date with Fleur," Clemency said, arching her back on Hugo's white leather couch before cracking her knuckles.

"Disgusting," Hugo said.

"You didn't like Miss. Fleur? I mean, darling, she has blossomed from a wilting flower into a rose."

"Not Fleur. Cracking your knuckles - it's a disgusting habit."

"So I'm disgusting and she's?"

"She took my breath away," Hugo admitted. "She was so hot, radiating sex appeal like a beacon. She turned me into a blubbering mess."

He slid next to Clemency on the couch. Their knees brushed together as Hugo leant forward and poured two steaming mugs of Harney and Sons vanilla tea.

"Those are big words for a little boy," Clemency purred.

"Alright, enough teasing. You sent me into that library unarmed. I had no ammunition, no clue what to say, do or how to act when I laid eyes on her."

"Who knew libraries could be such dangerous places?"

Hugo ran his hands through his hair. The afternoon sun filtering through the bay windows made the subtle streaks of auburn in his dark hair glow in the light. His eyes bounced of the rays shining deep amber.

"She has you wound up tight as a cuckoo clock. I've discovered a woman who can make you go mad with lust!"

"It's not lust."

"Love?" Clemency feigned shock. The way she bounced her head, her voice smooth like a kitten, reminded Hugo of old-world movie stars, like Delphine Seyrig.

"I don't know what it is. You're right though; it's making me crazy. Doing my head in. I mean when I first met Fleur, I thought she was the one. My sweetheart. The first girl to capture my heart, but then something about the whole relationship felt empty, like part of the puzzle was missing."

"I know what it was."

"You do?"

"Of course - you're a guy. It's obvious, isn't it?" Hugo shot Clemency a look saying, if it were so obvious, he wouldn't be confused. Clemency sighed, and looked at him as though he were a cute, docile puppy dog. "You weren't attracted to Fleur at the time."

"Yes, I was. I loved her. She stole my heart."

"Heart yes, penis no."

"That's ridiculous."

"That's men. Fleur was all books, glasses, and puppy fat. Plus, the girl couldn't pull a matching outfit together to save her life. She was a walking disaster. Sweet, yes. Sexually attractive, no."

"She was never ugly, if that's what you're implying."

"Not ugly but you were out of her league, what with your roguish, aristocratic good looks, even if you were a perpetual bookworm."

"I was a late bloomer and you know it. More interested in comic books than looks."

Clemency ignored Hugo and continued to tell him of the fatal flaws that had left him single and alone. "All men want to marry their mothers, dressed in the body of a supermodel. Someone nurturing, caring to his every whim, and looking like she just stepped out from the pages of Vogue magazine.

"That is not true. What about men who don't know their mothers? My mother was a model and I barely know her. What about gay men?"

"They want their Daddies."

"That's ridiculous. You are ridiculous. I can't believe I thought it was a good idea to invite you over to my house for advice."

"Who else could you invite? Yves-Jacques and that hideous money grabbing fiancée of his? He's terrible when it comes to understanding women. Treats them all like slabs of meat. Face it - you need me. Solid advice from a solid woman."

Hugo snorted. "None of your advice makes sense; it never does. By the way, did Yves-Jacques tell you he set me up with a woman in London?"

"Oui, I'm sure it was a catastrophe."

Hugo grunted. "She was nice, sweet even. The sort of woman I'd like to be friends with. But compared to Fleur, well ughh, I feel so confused. How am I supposed to ever move on?"

"Open your mind, mon chéri. If Fleur was so perfect, then why did you kiss me all those years ago and ruin the relationship?"

"I had to be positive there was nothing between us. Clear my head so that as my and Fleur's relationship progressed I wouldn't have three kids, a beautiful house, and hit midlife, only to realise that I was always in love with my best friend."

"That's a lie."

Hugo was shocked. It was the story he'd consoled himself with for years and now, Clemency, dared to shatter it? "It's what I believe."

"We all tell false truths to make us feel better about the world we live in, about the cruel terrible people we really are."

"My best friend thinks I'm cruel and terrible?"

"Not everything I say refers to you."

Clemency took another sip of the sweet smelling vanilla tea. Hugo let his tea cup warm the palm of his hands as he watched his friend, entranced. He'd never seen Clemency look so open, so vulnerable, as though she were on the verge of spilling some secret that had been winding her up like a rope.

"So why did you kiss me all those years ago?"

"I just did."

"The truth."

Hugo let out a deep breath. "Because when you walked into that party, I watched how every man, woman and child turned to look at you. It was like all the air was taken from the room and twisted in a cyclone spinning round the dress you were wearing. The one made from layers of lilac tulle."

"The Chanel one," Clemency whispered.

"Because in that moment, no one existed in my world, but you. It felt more real than anything I had experienced before, and I thought - for a second - I didn't love you as a best friend. Maybe I was *in* love with you. And now you know why I am going to hell. I can't keep my eyes on one woman."

Clemency's blonde curls didn't jangle around her face like normal. They were still, as if no breeze could ever lift them because they weighed a thousand pounds of gold.

"And when we kissed?"

"I realised the truth. That you're my best friend - nothing more. Even though I'll always love you, it'll never be that big love. The one I'm hunting for."

Clemency shook herself as though recovering from a hazy daydream. "I think you remembered me. You saw through my Chanel. The beautiful woman who'd make a terrible mother, looking at recipe books makes me cross-eyed, cleaning is the most boring thing in the world, I don't even like grocery shopping," Clemency shuddered.

"I remembered you, my funny, vibrant, smart, catty best friend. Clemency, what's this really about? I love you, who you are; you're an amazing woman. I wouldn't change you for the world."

"I know how men think, Hugo. That's why every time I date a new guy I give him this," she ran her hands over her petite body, smoothing her white dress. "Why I order meals and pretend I cooked them, why I have my laundry set up like I just folded the linens. Why I pretend to like children."

"Clemency. No guy will ever give you the love you deserve." Hugo didn't know how the conversation had twisted to him giving dating advice.

"He can't?"

"That love - that really big love you're looking for - it comes from within." Hugo pounded his chest like Tarzan and he looked just as fierce and brave. He'd just had a major insight. Turning his words back on himself, he realised that no woman could give him what he was really looking for. He needed to learn to love himself.

"I don't believe you," Clemency said, standing up, brushing the corners of her eyes as though trying to hide invisible tears. She picked up her pale blue Birkin.

"Where are you going?" Hugo asked.

"Out."

And before Hugo could stop her, Clemency had evacuated his apartment. Hugo felt the clap of thunder as the front door slammed. He was still just as confused about women. He hadn't even gotten Clemency's advice on the ones haunting him: Fleur, Sophia, and now Tabby. His life was a mess and he needed an escape route.

CHAPTER SEVEN

CHOCOLATE AND BIJOUX

"I'm winning," Clemency sung as she squeezed into her chair. Angelina's, Paris's most famous restaurant for hot chocolates and cake, was buzzing.

"Bonjour," Poppy smiled, trying her best to win Clemency over. Her 'to be' sister-in-law scanned her attire.

The hum of excited tourists filled the air. "It's so noisy here. Remind me why you wanted to come?" Clemency glared at her brother.

"Poppy wanted to see the place."

"I read about it on TripAdvisor. It's something of a Parisian institution. Isn't this the most exquisite restaurant you've ever set foot in? I feel like I'm about to dine in a jewellery box."

"It's beautiful, I guess." Clemency shrugged as though the beauty of the restaurant with its high ceilings, gold painted cornices and moulding, and cakes that sparkled like exquisite jewels behind lit glass windows was something she saw every day.

"It was a famous haunt of Coco Chanel, Audrey Hepburn, and Proust. It's so glamorous; I can't wait to taste the Mont Blanc meringues decorated with ropes of chestnut puree. They make the best hot chocolate in Paris. I read about them on this great blog."

"Fascinating," Clemency said, sounding the least bit interested.

"You haven't *won* anything, yet," Yves-Jacques said returning to the original subject, pulling at the collar of his pink linen shirt. "So at least prétendre to be nice."

"Oui, if you insist," Clemency said. Dressed in a cream merino skirt and loose cashmere jumper, her blonde curls pulled back into a tight chignon, Clemency oozed glamour. She made Poppy's outfit of jeans and a puffy pale blue parker look, and feel, disastrous. "The building is beautiful; our mother used to take us here for hot chocolates when we were little. I loved it. Now, I feel it's like going to the zoo, foreigners staring, trying to figure out who's French and who isn't. They spoil the surrounding natural beauty."

"But you look beautiful. The only reason people look at you is because you are so French looking," Poppy said.

Clemency half-smiled as she took a sip of water from the glass the waiter had poured for her. "I thought darling Hugo was joining us?"

"He is, in half an hour. I thought we should meet earlier, discuss our progress. I think Hugo seems happier. I mean, he shaved before he left for England; that's a good sign. And despite you thinking that you've won our competitive little bet on the side, Clemency, the truth is I think I've already won."

"You didn't say anything," Poppy said, pulling her eyes from the luxury of Belle Epoque architecture.

"I wanted to keep it a surprise. I think Hugo's slept with the woman I set him up with in England."

Clemency laughed, a delicate tinkling laugh as light as a bird. "Who cares who he sleeps with? The bet is which woman will steal his heart."

"I thought we were just trying to get him out of his rut?"

"No!" Poppy said.

"Non!" Clemency exclaimed.

"That's disgusting, Yves-Jacques. I thought Frenchmen were romantic?"

"Having second thoughts about the wedding?" Clemency asked Poppy.

"No, it's just I thought we were trying to rebuild Hugo's love life, to find him someone he wants to live for. Someone who makes him complete."

"The moment we slept together, I lost my heart," Yves-Jacques said to Poppy.

"Well, I guess that's sweet."

"We need some guidelines. How are we going to choose a winner?"

"The winner," Poppy said, "is whoever chooses the woman, Hugo falls in *love* with."

"It has nothing to do with who he sleeps with before her," Clemency added.

"Because we wouldn't want to take advantage of a woman," Poppy said.

"Exactly."

"But we will manipulate them to fall in love with our Hugo?" Yves-Jacques inquired.

"Who's being manipulative? You either love someone or you don't. We're simply making our friend happy."

"Yes," Poppy said in a voice that indicated she was trying to reassure herself of their great plan.

"Okay," Yves-Jacques said. "I think it's best I agree with you both. Now we each name the woman we've chosen for Hugo."

"Well, I picked Sophia Rupert; he met her out of his own accord. She's a New Yorker and soon to be a foreigner in Paris, like me! She's coming here to learn how to cook and explore the city; it's natural. Real. It's what love is supposed to be - two people meeting by chance."

"Oh, and you haven't helped them out at all?" Clemency asked, eyes wide, all innocent.

"Well, I may have booked her hotel and offered to give her a lift from the airport."

"I don't think we should be interfering in Hugo's relationships more than we need to," Clemency said sternly.

"But I didn't. I was trying to get them together."

"And you did. So now I say we take a step back and watch what happens. Let's not interfere more than we need to, that would be manipulation."

"I'm afraid Clemency does have a point, Chérubin."

"But, Sophia and I are going to the Louvre together."

Nerissa Marie

"Tell her you've gone home to Australia," Clemency said. "I'm sure she won't mind."

Poppy scowled.

"And you, Clemency, who have you chosen?" Yves-Jacques interrupted before things became too heated between the women.

"Fleur Lachapelle."

"Non! That's not allowed."

"Who's Fleur?" Poppy asked.

"Hugo's first love. He never quite got over her," Clemency purred.

"Why did they break up?"

"Yes, Clemency, would you like to tell us what, or should I say who, came between Fleur and Hugo?"

"Non, it's beside the point."

"It sounds like a good story," Poppy said, hoping some girl talk would help Clemency warm towards her.

"Oh look, here's Hugo," Clemency jumped up from the table and waved to Hugo. "Don't want him to wait in the queue out front. I'll bring him to us."

Wrapped in a warm cashmere grey scarf, with his dark hair curling at the edges and eyes sparkling like a naughty schoolboy, it was hard to imagine why no woman had ever committed to Hugo.

"We were just talking about you," Clemency said as he kissed her warm cheeks and sat down beside her.

• 83 •

"I've rethought the Tabitha situation," Yves-Jacques said just before Hugo's gorgeous rump felt the Louis chair.

"I didn't realise we had a situation?" Clemency said.

"Her name's Tabby," Hugo said.

"Wonderful, bring her to Paris," Yves-Jacques said. "I'm sure there's a spare apartment she can stay in during her trip. Let me sort out the details. Tell her we think her art is fabulous and we'd like to support her rise to success," Yves-Jacques concluded, looking happy with himself.

"Her art is jewellery. Don't you want to see it first?"

"Doesn't matter, Hugo. The important thing is I trust you. I mean, you trust me enough to let me manage your family's property portfolio."

"Yes. I guess."

"So make the call."

"Oui, I'll do it."

"How do you think she'll react to the invitation?" Clemency purred.

"She'll be ecstatic, I'm sure."

"I mean, what woman wouldn't want to move to Paris to have their very own jewellery line funded?" Poppy said.

"Sounds like you're investing a lot in this business *relationship*," Clemency's bright blue eyes hovered over her brother.

Was it just Hugo or did his friends seem a little jumpy?

CHAPTER EIGHT

AU REVOIR NEW YORK

It had taken several long conversations with Ollie before Sophia had decided that what she needed was a holiday. A trip to Paris, Ollie had advised, 'would soothe her soul.' He hadn't been too keen on the idea that Sophia would just disappear on Charles. However, after some consideration on the matter, the two of them concluded that Charles wouldn't notice Sophia's absence, and if it did give him a fright, maybe he would dedicate more time to their crumbling marriage. Besides on her way home from Paris, she could spend some time with much adored Mummy and Daddy.

Sophia knew if she informed her husband of her intended trip he would ask all sorts of questions and she would soon find herself spilling the beans about Hugo, and there was nothing to tell. Yet.

Feeling a little guilty, Sophia left a note on the marble kitchen bench reading: *Gone to Paris and England, be back in one month, need to think about our marriage, the A-cup bra incident, and what I want for the future.* Sophia picked up her trusty Louis Vuitton case and headed for the glass, gold framed doors.

"Have a good trip," Paul, her friendly doorman said, winking as he bowed his white and gold rimmed cap.

"Thank you," Sophia replied as the doors swung open to reveal a glorious, sunny New York day.

Sophia had always liked Paul. He wore a cheerful smile, though deep down she felt embarrassed that someone else knew how many nights she spent alone at home, waiting for her husband. Sometimes she felt as though this middle-aged doorman knew more about her day than her husband.

What would Paul think if he knew she was doing a disappearing act on Charles? Best not to find out.

"Taxi," Sophia threw her left arm into the wind and waved. A yellow cab screeched to a halt.

"Sophia? Sophia!"

One red Salvatore Ferragamo shoe raised in midstep crashed down to Earth, straight into a puddle. Water soaked into the shoe's silky fabric. "Eeeewww."

Sophia's heart begun to pound and her breath ran short, her lungs tightened, constricting with anxiety. Her mouth opened, her tongue felt dry and solid like a brick.

"Darling, what's the matter with you? Why haven't you answered me? I've been calling all day but you didn't pick up your phone. I thought something was wrong."

Charles. Red hair that had grown out in the last few months flopped in front of his face. He looked smart in his charcoal suit. Sophia liked the plaid pale blue shirt he wore underneath. Charles looked good. He also looked worried.

"What are you doing home? I thought you were at the office today."

"I am, I was. I thought we could go for lunch. Last night you were talking in your sleep."

"Really, what was I saying?"

"Nothing I could make out. I think you were speaking French. I thought I'd better check up on you." Charles stopped short. "Why are you carrying my Louis Vuitton suitcase?"

"You were worried about me?"

"Of course I was. You've been distant lately."

"I've been distant? How can you say that - when you're never home? Besides, you're the one who never bothered to explain the *A-cup bra* situation to me."

Charles's cheeks flushed hot pink. "Where do you think you're going?"

"I'm leaving, Charles."

"For a short trip? To visit your mother? England?" He looked hopeful and lost, as reality crashed down. Horns blared; the sound of car wheels grating along the road, people conversing as they flashed past in a rush melted into the background.

"Paris."

"Paris? Here, taxi, stop. You need to unload the boot; we don't need a cab anymore. Paul, come and grab madam's suitcase. She's not well."

The driver grumbled. Sophia stuck her head in the window. "I need a cab. Stay right where you are."

"Then hurry up, lady. I don't got all day."

"I'll pay double." Sophia pulled her head from the window. She smiled an odd smile at Charles, and a single tear caressed her cheek. "I didn't want to hurt you. I'm doing this for me. It's selfish, I know."

"You can't just leave! You're my wife." Charles turned his privileged nose to the sun. Sophia loved the way it rounded like a pebble at the tip. "What are you going to do in Paris?" His moustache quivered in the light.

"I'm going to Paris to learn how to cook. My lifelong dream. Then i'll visit Mummy and Daddy on the way home." She didn't mention Hugo; that was a need to know basis - the man who turned her real *Parisian Dream* into a reality. "Goodbye Charles," Sophia said, climbing into the yellow cab.

Charles ran forward and grabbed the cab's window as the engine purred and began to pull away from the curb. "Sophia, things can't end like this. It's not proper. Besides, you don't know how to cook; all you do is eat!"

"Then come." For once in his life, Charles, the man Sophia loved to hate, was rendered speechless. "Come to Paris with me."

"Now?"

"Our lives aren't slowing down. For so long I've felt like the pause-button is controlling my life, whilst the world moves on around me in fast-forward."

"Sophia, don't leave, not like this."

"Come."

"I have to work."

"We have enough money. Let's do something adventurous together."

"I can't."

Sophia felt her insides closing down. For a moment, she had felt the warm spark of hope, maybe Charles would do something spontaneous.

"Then forget you ever knew me. Because I am ready to live."

CHAPTER NINE

MAGNIFIQUE PARIS

ophia sucked in a great gulp of Parisian air. It tasted like French toast, croissants sprinkled with cinnamon, and a mug of hot chocolate. The flight had taken what seemed like a million hours. Her eyelids felt like heavy weights. Still she'd taken a first-class trip to heaven and arrived in style.

"Madame, we're here," the chauffeur at the helm of the black Mercedes turned to Sophia. The driver seemed nice enough; still she was a bit disappointed to have received the text from Poppy, Hugo's friend, when she'd touched down in Paris, saying she couldn't meet her at the airport, but had generously organized a chauffeur.

"Fabulous," Sophia replied, peeling her eyes away from the luscious building before her. It was early evening and the gloomy grey Paris sky didn't threaten Sophia's sense of awe as she arrived at the Ritz's doorstep. This place should be the eighth wonder of the world, Sophia thought, delighted with her new lodgings. Lights, tinted with warm golden rays, shone up the sides of the white stone hotel. "Magnificent."

"Let me get your door, Madame." The driver hopped, skipped,

and jumped to Sophia's door. As her rear rose from its cushy, cream leather seat, he slammed the car door, propelling her onto the streets of Paris.

Sophia stepped forward, empowered, ready for fun, excitement, and adventure. The first day of the rest of her life.

"Je suis maison. I'm home." She repeated in English.

"Madame, I am so sorry. Embarrassant."

"For what?" Sophia squinted at her fair-haired driver, whose face was lit with a horrified expression.

"I had no idea."

No idea? Did the young chap know Sophia had just walked out on her marriage, escaped New York for a Parisian dream – and the chance to see the hunkiest man Sophia had ever met?

"It's okay," Sophia assured the driver – along with herself. "I'm capable of taking care of myself. Everything is under control." Sophia beamed her most self-assured, trust-me smile.

The driver's face didn't flinch.

"Your skirt," he mumbled.

"My skirt. Jupe. I'm speaking French already! Yes, it's lovely isn't it? Vintage Yves Saint Lauren, very French chic. Merci. When I saw it I said, 'oui, that skirt belongs in Paris'. It's made for cobblestoned streets and sidewalk cafes." Sophia looked down to admire her pastel pink silk skirt. She loved how it hugged at her body with such lightness it felt like wearing air. "My skirt." Now it was Sophia's turn to look horrified. "I was wearing it a minute ago." She touched her thrumpy, white calves. Elastic from her stockings gripped her thighs. Her legs felt like ice. Naked ice.

Twisting to the Mercedes door, Sophia swore as she caught the glimmer of her designer skirt, clasped in its jaws. The Mercedes now looked like a naughty puppy, one that had stolen her favourite piece of clothing and slashed it to bits.

A man with white blonde hair and black shades, looking very much like Karl Lagerfeld, looked down at Sophia from the top of the steps. His entourage included a thin woman who glared at Sophia as though she disrupted the beauty of Paris. Another fellow carrying both a briefcase and child winked at Sophia as he passed, followed by a stream of porters and stacked luggage.

"I have a, how do you say, solution?"

Sophia's driver - while she'd been standing mummified, suspended in shock - had slipped to the front of the car and removed several tourist maps. With nimble fingers he unwrapped the paper and twirled the maps around Sophia's waist. This was not how she'd planned her debut stay at the Ritz.

"Thank goodness I wasn't wearing a dress," Sophia joked. The driver didn't bat an eyelid. Sophia decided it might be best if she kept her mouth shut or, better yet, her eyes closed. She took three deep breaths. "I choose to think positive thoughts." Sophia said out loud. She'd been engrossed in Louise Hay's, *You Can Heal Your Life,* on the way over and knew this utterly embarrassing moment would fade into the oblivion of all such moments. "I am a positive, empowered woman."

"I'll take your bags, Madame?" The driver asked.

"Yes, please see to my bags," Sophia said. With the confidence of a French princess, she marched up the steps of the Ritz.

After checking in and bolting to the lifts with her map skirt in place, she breathed out. Just as the doors were about to close, the white haired man she'd seen on the steps jumped in beside her.

"Bonsoir," Sophia said, aware that hiding in the corner of the lift wouldn't make her invisible.

As it reached the second floor, Sophia's lift companion turned to her. Black glasses blocked all expression on his face but the light tilt of the corners of his lips made Sophia think he was smiling. "The look suits you, so feminine, so real, so chic. Maps, a statement to the arts, travel, culture - you look magnifique. Perhaps I shall draw inspiration from your creativity in my next collection."

"Next collection? Me? But of course. Wait, it's you! My style icon, Karl Lagerfield." The lift door shut behind Karl as he exited on the third floor before Sophia could ask for an autograph or a French, two cheek fashion air kiss.

She thought she heard the rumble of laughter as the lift shot up, but who could be sure. One thing she did realize was that her shock had made her forget her skirt and she'd been doing all the talking with her hands. A trail of maps swam at the shores of her feet.

* * *

By ten a.m. the next day, Sophia had consumed three croissants, two Pain au Chocolat, Croque Monsieur, and one small serving of escargots. Feeling rather full, she decided to walk to the Arc de Triomphe, rather than take the *Hop-On Hop-Off* bus, which she'd bought a day pass for.

Ollie rang as she was walking past a delightful display of macaroons, which sung to her from a bakery window.

"Darling, how is Paris? Are you fluent in French already? How's the food? Have you eaten in all the fabulous restaurants? Better yet, how are the men? I've heard Frenchmen taste divine."

Sophia couldn't help herself. She laughed out loud. Just hearing Ollie's voice made her feel better inside. He was like a big bowl of fresh double cream you planned on eating scoop by scoop in front of, *Breakfast at Tiffany's*, on a Friday night. No one in the world knew her most intimate thoughts better than Ollie.

"Alas, I can't tell you. I haven't tasted any Frenchmen, but I think I met Karl Lagerfeld in the lifts at The Ritz."

"No way! Tell me everything."

"He was just like in the fashion magazines, a style icon. Cool, calm, collected."

"What were you wearing?"

"Oh, nothing really," Sophia said with a grimace.

"Did he introduce you to any seductive male models?"

"No! You shouldn't even be suggesting such things. You know I'm a married woman. Well, that's if Charles still loves me and wants to salvage something. I left my marriage behind in tatters." Sophia tried to keep from crying, but a tear slid down her cheek like a cold wet ice block.

"Charles is so bland. I can't imagine he'd be the slightest bit exciting in bed. Promiscuity is just what the doctor ordered. I think I should enrol in medical school and become an expert in happiness! Imagine all the doctors I'd meet!"

"Charles is not bad in bed! When he's not distracted, that is." Why did Ollie insist on bringing Charles up in conversation? She was halfway across the globe. Still it was impossible to escape guilty thoughts about abandoning her husband.

"We all know how *busy* Charles is. Honestly, darling, there's no denying that you married a pretentious twat. Charles treats his business as though it's the leading lady in his life and you know it. He can't see what he's got in you: a woman who loves him, who'd die for him. If you did shack up with Prince Charming over there, it'd teach him a lesson. You are not a woman to be trifled with. You are a woman of principles and moral standards! That you are a woman who demands, no, deserves to be loved."

Sophia went quiet. She knew that - although not everything - some of what Ollie said was the truth. Charles had neglected her since the day she'd said, 'I do'. It wasn't that he didn't want her to be happy, or didn't want to spend time with her.

Charles Rupert loved nothing more than to win. Sophia had been won, and although she hated to admit it, she felt like she'd been shoved onto the back shelf with one of his old football trophies. He polished her on occasion, when she took his fancy, then returned her to the shelf where he could gaze upon his victory from a distant standpoint. After the *bra-in-suitcase* incident, she'd been pushed to the back of the shelf, a new trophy in sight.

"Sweetie, why are you so quiet? What are you thinking of? The horrors you got up to last night! Could it be that my Cinderella has fallen off the pumpkin carriage and met her prince?"

"That's not how the story goes. Cinderella is single. Charles and I, well, I don't know what we are right now."

"Everything needs embellishment; make your life sparkle darling."

Sophia walked past another bakery opposite Jardin des Tuileries Park. The window was loaded with bagels and croissants.

"How's Hugo? Describe what the stud looks like naked."

"Stud?"

"It's part of my new repertoire. I'm dating a new man, Jamie. He's from Texas," Ollie added, as though this explained his new fancy to rodeo language.

"There are no men in sight. There's a mother wheeling a toddler in a pram up the street, a sweet elderly couple with paper thin crumpled cheeks sharing a bagel on a park bench across the road."

"Embellish, darling, embellish."

"I haven't seen Hugo yet. We'll meet in the next couple of days; he's been sending me texts. I'm keeping things casual. He's been in London."

"I'm starving for some delicious gossip."

"The only delectable thing in sight is a tray full of macaroons. They come in the most beautiful colours: lilac, pale green, pastel pink with gold leaf glitter. Mmmm, délicieux."

Ollie groaned, "I should've known."

"Wee monsieur," Sophia retorted. "You're not the only one with a new repertoire."

"I am soooo jel. If I weren't so busy with the Haberdashery store I'd have come with you. Keep me posted on the man front. Remember, cheating overseas is not the same as cheating in America. You're in a new country; there are new rules."

"According to whom?"

"Me, darling. Call me Dr. Love. I'm sure Charles sticks to them every time he leaves the state."

"Charles has never cheated on me, Ollie." A lump formed in Sophia's heart that burned. Why was she bothering to defend Charles? Did she even love him anymore? Did he love her?

"And how would you know? You said yourself he's always too busy for sex. That means one thing. He's getting it from someone else."

"Ollie! How could you? I know you and Charles don't see eye to eye on everything. But do you need to rub his face in the dirt?"

"Don't I? Everyone's heard the rumours."

"Are you on about Charles and his secretary again? That's nonsense. How many times do I have to tell you? The young woman was found with her pants down in his office as a bee had climbed into her pants and stung her! She was trying to change her outfit."

"Whilst he watched? How often have you even seen a bee here? New York is concrete jungle, not the Amazon."

"Let's not get into this now, Ollie. I'm in Paris. I want to relax. I need to have fun. I need to figure out what I want in my life for a change, instead of worrying about what everyone else thinks."

"Yes, you do. You need to open your eyes and realise the world is your oyster. I'm proud of you and I wish I'd come with."

"Miss you too, darling. I have to go…"

"Mwah, love you loads. Remember what I said. Let your hair down, have fun, do something dangerous. I want you to be happy."

"I am happy," Sophia replied, lifting the corners of her lips in a false smile, imagining that Ollie was before her.

"Don't play the happy card with me, darling. I want you to find joy from within."

"I'll do my best. Bye."

"Toodles."

Sophia hung up, muting Ollie's exaggerated kisses. She loved the man but there were times when he made her feel as naïve as a puppy.

CHAPTER TEN

THE HEART OF ART

"I want the vintage cherub sconce, on the right wall. The right!" Fleur ran her thin pianist fingers though her short black hair; it was in desperate need of a trim. If she weren't careful, blonde roots would start to appear at the tip of her scalp.

The furniture removal company Luxe Magazine had hired to disentangle Diego Piucci Palomo's apartment were clumsy and grumpy. On an average day, this would have driven Fleur crazy. But today, Fleur was in a good mood.

Last night Hugo and Fleur's date had been unbeatable. When they'd broken up six years ago, she'd vowed to change her life and appearance so if they ever ran into each other again, he would be stunned by her beauty and success.

"Can you pass me that painting?" Fleur nodded to a giant piece. The background colour was white, splashed with pastel tones and a giant red ankh stood out from the front. "We'll hang it above the couch. Where is a tradesman when you need one? Chantal, pass me the drill; I'll hang it myself."

Her assistant was quick and sharp. Fleur knew if she left

Chantal alone for too long, she'd busy herself with the task of taking over her head interior stylist position in the magazine.

"Maybe I can be of assistance?" A male voice floated through grunts of men maneuvering a huge marble coffee table into the centre of the room. The man was tall, chubby but not fat, and a large black beard wrapped around his square chin.

There was something familiar about the figure before her, but Fleur was in too much of a hurry to figure out what it was. Sure he was gorgeous, with exotic good looks but Fleur was positive she'd remember him if they'd met before. "That drill over there; use it to create a hole for the wall plug so we can hang this picture above the chesterfield."

Chantal ran for the drill and passed it to the builder with one swift movement. Her eyes were wide and she panted at his feet like a puppy. She's acting as though she's on heat, Fleur thought.

"So you want the painting hung here?" The builder asked, standing on top of the old chesterfield, which had deep cracks running down the leather.

"Up a little higher and a little to the left."

The drill cut through stone walls, sounding like thunder.

Fleur darted from left to right, throwing cushions onto Louis Chairs and moving furniture around as though she were playing with a doll's house.

"Do you always change so much when you do interior photo shoots?" The builder asked. He poked a large screw between his lips and recovered a hammer from under the couch.

"The brief was for a French minimalist artist studio. It looks as though a bomb went off ten years ago and no one's bothered to clean up, ever."

"Maybe it's the artist's way of spreading his wings."

"It's an artist's impression of hiding who he really is so he can escape from the world into this hovel and pretend he doesn't matter anymore."

"You presume to know a lot about the artist."

"I don't need to. The art does all the talking."

"You haven't used any of the nude figures."

"They look like pieces done by a middle aged man who has no refinement and the only joy he can find is through sensual pleasures."

Chantal snorted into her coffee. Fleur turned and glared at her assistant who turned and busied herself fluffing large black and white cushions, scattering them about on the floor as makeshift seats.

The builder didn't laugh at Fleur. He set his big brown eyes on her pinched, scowling face, studying her shrivelled, prudish soul from the inside out.

"You seem like a woman who has been greatly hurt by men. For that, I am sorry. Art is not supposed to bring joy; it's supposed to make people feel. To touch something deep inside. Your reaction would give any artist confidence. Thank you."

"Well, it shouldn't. Half of this stuff is overpriced junk; the other half - let's just say you wouldn't find it hanging it in my living room."

At this, Chantal made a strangled, gurgling sound. Fleur

didn't have time to ask her what the matter was because the photographer and his crew had arrived. A flamboyant flurry of people, all dressed in black, with the photographer alone in black boots, red pants, black leather jacket, and a red beret. The instant he laid eyes on Fleur, he swept across the room and kissed both cheeks.

"Fleur, darling, it's been what - three weeks? Where have you been hiding?"

Fleur blushed, thinking of the weekend she'd spent shacked up in Hugo's luxurious apartment.

"I've been busy with Luxe Magazine, Michel."

"Liar. You're glowing. Whatever, or whomever, you're taking, I need some of him. Spill, who's created this daydream before my eyes?"

"Daydream?"

"You never wear pink, Fleur. You belong to the black fashion crowd."

"Look, I understand what you're saying, Michel. But people change. I've changed."

Michel snorted. "Looks to me like you've fallen in love. You've lost your haughty glow; you're blossoming into a sweet rose."

Fleur rolled her eyes. She shot Michel a look that said the ice maiden lives on, and went to busy herself with the rest of the shoot. She knew that in Paris everyone had a reputation to uphold. She'd worked hard for the past fifteen years, cultivating herself into a force that could be reckoned with. No matter what Hugo offered her, Michel seeing the change in her demeanour was not a good thing.

She hadn't come this far to lose sight of the big picture. Fleur Lachapelle had dreams and ambitions that no man would interfere with.

Straightening out the leopard print rug laying in a dishevelled flop on the living room floor, Fleur put her hands on her hips and began to hum to herself. It was a gorgeous rug, woven from soft wool. She'd be sure to find Diego after the shoot and see if he could find it in his heart to part with the dear old thing. It would look amazing in her bedroom.

Thinking of bedrooms, she set off wandering through the kitchen made from white washed wood, marble bench tops and a chandelier hanging over the island bench. Pieces of artwork lined the bench, laying in a scattered mess against the wall; the sink was full of paintbrushes and smelt like turpentine. At least this room wouldn't need any modification.

She found the bedroom and gasped when she discovered Hugo, sitting on the bed. He looked like he was waiting for her, from the dark recesses of her dreams. Hair tied in a loose ponytail, his silver rings glittered under the light, capturing specks of dust from the open bay wood framed, white window.

"Hugo?"

"Fleur?" He answered in unison, in his husky, sexy voice.

Fleur ran her fingers down the pink silk dress she was wearing. Her black calf length boots, tops hidden by a soft rim of black lace at the bottom of the dress clenched her thighs, cutting off her circulation. She stood dead straight and still it was all she could do to prevent herself from collapsing onto the circular bed.

"What are you doing here?" She pushed her black bob behind her ears and tried to pat down her hair. She needn't have bothered; her hair was neat as a pin. "Have you been stalking me?" She added in a soft flirtatious tone.

"I have - you left your diary at my place. I thought you might need it." He handed her a worn leather book. "I met Diego as I was coming in and he said I could wait for you in here. A retreat from the madness." She softened and a soft pink blush crept up her neck and flushed her cheeks. She felt like a schoolgirl, unable to compose herself. "Would you like to grab lunch?" Hugo asked. His white semi-see through shirt clung to his thin waist and Fleur could see the outline of his sparrow tattoo resting on his chest.

"Since you're here, can you help me put this bed together?" The black sheets sat in a crumpled mess and a black fur stole dangled on the edge of the bed.

"Of course. So are you available for lunch?"

"I can't. I have a feeling this photo shoot is going to take all day. We could tomorrow?" Fleur replied, her tone losing its harsh edge.

"I like a woman who's in control." Hugo winked. "If only this were my room."

Fleur blushed. What was wrong with her? Hugo was acting so sleazy but it made her want him more. She had to regain composure.

"It takes more than a wink to get me in bed," Fleur muttered. "Come on help me make it, we'll be photographing this room."

"You're different, you know," Hugo said.

Together, they pulled the base sheet, tucking it under the circular mattress. Fleur couldn't help thinking this is how life would be if they settled. They'd share a bed every night. Every morning they'd make it together.

"How so?"

"Your hair is much neater. I always remember it being curly."

"I straighten it every morning."

"It's not just your looks, though. It's like you know what you want. Sometimes, and I don't mean this in a bad way, you used to follow me round."

"Followed you?"

Fleur knew Hugo didn't mean it in a negative way. There'd been a time when she'd hung on his every word. He was smart, funny, and seemed so mature. Perhaps that's what happened to men who'd lost their father at a young age - they didn't have a choice, they became the man of the house. She'd always admired Hugo as a young writer with ambitions. He was her own Ernest Hemmingway.

"You seemed naïve of the world. Now, I find myself looking at you, wondering what to expect. What you're going to do next. I'd always guess before; now I don't have a clue. It's like when I asked you to lunch earlier - I expected you to say yes. The old Fleur was always free for lunch. Now you're different.

I like that you're in control. Some people spend their whole life drifting. Hell, I feel like I'm bobbing around the ocean on a tug boat all the time. You cut through the waves like an ocean liner; it's sexy."

They locked eyes. Chantal broke the spell by coming to the bedroom door. "Michel needs your advice on some books he wants to place on the coffee table - something about fairy tales by Hans Christian Andersen or a guide to Chanel."

Fleur headed to the door. "Let's go with the fairy tales. Everyone needs to learn to dream. Oh and Hugo," she said, turning back.

"Yes?"

"I'll call. Tomorrow. Let's have dinner."

"Sure." Now it was his turn to flush pink.

"What's he doing here?" Chantal asked as they waltzed through the kitchen. A big jar of kombucha sat brewing and growing on the countertop.

"He's a friend."

"Isn't he the guy that was dating Arabella Sparks? Do you know how many times I've fantasized over him?"

"Chantal, this is a business environment."

Chantal went on. "What are you two meeting for? Do you think Luxe magazine will feature his house? Is it a business date or a date date? If you're meeting for business, which I know is your priority, do you think you could give me his phone number? You'd be doing me a huge favour."

"No, Chantal. We're meeting for business and that's it," Fleur lied. She didn't want to admit that she, too, was dying to rip Hugo's clothes off. "I knew Hugo before he was famous. He's an old associate."

"Okay then," Chantal said. Her cute puffy cheeks withdrew as she chewed on the soft flesh, suppressing agitation. "Well at least you have a hold on the magazines image of professionalism."

"What's that supposed to mean?"

"The way you handled Diego in the living room was quite impressive."

Diego, the living room. Oh no. Fleur had been so distracted. Did Chantal mean to say the builder had been Diego? They hadn't been introduced when she'd arrived thirty minutes late, landing in a whirlwind of interior design dramas. Where had her finesse gone? She always researched the famous people's houses they would be photographing before she arrived. She was never late. She felt sick.

Chantal's blue eyes flickered with a hint of malice. "You did realize who you were speaking to?"

"Of course." Fleur's dress felt far too tight. She needed air.

Chantal's warm hand clung to the side of Fleur's elbow. "This way. Diego's waiting for us in the lounge."

* * *

Sophia was thinking about food. Most people she came across said that in life there were three great joys: food, shopping, and sex. Having never been the world's greatest shopaholic, and as seven years of marriage changed the term *sexual lust* into *sex is a must* - when your husband is in the mood. Food had become Sophia's big love.

She chewed on her dark auburn hair, pondering where and what to eat? In Paris, you were never far from something delicious. Smelly Camembert, fresh baked bread, warm chocolate croissants, panna cotta - smooth as angel wings - and flambé pancakes.

Sophia wasn't in the mood for anything French. She wanted hearty comfort food: Nachos to be precise. Nachos with crunchy corn chips coated in layers of melted mozzarella and blue cheese, topped with rich kidney beans, sour cream, and guacamole. She'd spent hours imagining Paris, decadent food, beautiful vintage shops, art so majestic that if Mona Lisa climbed from her frame in the Louvre, she'd look about and think she'd died and gone to heaven. Sophia had arrived and all she could think about was her Mum's macaroni and cheese, pizza, and nachos.

Without thinking, she picked up her mobile and dialled. She wanted to spend a day with Hugo; a guilt free day where no thoughts of Charles would wriggle into her mind. She wouldn't scold herself for consuming loads of junk food. A day of indulgence.

"Hello," a husky male voice answered. Did all men always sound this sexy, thought Sophia or just Hugo? She thought of his golden green eyes and long lashes battering out sunlight. His voice was raw; he'd either been having sex or had just woken up. "Hello?"

"Hugo. It's me, Sophia. How are you?"

"I've been visiting a friend at an artist's studio."

Sophia breathed a sigh of relief. So he wasn't having sex. I mean, who knew with a man like Hugo? Charming, funny, rich. Women would be drawn to him like fireflies to stars.

Hugo's throat made a low growl, which Sophia thought was

devilishly sexy. "How's the city of love treating you?"

Sophia rolled her eyes. Flirting. A grown man was flirting with her. Her stomach felt as though a small bluebird was doing flips inside.

"Paris is beautiful. I was wondering, if you're not busy writing today, would you like to meet up? I know it's earlier than we'd planned but I'd love share the joy of discovering Paris with someone. I know you've seen it all."

"I'm free actually." Sophia released the breath of air that had formed a tight ball in her chest. "Until I've seen the sun in Paris, through your eyes, I haven't seen it at all."

Sophia's eyes skimmed down over her curvy body. She felt confident in the tight fitting white dress she was wearing. It clung to curves and pretty pink bows had been sewn around the bottom. Yes she felt very feminine and attractive. After applying several swishes of blue black mascara to her long lashes, and a coat of beige high sheen lip gloss, she felt confident to meet Hugo.

Burying all thoughts of Charles to the dark recesses of her mind, she paced back and forth at the base of the Eiffel Tower. It had been a rather silly place to agree to meet, filled with tourists and children running through the crowds, bursting with excitement. Would Hugo even recognise her? It had been a couple of months since their meeting in New York.

How could she compete with the bevy of young women looking like models in their skinny jeans and tank tops that seemed to flood the streets of Paris? She felt dowdy and old. In reality, it didn't matter how she felt because nothing was to happen between her and Hugo. She was a married woman, for heaven's sake!

That's when she saw him strolling through the crowd, a bunch of pink tulips wrapped in brown paper, draped casually over the arm of his sharp fitting grey suit. A green and blue striped shirt with the top buttons opened showed the smooth skin of his tanned chest. His hazel green eyes creased at the sides, and he smiled at Sophia as he approached. Sophia felt the corners of her lips rise as she burst into a smile, warm and bright as the sun.

"Bienvenue à Paris!" Hugo said, kissing Sophia on both cheeks.

He thrust the tulips into her open arms. They smelled divine, and Sophia felt herself grinning like a Cheshire cat. She didn't know what to say! Flowers - how romantic - once you've been married for seven years, simple things like a bunch of flowers can make a woman feel like she's just received a noble prize. Sophia knew how to appreciate the finer things in life.

"They're beautiful; thank you!"

"Not as beautiful as you. I'm so glad you came to Paris. We're going to have so much fun together. How about we escape the crowds and head somewhere more intimate?"

"That sounds lovely," Sophia said as she looped her arm through Hugo's, discovering a flirtatious confidence she didn't even know she possessed. "Where should we go?"

"I know just the place," Hugo said as he slipped his arm out from Sophia's and slid it around her waist.

"This place is gorgeous!" Sophia exclaimed as they arrived at a darling little tea and cake house. The walk hadn't taken long and the conversation had drifted by like a gentle breeze. For that,

Sophia was grateful. With Hugo, Sophia felt their friendship was blossoming into new levels. She considered the title: Sophia De La Laville; it sounded so romantic and exotic. But one must not get ahead of oneself, especially when one is already married.

"What was that?" So caught up in her own thoughts, Sophia had disengaged from the flow of conversation.

"I said this place is called La Pâtisserie des Rêves. They're famous for their Saint-Honoré cakes."

"It looks divine!" Sophia said as they entered the cake shop and her eyes danced with glee at the assortment of scrumptious looking cakes before them, all housed under glass domes. "They're all so pretty - it's hard to choose. You know the way to a girl's heart, Hugo!" She sighed with glee. Paris was full of delightful surprises.

They both ordered cakes and Hugo selected a red pepper & mint tea to share.

As Sophia sat, sipping tea and nibbling vanilla cake, she felt the warm gaze of Hugo's eyes upon her.

"Don't mind me," Hugo said. "I'm just admiring the wondrous, confident creature before me. After wandering through the streets of Paris together, I feel as though we could be a married couple."

"Married?" Sophia hoped her blush wasn't giving too much away - such as skeletons in the husband closet.

"I don't mean to sound presumptuous, but I feel like we've known each other for years. You're a wonderful woman, Sophia. Any man would be lucky to have you in his life. You're so full of positive energy and vitality."

"Thank you. I'm not used to such compliments. My hus... friends aren't quite as romantic as French men."

Hugo smiled a knowing smile. Sophia wondered what he was thinking. "Tell me something about you, something I don't know."

"Like what?" Sophia asked.

"What sort of men have you dated in the past?" Sophia flinched at the question; she felt her face blush scarlet. "Do you want children? Where would you like to live in the world?"

"Those are big questions."

"But it's good to discuss the things we wish for. How else will we reach our goals? I'm ready to settle down; I want a family, children of my own."

"Well, I would like a family," Sophia confessed. "I've always loved the thought of having two little girls. I thought men didn't like to discuss these sorts of things on second dates?"

"Maybe I'm not like most men."

"We'll have to wait and see."

"Let me take you for dinner. I know this amazing restaurant that you'll adore."

Sophia smiled happily, "Sounds wonderful. I have a feeling Paris is going to be better than I expected."

"To Paris!" Hugo said, raising his tea cup.

"To Paris," Sophia smiled and they made a very special tea cup toast.

CHAPTER ELEVEN

MORTAL HEARTS

One week later...

*T*abby and Hugo had been walking around Père Lachaise Cemetery for hours. When Hugo had asked Tabby out on her first day in Paris, she'd wanted to see the city's most famous graveyard. The cycle of birth and death in cemeteries always felt so natural. Père Lachaise didn't reek of agony, lost loves and pain. It had a subtle, vibrant energy. Weeds poked their way through cracks in tombstones and birds chirped picking at worms having a splendid time in this rare garden created from life and death.

It always surprised Tabby that when people, *living* people, thought of death, they didn't freak out, go on exotic holidays, quit their jobs and do something exciting and spontaneous. She felt people were so afraid of not fitting with the living that they shackled their souls, finding it easier to become the walking dead. It was the one fear haunting her own life. She wanted to be free; so why wasn't she happy?

Dressed in white Doc Martens now covered in a light spray

of mud and city dirt, no makeup, a denim skirt and black T-shirt that read, 'My Spirit Animal is a Goth Teenager,' Tabby, for the first time in a long time, felt at home.

The graveyard was quiet, not a soul in sight - or a visible one - except Tabby and Hugo. They had their own little world. The truth was Tabby was craving being away from people and around something green and quiet - a place where she could relax and let go, like she did when she visited her Dad at his little cottage in the Lake District.

"Why did you want to come here?" Hugo asked as he walked by her side. His soft leather loafers crunched over leaves.

"I like graveyards; they make me feel safe. When I walk through a cemetery, it shows me the fluidity of life. How fear is all that's holding us back - fear of death, fear of rejection, fear of lack. Yet everyone on Earth is doing the best they can, with the knowledge they have. If we weren't meant to be living, our air supply would be stolen, and we'd be buried six feet under. Graveyards remind me to live."

"That's wise," Hugo said. He was surprised that Tabby, who seemed so tightly woven in a net of rebellion and unexpressed resentment, would be so open with him. That she would think so deeply about life.

"People are so afraid of what's displayed on TV killings and murders, unexpected dangers. But I believe that life is here to support us. Residing in fear, is what keeps us stuck. Everyone is born with a destiny; everyone has greatness inside of them. People are inherently good. It's a matter of perspective. Anyone raised with good values, with self-respect and unconditional love, spreads a wave of goodness across the land. I wish TV showed things promoting self-esteem and self-love; then we could educate people in one generation about the power of love. We could transform the planet. I think everyone should boycott television until the networks start to promote love."

"An idealistic view. So were you raised in a household like the one you describe?"

"Far from it. Mum and Dad were always arguing. Mum had an affair when I was fifteen with Ravii, the King of Curries. He's friends with your friend, Yves-Something."

"Yves-Jacques."

"That's it, the one who set us up. According to mum, Ravii leases factories from him. Ravii owns the largest distribution networks of premade curry sauce in the U.K."

"Impressive."

"Mum was impressed. Dad wasn't. She left him the cottage in the Lake District when she moved with Zen and me to London. Country kids, in the city."

"Zen? Is that your brother?"

They looped their way through the gravestones. The air felt cool on Tabby's skin and tiny goose bumps tickled her arms.

"Was."

"Oh, he's not with us anymore?"

"He killed himself. Eleven months ago."

"Tabby, I'm so sorry."

The picnic basket Hugo carried felt heavy. He felt protective. Tabby was a woman, yet she felt so young and fragile. He wanted to scoop her into his arms and shelter her from the winds of life. Feel the beat of her heart against his chest and flood her with the warmth of his body. Make her whole again. He hadn't intended on feeling this way.

"I know it was a rash decision accepting your offer to come to Paris and start my jewellery line. I needed a change of scenery. Zen was the good one. He taught me about love. Since he left, I've lost my moral compass."

Why was she spilling her heart to Hugo? She supposed it was because of the amazing offer he'd given her. He needed to know what he was getting himself into.

"I'm sure you're a good person, Tabby."

"I've lost the capacity to love, to feel. I've been sleeping with a married man, and I don't even care."

"You're still breathing."

"So?"

"Everyone does things they feel guilty or ashamed about. There's a time when you need to let go. You're the one talking about greater destinies. Perhaps you just don't know what yours is yet."

Dark grey clouds loomed overhead, and green weeds licked tombstones as if hunting for life they would never find. It was all very morbid. A light splattering of rain made Tabby's normally straight hair curl at the ends in messy flyaway tendrils.

She looked across at Hugo. He was sweet. Carrying a bottle of red wine in one hand, and a picnic basket full of goodies he'd prepared the night before for their date. Sitting on an old concrete tomb, cold and grey, Hugo looked so alive. He lit a cigarette, and a puff of grey smoke swirled around his face, getting caught in the brown locks of hair twisting beneath his chin.

He was beautiful; Tabby couldn't deny that. He looked as though chiselled from stone. There was something about him that made women stare. She heard women whispering things like, 'Beau, Il est très sexy,' as they strolled through the city streets. Tabby wondered what he'd look like naked, lean and muscular, skin so golden it reminded her of weeks spent holidaying on tropical islands.

"What are you thinking about?" Hugo asked. The sun was setting overhead and it rested on Hugo's eyes, making them shine a deep, rich golden green.

"You," Tabby replied.

Hugo tapped the tomb and slid to the side, offering her a seat. "I won't bite," he promised.

"But will they?" Tabby raised her white blonde brows and jutted her head toward the tomb.

"Can't promise they won't."

Tabby laughed and came to sit beside Hugo, resting her chin on his shoulder. She could feel the hard muscles of his torso, and he twisted his body and slung his arm around her waist. Everything he did was smooth, nothing like guys she'd been with before who were awkward, clumsy, and rough.

"I was thinking about you, too," Hugo said.

"Oh yeah?"

"I was thinking how glad I am you came to Paris."

"And?"

"How when I'm around you, I feel like I can be myself. I haven't felt this way in a long time."

Tabby wriggled a little closer; Hugo smelt like smoke, sandalwood, and peaches. She went to nuzzle her chin further into his shoulder, but with his left index finger he reached over and lifted her chin to meet his. A warmth flooded through Tabby's veins and at the same time, she felt the chill of goose bumps prick her skin. Like anything could happen.

Hugo pressed his lips to Tabby's. His mouth was hot and her body burned like a candle's flame. She slipped her hands up underneath his shirt and felt the smooth, rawness of his skin, muscles crunching into her hands as he pulled her closer.

Tabby liked the way Hugo's arms felt, strong and unyielding. Like she was a delicate flower, but that he wasn't afraid to let go. To grab her with all his strength and hold her tight. Hugo ran his hand through Tabby's hair and she kissed him harder still. Only when her lungs began feeling as though they would collapse if she didn't come up for air did Tabby pull away.

Hugo rested his forehead on hers and whispered, *"you're the one."*

Tabby didn't reply. She could feel the essence of his words flooding through her body like warm cocoa, lifting her spirits so high they would soar through the sky with eagles. 'I feel it, too.' She said in her mind, hoping it was loud enough for Hugo to hear.

Chapter Twelve

MENAGE A QUATRE?

"Have you decided?" Poppy, dressed in tall tan boots with red flowers on the side, a knee length black dress and a dowdy old grey angora jumper, stared at Hugo. Expectation gleaming in her powerful grey eyes.

Clemency had been so cool with his latest love triangle; he hadn't expected the menace pulsating from Poppy. He was having serious second thoughts about having invited her and Yves-Jacques for dinner.

"Decided what?" Hugo replied.

"Which woman you're going to date? You can't just string three women along at once, you know?"

"I never intended on stringing all three along. It's harder than it looks. I don't want to hurt anyone."

"See, he's being compassionate," Yves-Jacques said. "Would you rather he shatter the hearts of all these woman?"

"I'd rather he came to a decision and stopped avoiding the pain of breaking up with people."

Poppy scowled. "I'm going to the bathroom and I hope you rethink your stance on ménage à trois if you expect me to go through with this wedding." She swept down Hugo's corridor in a swirl of custom French floral perfume that Yves-Jacques had purchased as a gift.

Yves-Jacques flopped down onto Hugo's couch and ran his hands through his hair. "She's driving me crazy."

"She seems a little more stressed than when we first met," Hugo admitted.

"It's this wedding. Clemency is being vile. She went to see Mother in Monaco and has her convinced my marriage to Poppy is a rash mistake."

"Is it?"

"I love her. I need a strong woman who can handle my sister and mother, as well as me. Poppy's more than capable. She *was* funny and relaxed before she began organising this wedding. There's a month to go. We have one-hundred and fifty guests flying to Monaco for the ceremony. I can understand why she's stressed. I think her stress is fear. If I talk about weddings for one more minute, I'll explode."

"She seems pretty upset about my love life."

"I know; it's like Poppy thinks that you not choosing a woman is *my* fault. Like I got you into this mess! As though it has nothing to do with *her.*"

"Why would she even dream that?"

"I have no idea." Yves-Jacques looked down at his shoes,

mumbling his words.

Hugo felt abashed, he needed to be supporting his friend. "I'm the only one responsible for my relationship dramas. It's not like you can choose who you in love with. You're so lucky to have found Poppy, she's a wonderful woman and I know that you two will be happy together."

"If we survive this wedding, we can achieve anything. I'm so lucky to have Poppy. Between us, have you chosen a leading lady?"

"It's so hard. They are all such incredible women. Tabby is strong and independent. She's dealt with a lot of pain. I find myself wanting to take care of her. She's also incredibly beautiful. Sophia is light and enigmatic, but for some reason I feel like her heart isn't in it. I'm her French fling; she can gossip to her society friends about me when she gets back to New York. I don't know what it is, but I know she's holding something back."

"Fleur?"

"Fleur is insanely beautiful. She's like a beautiful memory of when I was happy. But do you not think maybe there was a reason things never progressed between us? Do you think God had other plans for me? Everyone can lament over past loves, remembering good times; it's an easy habit - but is it healthy?"

"I don't know friend. Amour!"

"Who do you think I should choose?"

"Seems like you're leaning towards, Tabby."

"Hmmm, my feisty kitten. Her name is perfect, an untamed tabby cat. I'm taking Sophia to Le Meurice for dinner tomorrow night."

"Good. It will give you two some time to connect and get to know each other better. Have some fun - you're technically single - so if the mood feels right, don't hold back. I've been looking at her photos on instagram; she is a belle femme, and you are young."

"I don't want a fling. I want love."

At that moment, Poppy returned, wearing an even bigger scowl than when she'd left. "Your mother's sent me a text asking me to change the date of the wedding because her hairdresser can't fit her in on the day!"

CHAPTER THIRTEEN

LOVE AND COFFEE

scaping the clutches of Hugo's apartment, Sophia walked as fast as she could across the cobbled pavement. A little too early, according to the cloudy fog of her brain and the dark sky. She needed to think - an impossible task when your head is still swirling around last night's wine.

The restaurant had been good, the wine heavenly, and Hugo. Oh! Her body warmed at the thought. He was so handsome naked. You never knew what a man looked like till he was stripped bare of his clothing, did you?

Hugo was like a God. His body, hard and chiselled, his six pack rippling in the candlelight of his bedroom. He'd awakened a carnal lust in her. Charles had never made her feel so alive. Kissing the curves of her body, Hugo's breath, warm and ragged. Sophia had felt like a sparkling crystal.

Her cooking class at Le Chef Délicieux would begin in an hour. They were making macaroons. French cooking was fantastic! She needed a shower to freshen up. Perhaps she could allow herself to luxuriate in the scent of Hugo, just for the morning. She felt strong and free like, Samantha, on *Sex and the City*. She was a sex goddess!

Ollie would want to know everything. What Hugo had been wearing, how he smelled of cloves and peaches. The way his hair stuck out in all angles and curled at the ends when he slept. The gentle sound of his breath blowing against her cheek as he cuddled her like a teddy bear in the morning.

If only she could remember more intimate details. She needed a kick of caffeine.

Charles. What was she going to say to him? How could she explain that after seven years of marriage, not once had he made her feel so aroused as Hugo had in one night? It would tear him apart. Sophia liked to think of herself as a good person. She didn't want to hurt Charles, even if he had damaged the glass casing surrounding her heart. People were fragile and Sophia didn't like the idea of breaking anyone. Maybe that's why it had taken her so long to consider the realms of divorce?

With nowhere to go, Sophia decided to head to Le Chef Délicieux. She pulled out her map and looked at the star she'd marked indicating the school based in the centre of the Les Halles district.

It was a scenic walk and Sophia felt her body begin to relax as she surrendered to the beauty of Paris's tree lined streets. It was early so they weren't flooded with pedestrians. Sidewalk cafes and artisan food shops were starting to open and she walked past the high-tech Pompidou Centre, home to the National Museum of Modern Art on her way. In the big open square outside the museum, a lone street performer pulled juggling sticks from his black leather bag.

Le Chef Délicieux was housed in a beautiful stone building. A small staircase with pot plants spilling with tulips led to the entrance where a gold plaque read the school's name.

Sitting on the steps, cool air lifted her hair in a gentle breeze. It was enough to sit and watch Parisians stroll past her, oblivious of her presence as they began their day. She was here, in Paris, learning to cook, and she had an incredible, sexy lover. Could life get any better?

She looked across the opposite side of the street at ornate cream apartments with pretty pale blue shutters and flowerpots spilling colour that hung under windowsills. A man with a bushy beard and short black curly hair, standing on a tiny balcony was waving in her direction.

She looked behind to see if he was beckoning someone else. The door to Le Chef Délicieux stood firm. Turning back, he started to pull his hands towards himself. Calling her? She pointed at herself and he nodded and kept waving.

She picked up her handbag and, wishing she'd brought her white cashmere cardigan, approached the man with trepidation.

"Can I help you?"

His face seemed pleasant enough - smile lines etched into the sides of his eyes and a mass of soft wrinkles furrowed his brow.

"You're up early."

"Yes."

Who was this stranger and why did he presume to know her routine?

"Would you like a coffee?" Sophia's Romeo asked.

"Excuse me?"

"Would - you - like - a - coffee?"

"Excusez-moi?"

"You speak the English, non?

"Oui. Je suis un Américain." Sophia replied feeling very proud. She was speaking French - with a hangover!

"Well, would you like to come up for a coffee?"

He was giving her the funniest look. As though she was a little daft.

"I don't know you."

"Ah! Now I understand. You think I am a stranger. It's me, Diego, from Le Chef Délicieux. We made croissants in class yesterday. I partnered with the skinny woman from Belgium. The one with saffron coloured hair?"

"Yes, oh, I remember," Sophia lied. "Sure, I'd love a coffee."

"Excellent, open the door on your left. It's unlocked; I'm on the second floor, apartment number eight."

"Okay." Sophia made her way to the door. It felt odd accepting an invitation from a strange man into his apartment. He had a prime location for unsuspecting female tourists. "Don't be ridiculous," she chided herself. How was she to make friends if she was always afraid? He was probably leasing the place during his stay in Paris; he did have a Spanish accent after all. Maybe the school had organized it for him.

Diego flung the door open as Sophia reached the top step. "Welcome to my humble abode!"

It was not a holiday lease. That much was certain. The place reeked of oil paint, and artwork hung from every spare surface available - lots of nude art. Maybe this had been a mistake.

"You live here?"

"But of course."

"You're an artist?"

"Yes."

"Why are you at Le Chef Délicieux?"

"I need inspiration. My life is mundane. Paris is stagnant, grey skies, families sleeping under cardboard in the streets, endless museums."

"I think it's fabulous."

"Exactly!" Diego exclaimed, as though she could read his private thoughts. He was still wearing chequered pyjamas, Sophia realized. "Every morning I wake up, I get my coffee, and I sit on my balcony and I watch tourists flock to Le Chef Délicieux. I think to myself: they look happy, they are passionate, they laugh. I need that passion, so I signed up for lessons. I need inspiration to paint!"

"How sweet!" Sophia said.

"I moved to Paris ten years ago from Spain, after my wife and I divorced. Paris is home now. It has made me what I am today."

'Totally bonkers,' Sophia couldn't help thinking, but she didn't say anything. She just smiled at the pyjama clad, bearded man before her, whose body vibrated with passion. She was beginning to like him already.

"Come, I'll get you a coffee."

"Sounds great," Sophia said. In her foggy hung-over state, she hadn't noticed the layers of rugs covering the floor, full of exotic patterns and textures. The whole apartment was wonderful, wild and bohemian. This was the Paris she'd always dreamed of - fabulous artists and lovers.

"So, tell me what mischief did you get up to last night?"

"You presume to know a lot about me," Sophia blushed.

Diego passed her coffee in a beautiful handmade terra-cotta mug.

"I'm an artist. It's my duty to observe. You're wearing the same dress as yesterday."

"Oh, right."

"And you haven't brushed your hair. You look like the sort of woman who always brushes her hair."

"Truly?"

"Yes."

Sophia turned to Diego and changed the subject. "So, you're single?" Diego nodded. "Any leading ladies?"

"Besides you?" Diego asked, eyes twinkling.

Sophia rolled her eyes. Her long lashes batted together, fending off the compliment. She had enough male troubles already and had no intention of adding another to the list. "Seriously, though. Are you happily divorced?"

"What do you think?"

"You've got an amazing apartment. Two adorable children," Sophia eyed the photographs and drawings of two dark eyed boys covering Diego's fridge.

"That I hardly ever get the chance to see," Diego interrupted. "My bambinos live in Spain."

"I can't imagine how hard that would be."

"It feels like having your heart ripped out and being forced to eat it."

"That's disgusting."

"It's true. My bambinos come stay with their Papa over the holidays. I spend the rest of my time wishing they were here. But I must admit the best thing about living alone is no one complains if you don't do the dishes, make the bed, or sleep in till one. I've been forced to get to know myself."

"Sounds wonderful, besides missing your children so much." Sophia looked across the looming mass of dirty dishes lining the wooden countertop of Diego's kitchen. "If you fell in love again, would you remarry?"

"Never. Marriage is like a disease. It's poisonous to the shell. Puts us in a cocoon and eats away our very essence. No, I would never remarry."

"Okay," Sophia said, digesting Diego's words with some difficulty – everything he said was so accurate – but tasted bitter.

Sophia smiled. Conversing with Diego felt like a summer breeze. Easy and relaxed. She felt safe being honest for the first time in her life. With strangers, you don't need to pretend to be strong. Before long, she found herself confiding her own history, starting with her marriage, the 'a-cup bra' incident, and meeting Hugo. Her fears, her dreams.

"Do you think I should get a divorce?"

"I think you should do exactly as you please," Diego replied.

"Yes, but you said..."

"Everyone has to make their own choices; my beliefs don't have to be yours."

"I know, but still. "

"You want me to make the decision for you?"

Sophia nodded glumly.

"What a terrible burden, my darling. I suggest you sit back, relax, allow the dust to settle. It's funny, sometimes when we aren't looking for answers, everything becomes clear."

"I hope you're right," Sophia huffed.

"You can't mope forever. Seasons change, winter ice melts, spring buds bloom. I think we all go through hard points in life to learn about ourselves. When the sun comes out, bask in the warmth of its glow. We learn to appreciate and have gratitude for the good things in life. When you look for goodness, it will begin to sprout all around. Next thing you know, you will be dancing in a garden of gratitude, filled with roses and orchids and wonderful scents and experiences you've never dreamed of."

Sophia nodded; she wanted to believe Diego desperately. "We should head to class, it's starting in five minutes."

"You run ahead, you've given me the gift of inspiration. Today, I paint."

Chapter Fourteen

DEEP WATERS

*T*abby lent down on the wood of the park bench, placing her head on Hugo's lap. Hugo curved his body and ran his fingers through her wispy hair. The grey wool from Hugo's pants felt soft on Tabby's neck, like a pillow.

She snuggled her head, eyes closed, getting comfortable. Wiggling her back in an attempt to make the wood from the park bench softer. Then she looked up to see the soft cream cashmere of Hugo's jumper melting into her hair. Hugo's strong jaw jutted forwards; Tabby stared at the gentle brown birthmark resting on the baby soft skin underneath his chin. Further up, the oak tree canopy towered above, its leaves splitting to reveal grey sky and specks of sunlight glittering like diamonds.

"I don't think I've ever felt more relaxed," Hugo murmured.

"Really?"

"Never. You bring out the best in me, Tabby. Make my world slow down. To the point where I can feel the chill of the wind and the warmth of sunlight when it escapes the clouds grasp."

"You're very poetic."

"I'm a writer and you're a poem - ducking and diving in and out of my life. I never know what to expect when we're together. Except that for one day, I'll be able to smell the roses."

Tabby nestled a bit deeper into Hugo's lap. His fingers ran through her long hair, gliding over her scalp, and she felt like a contented puppy.

"I think you help to ground me. I feel centred when we're together."

"Then it's settled; we're perfect for each other. You're my medicine; you've help me heal, made my heart start beating again. I can feel it sparkling from your warmth." Tabby sat up, pulling away from Hugo's touch. "Did I say too much? Do you want me to play the romance game a little more?"

Tabby laughed. "You read into things way too much, Hugo. I got up to do this," she whispered.

Leaning forward, Tabby breathed in the scent of clean grass, the warmth of Hugo's breath, his sandalwood cologne. She pressed her lips to Hugo's. Cherry gloss collided with the smooth, natural plump pillows that were Hugo's lips. Wrapping her hands around Hugo's neck, she pulled him closer and kissed him deeper. Feeling the beating pulse of his heart against her heart. Soft swirling tongues danced back and forth.

Tabby felt her innocence, like a schoolgirl with a crush. The fear of rejection or loss drifted away, and the world stood still. As the dance of love began to pirouette around the bench.

"I never expected this," Tabby said.

"Neither did I," Hugo replied.

Hugo's hands ran up Tabby's back, slipping underneath her black leather jacket. A grandma with white blonde hair, walking a grey whippet, caught Tabby's eye and winked. She felt her cheeks flush pink.

Pulling away, Tabby looked into Hugo's eyes. The desire to nibble his chin pulsed through her body. Hugo was the most delicious man Tabby had ever kissed. With him, she felt safe. Hugo's liquid amber, grey green eyes took Tabby's breath away. Tabby knew what she wanted.

"I love you." The words slipped from her lips before she had time to collect them, rearrange them into something more sensible or zip her mouth.

"You do?"

How could three simple words create such joy – and cause so much damage?

"Oh no. I've done it; I've said too much." No guy likes a woman to make the first move, Tabby thought bitterly. I've thrown my hands on the table and landed an empty hand. Wait, stop with the negativity; he hasn't exactly replied - has he?

Daring herself, Tabby took in Hugo's straight jaw, yummy lips, the soft curve of his nose, fine lines dancing at the edges of his eyes, then the concern flooding them as he took in her clingy state.

"You know you mean the world to me, don't you?"

"Mmhmm," Tabby replied. It wasn't an 'I don't love you,' but it wasn't a 'let's get married and have babies' either.

"Tabby?"

"Sure, whatever. I shouldn't have said anything. Can we just forget it?"

"No." Tabby's heart sunk. "But I'm glad you said it."

Then why couldn't he offer Tabby the same words in return?

Hugo went on, oblivious to Tabby's distress. "I've got a lot going on in my life right now. I'll be in Monaco over the weekend; helping a friend. When I get back, we can talk some more. I'll take you to Le Nemours for supper. Would you like that?"

It's over, thought Tabby. Damn it. How could she have been so stupid? You find the right guy and then you go and chuck all of your emotions on the street - your heart is bound to get run over.

"Sure," she lied. Hugo needed time to think. Love does not need time - it needs words - thought Tabby.

"Good." Hugo sounded pleased - but who wouldn't be when they've just had their ego back-scratched by a swooning lover. "In the meantime, I have a present for you."

He reached into the pocket of his pants and pulled out a long, red velvet box.

"What is it?"

"Cartier, for you."

Tabby flicked the box open - it felt so smooth in the palm of her hands - to reveal a diamond choker.

"It's beautiful."

"When I saw it, I thought of you. I know that you make your own jewellery, but I couldn't help thinking that the next time I see you, I want you to be wearing something I gave you. I want you to belong to me."

Hugo's soft lips pressed into Tabby's own. She wanted to pull away. But she couldn't. She wouldn't. Damn Hugo, he tasted so delicious. Climbing back aboard the roller coaster, Tabby cursed, her voice was muffled by the pressure of Hugo's kisses.

CHAPTER FIFTEEN

CHAMPAGNE KISSES

*T*abby licked her lips and took a swig from the bottle of Moet sitting on the table beside her at Le Nemours. Tourists flapping maps like wild geese walked back and forth, trying to find the Louvre. Lost in the city of love. Two champagne glasses sat empty on the rickety table.

"Madam, may I pour you a glass?"

Tabby raised her eyebrow and took another swig from the bottle.

"Don't worry, darling. Unless you'd like to join me?" The waiter's cheeks flushed pink. Gel from his neatly parted hair - slicked to his scalp like a swimming cap - formed sweat-like particles around his earlobes and at the base of his neck. He reminded Tabby of a lizard in a formal suit. "I'm sorry. Am I making you nervous?"

The waiter shook himself from his paralysed stupor. "Non. I am very busy, that is all." He pulled on his white necktie.

"Run along then," Tabby barked.

The restaurant was bustling. A man wearing a red suit that

made him look like a giant tomato hit the back of Tabitha's rattan chair.

The waiter blinked. "If you're not going to join me, then leave me alone." Tabby waved her hand, shooing him away.

Tabby pulled out a cigarette. She pushed the tip of her heel into the cobbled pavement. Sitting in her favourite jeans and a black singlet top, she felt like a fool. The Cartier diamond necklace Hugo had given her clung to her neck like a collar. She was on a leash, strangled by her love for Hugo, sitting like a dog waiting for snippets of affection and treats.

Life was a giant whirlwind. Like Dorothy in *The Wizard of Oz*, she'd been swept off her feet and landed in a foreign place. Leaving England, coming to live in Paris. Her jewellery designs were starting to take flight. Hugo had promised they'd begin production in the next two months once she'd perfected the designs.

White blonde hair fell in front of her eyes. She stuck a piece between her plump blood red lips. Tabitha could smell the melted butter pasta with blue cheese the couple to her left were enjoying. The young woman's skin flushed and she giggled at every word flying from her lover's mouth. Tabitha had been in Paris for a month and still she couldn't understand a word.

However, when Hugo spoke French, every syllable that dropped from his lips tasted like French champagne and made sense. They spoke the language of love.

Warm hands closed over Tabby's eyes. Hot air caressed her earlobes; lips tickled the skin.

"Guess who?" A voice as soft and smooth as butter whispered.

"Hugo. I know it's you."

"Kitten. Forgive me for being late. I wanted to surprise you." Hugo plonked an enormous bouquet of white roses in front of Tabby. Their sweet, floral smell made the tension flow from her body.

"You're an hour late."

"Traffic is a bitch."

"You've been gone all weekend. You didn't even call. I don't wait for men."

"You waited for me."

He kissed her lips and drew Tabby in - like a spider kissing a fly. She was tangled in his web. Hugo glanced at the empty champagne glass.

"Only to tell you never to talk to me again." Tabby felt breathless and dizzy from the heat of Hugo's kiss and the champagne.

"Kitten."

It took all of Tabby's strength not to melt into Hugo's arms. She should never have mentioned the L word. Once you handed it over to a man, it was like they thought they owned you. Outrageous!

She stood and grabbed her black Swarovski clutch from the table.

"Mon amour, stay." Tabby was no angel. She glared at Hugo. "Give me one more chance?"

Tabby stared into Hugo's eyes. Did he love her? Was he playing her for a fool? Tabby's mother always told her that if you cried more tears for a man than you laughed, you should dump the bastard and move on. That your intuition was guiding you in another direction. What she didn't say was how hard that last step could be.

How could she dump Hugo when she adored him with every fibre of her being?

"It's over." Tabby tried not to melt into Hugo's puppy dog eyes. If she weren't going to dump him now, she could at least put him on the hot seat.

"If you insist on leaving, take my coat." Hugo slipped out of his custom pale grey Hugo Boss suit jacket and wrapped it around Tabby's shoulders. So light, its touch felt like rolling grey clouds floating in the night sky. He kissed her cheeks. "Je t'aime."

Tabby bit her lip. Maybe things would be okay in the end. However, it was in no way acceptable for Hugo to have left her waiting for him for over an hour!

"We're not over. We've just begun. You're scared but you need to learn to trust me. I'd never do anything to hurt you, kitten. I had a business meeting earlier and there was traffic, that's all."

Tabby didn't reply. She was stronger than Hugo thought. At least she hoped she was.

Tabby didn't look back to see Hugo take the empty seat at their table. Or the pretty French waiter that approached the minute she'd taken a step across the cobbled paving. The moon lit her path through the cobbled streets on the way home. She'd found her place in the world. Paris was home, a fresh start, and yet - she'd never felt more lost.

CHAPTER SIXTEEN

LOVE IS ON THE MENU

"Chop, chop, chop. I vant these herbs so small and fine they're the texture of soup. That's it, Sophia, flick the wrist, flick, flick."

Francois, Sophia concluded, was a born slave driver. Her black eyes cut sharp like the blades as she watched beads of sweat glistening upon her pupils brows. François' beady eyes bulged; her arms were slender, muscular, and her pale blue shirt clung to the folds of skin hanging loose around her apron.

Sophia had always believed the saying, 'You are what you eat.' Should have been - you look like what you eat. Sophia herself was soft and round, like a bowl of frothy, white chocolate mousse.

Francois bounced through the room, critiquing everyone's cooking. We're her tadpoles, Sophia thought to herself.

"Sophia, flick your wrist! Diego, make the knife bounce. Susanne, I love your enthusiasm, but soften your slicing motion. We need to extract the flavours, let the oil ooze from the marjoram."

Glancing at Susanne, Sophia took a guess at the woman's

favourite food. She had mousy brown hair, streaked with grey. Weathered skin creased at her eyes in soft folds and she was so small and petite, she looked as though she could eat a dozen raisins a day and survive. Sophia decided on pigeon. With her bony nose and the soft flapping noise her batwing top made every time she brought down the knife. Despite her size, she was doing well murdering her herbs.

Upon arrival at Le Chef Delicioux Culinary School, Sophia had been shocked to find a bunch of tourists. She had been expecting to find a class full of glamorous Parisians and folks from the country who'd taken the time to fly or drive into the capital to perfect the culinary arts.

But she had made some friends; there was Susanne, the fifty-eight year old Greek-American divorcee. An eighteen year old German exchange student that wore so much makeup Sophia had seen drips of sweat and foundation drop into vegetable ragout. Her less than enthusiastic boyfriend was more interested in texting on his mobile than listening to a word Francois said. Three Australians and one vegetarian from Holland made up their entire class - plus Diego, the only local.

Thank the heavens for Diego. He was her cook in shining armour. When Sophia glanced at Diego, and he smiled at her, she knew he understood. Today's class had been breezy; she'd made a perfect cheese soufflé, and now she was perfecting the art of homemade vegetable stock that would be the base of her soup.

François slipped out into the freezer and Diego came to stir Sophia's stock.

"Smells divine. You should come and cook for me one night?"

"You're such a flirt, Diego," Sophia grinned. She liked how he made her feel. No expectation. Just fun, relaxed.

"I know. It's true. But if you won't cook for me, will you let me cook for you? I've met a gorgeous woman, an interior designer and I'm thinking about asking her on a date and I need some advice on how to woo her. So you don't have to worry about me falling in love with you," he winked. His dark brown hair curled around his temples, and chest hairs popped from beneath his black and grey paisley shirt.

"We can cook together," Sophia said.

Francois returned with a large stainless steel table with wheels underneath; she rolled out a row of pheasants. Dead pheasants. They stunk. Sophia looked around at her classmates to see if they were feeling queasy at the sight. Only the blonde Dutch girl, the vegetarian, looked a tad uncomfortable.

Sophia smelt rotting carcass, blood and faded life. Francois asked each student to collect a bird. Grabbing it by the feet, Sophia held up the bird. Francois was ripping feathers from her pheasant, nodding as people began the same twist and pluck motion.

The bird made popping noises as Sophia tore the feathers loose. Plucking the bird was easy, but the smell, Sophia gagged. She bit back the vomit creeping up her neck like an untamed monster. Sophia threw her carcass onto the marble bench. Her feet slipped over the polished concrete as she ran for the toilets. She would never make it in time. She turned back and vomited into her soup pot.

* * *

Tabby punched Mia's mobile number into her phone, shaking so much that if she didn't hold the phone with two hands, she'd drop it.

Mia answered, her voice spiky and brisk, like the silver studs that coated her favourite tan leather jacket. "Hello?" Pause. "Hello?"

"Mia! Don't hang up. It's me, Tabby."

"Tabstar! How's life? Are you missing me desperately?"

"Horrid and yes."

Hearing the sullen notes hovering in Tabby's voice, Mia's tone softened. "What's wrong?"

Tabby inhaled. How could she explain to Mia that she'd fallen in love with her business partner? She'd know what to do; Mia always did. Even if - Tabby felt sure - it would involve the sacrifice of her own ego. "It's Hugo."

"What's he done?"

"Why do you never presume that I'm the cause of the problem?"

"Because I know deep down you have a good heart."

"I think you overestimate my value."

"And you underestimate your true worth. So what's Hugo done?"

"I've fallen in love with him. He's supposed to be my business partner, and I've gone and blown everything."

"That's not so bad."

"I told Hugo, I love him."

"Tabby, that's wonderful. Paris has been good for your soul. The girl we never thought would love again has blossomed! How does he feel about you?"

"Hugo's been seeing other women."

"He what?"

"At least, I think he has been."

"The bastard."

"I know, right? I found messages on his phone."

"You went through his phone? That's not a very Tabby like thing to do."

"I had no choice. He gave me his jacket the other day after I'd been waiting for him at café Le Nemours for over an hour."

"You waited an hour? Tabby, what has happened to you?"

"I'm crazy in love. It's terrible. On my way home, it began to ring. The mobile phone, not the jacket. It was a call from some woman, Fleur."

"Go on. Did you answer?"

"No. But three hours later, Hugo got another call from another woman, Sophia."

"That scum."

"Am I on speakerphone?" Tabby asked.

"Richard's and my relationship has progressed. We no longer have secrets."

"Hi Tabstar." Tabby didn't like the way her name sounded on

Richard's lips. But if she kept Mia in her life, she was going to have to get used to it. "Don't worry about me. I'm invisible." Richard laughed; Tabby cringed.

"Go on. Did you speak to Sophia?"

"No. I didn't speak to anyone. I sorted through his messages, and I found declarations of love, sext txts, all sorts of stuff. It's sick. He's been three-timing me." Tabby didn't care who was listening anymore. She was so glad to share the burden.

"You need to come home, immediately."

"I can't. We're launching my debut jewellery collection in a month."

"I know how important this opportunity is for you, but do you want to go into business with a man who's already cheated you?"

"No, I mean, yes. I don't know what I want. Hugo's offered me an incredible opportunity. I can't waste it on a stupid crush."

"Do you think it's karma for sleeping with a married man? I mean, crazier stuff has happened."

"No!" Tabby said, before hanging up. "At least I hope not," she whispered to her apartment walls.

Her own mobile rang, and Tabby jumped away - like it was a dangerous wasp threatening to sting. Why, she thought, did anyone even bother to get a mobile phone? It was much easier to avoid people and bottle up your thoughts, rather than own a device that would allow you to spill the beans and your heart any moment you felt vulnerable.

It took three more calls before Tabby decided to pick up again.

"Tabby?"

"Yes?"

It was Richard; his voice felt almost soothing, void of the unstable emotion racing through Mia's. "Do you mind me giving an opinion?"

"That depends. Do you think I deserve to rot in hell?"

"I didn't say that!" Mia's voice was muffled in the background, and Tabby could hear Richard's breath as he paced their Battersea apartment. She could imagine him there, finger pressed to his lips, quietening Mia, striding past the teapots on the mantel place and the books rising from the floor as abstract coffee-tables.

"Do you still have the phone?"

"Yes."

"Take down the other women's numbers. Call Hugo. Act natural. Tell him you have his phone and you thought he might need it. He'll come running. When he does, count every bead of sweat that falls from his head. Pretend as if nothing's happened, then call the women. Arrange a meeting. You need closure; you'll never get it by running. Find out the truth and then come home. You can stay with us for as long as you like."

"No, she needs to leave now," Mia's sharp voice interrupted.

"It's your call, Tabstar. Do what's right for you."

"Thanks," Tabby replied.

Maybe Richard wasn't so bad after all.

CHAPTER SEVENTEEN

TEARS OF TRUTH

Fleur sat on the edge of Tabby's linen chesterfield sofa, her bottom resting on the armrest. The apartment was warm and tiny. Roses perfumed the lounge with sweet scents and a bag of warm croissants sat on the marble kitchen bench, releasing their aroma, making the place smell like a bakery.

Stretching out her long slender legs, Fleur picked at the rim of her knee-high white Chanel boots. Gold embroidery ran up the sides, matching her sequined rose gold vintage backless cropped evening dress. She opened her purse and pulled out a long Audrey Hepburn style smoking pipe.

"I'd prefer if you don't smoke in here," Tabby said.

"Everyone smokes in Paris." *The girl has no clue,* thought Fleur. "Fine, I'll smoke on the balcony," she hissed.

Tabby walked over to the small French doors leading to an even tinier balcony. She jiggled the door, and with a huff, puff, and mighty groan, it swung open. A sharp icy breeze slapped Tabby in the face.

"There you go."

Cars honked on the street below. You could hear the scrape of metal on metal as cars, bumper-to-bumper, squeezed past one another. Fleur tapped the tip of her cigarette and let ash spill out onto the street. You could see the tip of the Eiffel tower.

There was a loud bang as the apartment front door swung open. Fleur turned to see a buxom woman with long dark hair floating in soft ringlets around her face and down her back. She was carrying a large bag. Food? She'd be quite stunning - if she lost twenty pounds, thought Fleur. In an odd way, she reminded her of a younger version of herself. The bag barked. A dog.

"Hi ladies," Sophia said, taking in the two women. "Sorry I'm late." She dropped her bag to the floor; a French bulldog jumped out. She pulled out a bottle of wine and packet of biscuits. I didn't know what to bring. "Mr. Bean. Sit."

"Mr. Bean?" Tabby said.

"Yes, because he loves beans. I bought him yesterday. Paris can be lonely."

Tabby nodded.

Fleur stepped inside. "You don't allow smoking but rodents have free reign?"

"Mr. B is not a rodent. He's a French citizen. I promise he has excellent manners," Sophia said.

Tabby's blue eyes opened wide. Sophia saw Mr. B, humping Tabby's long plush pillow.

"Mr. B. No," Sophia commanded. "What can I say? He thinks you have great taste."

Fleur snorted.

"Mr. B, want a cookie?" The puppy stopped and ran to snatch the dog biscuit from Sophia's outstretched hand.

"I presume you're not expecting any more guests?" Fleur snapped.

"Just us," Tabby said.

Sophia thought back to a classic 1950's movie she'd seen many years ago as she eyed Fleur. She possessed an aura of regal importance. Fleur held herself with such elegance and authority; Sophia was spellbound. Well-maintained French women could be very intimidating, she surmised.

"Well, hurry up and tell me what this is all about," Fleur said, her French accent thick as smoke as she spoke English.

"Sure. Have a drink first." Tabby poured three glasses of wine and downed hers before sharing with her guests. "Down to business then, Hugo." Tabby began to shake. She hadn't planned how she was going to explain everything.

"Oh no, don't cry," Sophia shot up and wrapped her arms around Tabby. "What's wrong? Is something the matter with Hugo? Is he sick? Is that why you invited me here? I must say I was surprised to receive your invite, given as I've never met any of Hugo's friends before today."

Sophia had been mulling over the summons to this party all week. In secret, she'd been delighted. Living in Paris with a French lover was lonely when you didn't have any friends or family nearby. Poppy had never pulled through as a reliable friend. She knew it must have been regarding something to do with Hugo. Could he be in trouble? A drug problem?

She'd always known he was too perfect. Ollie had warned her

time and time again of perfect men. Maybe his mother had died, and he'd been too devastated to break the news? Begrudgingly, Sophia had not yet met Hugo's family. But Tabitha was English, so that squashed that theory.

It must be the C word then. Cancer. How horrible. How morbid. Poor sweet Hugo. He always acted so strong. Why hadn't he told her face-to-face? Sophia began to cry.

This stopped Tabby in her tracks. "Are you okay? I guess you must already know the truth of the situation"

"Hugo has cancer! He's all alone."

Tabby glanced at Fleur; the woman offered no support. Sophia continued to sob, pulling Mr. B's head tight into her bosom.

"No, nothing like that," Tabby reassured Sophia. With Sophia's outburst, Tabby, began to feel that maybe she'd overreacted to the whole situation.

"He's having an affair. No?" Fleur said.

"How did you guess?"

"Isn't it obvious? You are both his foreign whores. I knew the moment I received your invitation."

"Firstly, I am not a whore and secondly, if you knew about Hugo's indiscretions, why'd you come?" How could Hugo be attracted to such a bitch? Tabby thought.

"Curiosity. Who owns this apartment?"

Tabby swallowed her pride. It tasted like razor blades. "Hugo."

"My point exactly."

"We're business partners. I moved here to start my business."

"Hugo is not a businessman; he's a writer. He brought you here because he has enough money from his family to buy whatever he wants. He's like a spoiled child. One you can't say no to. I should have known he was up to no good. *On n'aime que ce qu'on ne possède pas tout entier.* You're in love with him, yes?" Tabby didn't answer, but she knew her cheeks were scarlet. "Look what your fortuitous move has bought you. This apartment, some expensive jewellery? You could've asked for some new clothes."

"Excuse me?"

"Your nose ring, your tattoos, and then you wear these clothes that look like they've been pulled from a trash can."

Tabby looked down at her outfit. Funky torn denim hot pants, black fishnets, a gorgeous oversized *I Love Paris* T-shirt, Hugo had bought her, and a black vintage leather jacket. Her hair sat in a chignon at the top of her head.

"It's French chic."

"I'm French, and you are definitely not chic."

"Who made you the fashion guru?"

"I'm the editor in chief of Luxe Interiors."

"Isn't that an interior design magazine?" Sophia asked, perking up. "I'm at cooking school with an artist who just had his apartment featured. What was that line you said in French?"

"Proust," Fleur retorted, which made no sense to Sophia.

"Tabby?" Sophia said.

"Don't call me Tabby."

"Why?"

"Because that's what my friends call me; to you, I'm Tabitha.".

Sophia began to sob, again, softly at first, until it grew into a deep guttural sound. Deeper and deeper. Like a lamb sent to slaughter, Mr. B howled.

"This is ridiculous," Fleur exclaimed.

"I didn't mean to snap, Sophia, I'm sorry," Tabby said. "We shouldn't all be crying over a man. I wanted us to meet so we could decide what to do. "

"I think we should be friends," Sophia sniffed.

"Wow, radical idea," Tabby said sarcastically.

Fleur pursed her lips together before opening them just a slither so her words could seep out in a gentle hiss. "I don't do friends."

"You don't *do* friends?" Tabby raised a brow and smirked. "Sounds very sexual, Fleur."

Sophia and Tabby giggled together.

Fleur's body stiffened. "I don't need friends because I don't need any more drama in my life. All women do is backstab, bitch, and betray one another. It's sweet and naïve of you to ask, Sophia. At some point, you'll wake up and realize all women are out for blood."

"I'm not naïve," Sophia said. "Come on, Fleur," Sophia said, rolling her eyes.

"Yes?" Fleur bit her tongue, waiting for Sophia's bullet.

"You're so thin, it's like your body is so full of rigid hatred at the world that it's been forced to eat itself. You're starving for affection and love," Tabby retorted for her.

"Thank you for proving my point," Fleur said. Fleur picked up her tortoiseshell Chanel sunglasses and tucked them inside her purse.

"You can't just leave," Tabby pleaded. "We need to sort this out.

"I can and I am."

"No one wants to be the girl that gets dumped," Sophia didn't want to admit it to the other women, but last night she'd tried to call Hugo, five times. He hadn't responded.

"No one has to be that woman," Tabby primed. "The best thing about us knowing that Hugo is cheating on us simultaneously is that we can dump him before he has a chance to leave us."

The front door slammed as Fleur escaped the cramped apartment. It was so hot in there; standing alone in the cold corridor she leaned her back against the brick wall and breathed.

"You're a terrible host," Sophia said, turning to Tabby before running to the bathroom, grabbing the cold porcelain rim of the toilet bowl, and vomiting up three glasses of white wine, two peanut M&M's, five bites of pumpkin and rocket salad, and one small serving of Camembert cheese.

"Really?" Tabby said to no one at all.

The meetup was over, before it began.

* * *

A delicious fraise bonbon strawberry candy marshmallow macaroon sat wedged between Sophia's thumb and forefinger. She'd no idea how it'd got there. But one would be all right.

Nothing was as sinful as sharing a man with two other women. Two women who looked like they hadn't eaten a crumb of bread in over a month. It wasn't as if she'd taken up smoking or some other hideous habit. Indulgence in a little sweetness was harmless.

With a whizz, pop, and fizz, the marshmallow filling exploded. Crumbling between her lips, her taste buds danced, hurrah! A sharp, hot, sweet sensation hit the back of Sophia's palate. She melted into oblivion. Staring at the pink box of macaroons from Laduree's, Sophia bit her lip and resisted the urge to scoff the lot.

On her way back to the hotel from Tabby's apartment, perusing Paris's streets had brought many sumptuous delights to her attention: Lingerie, bakeries, the scent of Arabica coffee coming from tiny cafes.

Nothing had spoken of sensual pleasures to Sophia as much as Laduree's windows on Rue Royal. The shop was a girl's best friend, at least a heartbroken girl. Macaroons reflecting all colours of the rainbow sparkled from the window. Luring, tempting. Well worth devouring. The green and gold windows were magnets for Sophia. Magnets of temptation, sinful treats, and unlimited passion.

Nine minutes later, Sophia stared down at the empty box before her. It still looked pretty, even with a scattering of multi-coloured crumbs layering its base. She licked her ring finger and ran it over the cardboard, stuck it in her mouth and felt the cool sugar melt against her teeth.

Sitting on a park bench a pigeon landed beside her, its wide brown eyes hungry, cooing for macaroon crumbs, anything. Sophia felt starved herself. Starved of affection. Full of macaroons. Devoid of love.

CHAPTER EIGHTEEN

SHARING SWEETHEARTS

"*It's* getting out of hand. I have to choose someone." Hugo sat at Yves-Jacques and Poppy's dinner table. The fire burned bright, illuminating and cutting into the hollows and shadows of his friends' faces.

"I told you so," Poppy replied.

Dressed in a lilac velour tracksuit, she was a lot bossier than she looked, thought Hugo.

Clemency glared at Poppy. "No one asked for your opinion. We're here to help Hugo. Not make him feel worse."

"I think we've done enough helping," Poppy snapped.

Clemency breathed out a sigh of exasperation, the tiny hairs on her grey mohair jumper shook. "And whose fault is that?"

"It's all my fault! I can't think. I can't write. It's driving me insane. My mind is a broken record. All I can hear is Fleur, Sophia, Tabby, running in repeat, over and over."

"The good thing is he's no longer moping over Arabella." Hugo winced, as though Yves-Jacques had cut him with a sharp knife. "Stop being so hard on yourself," Yves-Jacques said. Poppy smiled at him. Hugo was relieved he'd spoken up. The tension between Poppy and Clemency was starting to drain him of the little life force energy he had left. "Any man in your position would find it hard. Beautiful woman are the downfall of mankind."

"That's ridiculous," Poppy snapped.

"Honestly Yves-Jacques, with your naivety towards women it's a wonder Poppy even wants to marry you. No wonder mother is being so difficult towards the wedding; you're a boy and before you make such a life changing decision you need to become a man."

"You're all impossible," Hugo snapped. Three hurt, bewildered eyes turned to him at once. "I'm sorry. It's just hard to hear myself think when all I can hear is you three bickering. It's like there is this unspoken power struggle and you're all trying to strangle one another with words. Clemency, no one in your eyes will ever be good enough for your brother. Poppy is a delightful young woman; which you'll discover if you give her a chance and get to know her."

"Thanks, Hugo," Poppy said with smugness.

"Poppy, you need to learn to rise above things. Yves-Jacques can be a right pain but he does love you and it's expected that his family may be resistant and a little shocked at the suddenness of your plans to wed. They love him and care about him.

And Yves-Jacques, I don't have any advice for you other than to step back and let things heal. Everyone will come round in the end; you know they will. So stop acting like a pompous brat and start helping Poppy with wedding preparations. There were so many French spelling mistakes in the invites. It was obvious Poppy made them by herself."

"I help out!" Yves-Jacques said.

"I could do with some more help," Poppy admitted.

"Why would any of us take advice from Hugo?" Clemency retorted. "He's a complete wreck."

Three heads bobbed in agreement. Before Hugo realized what he was doing, his own began to bounce, in unison.

"What do you advise I do then?" Hugo said. He shivered, even though the room was being heated by the crackling fire. He'd left his jacket at the door and his organic cotton, black V-neck T-shirt wasn't enough to keep him warm. He twisted his merino scarf tighter around his neck.

"I'll go make us all hot chocolate, and we can figure this out," Yves-Jacques said, leaving the table. "Hot chocolate always helps."

"You must know which woman you want to be with?" Poppy said. "It's the sort of thing you just know, and if you don't then none of them are the one for you. You feel it in here," she said thumping the centre of her chest.

"The thing is, they're all perfect. You spend a lifetime searching for the perfect woman, then you find three."

"Love is the answer, Hugo. You used to love Fleur, non? Are those feelings still there?" Poppy said. She and Clemency exchanged a glance.

Hugo sat staring at the table as Yves-Jacques placed a steaming mug of hot chocolate under his nose. It smelt of cinnamon and cloves and warmed his face.

"Every time I see Fleur, it brings up all of my old feelings. It's like coming home on a rainy day. She's warm, smart and sensitive. She understands my obsession with books, she knows how I like my coffee."

"But?" Yves-Jacques said.

"I'm scared when I'm with her. When we split up all those years ago, there was so much pain. I felt like I'd never heal again, and maybe I haven't. Then there's Sophia."

"From everything you've said I think she's the one," Poppy cajoled. "Everything between the pair of you has flown naturally. It's real."

"It's real, all right. She's incredible, but I feel like she's hiding something from me, holding back."

"How?" Yves-Jacques asked.

"I don't know. It's like every time I ask her about life in New York, she acts all vague."

"Everyone has secrets," Poppy replied.

"I hope you're not hiding anything from me," Yves-Jacques said.

"It takes time to build trust."

"Hugo doesn't have the luxury of time right now," Clemency said. "What about Tabby?"

"The girl is mad. She's so much fun; in a way, she's my wild card. I never know what to expect from her. I never expected a relationship. I thought we were going to be friends, business partners. The other day in the park she told me she loved me."

"She what?" Clemency choked on her hot chocolate.

Poppy's mouth burst open and little spits of warm milk scattered over the table.

"That's deep," Yves-Jacques said. "You need to make a decision or someone is going to get hurt."

CHAPTER NINETEEN

SUGAR AND SPICE

Fleur ran her fingers through her silky soft, curling black hair. Three hours in the hairdresser, black dye to cover the blonde roots and she was a new woman. Her straight hair had been her signature look for so long. Proud she hadn't had a single split end in two years, Fleur fluffed her shiny locks. The floral Chanel hair mist she'd sprayed in it before leaving for dinner floated around her, mingling with the rich aroma of melted butter and sizzling garlic coming from the kitchen. She hoped Hugo would adore the hairdresser's magic enough to take her to bed and want to make love to her.

Candlelight shimmered, bouncing across the table, making the silver cutlery glisten. Stone walls added to the restaurant's intimacy, absorbing the chatter, turning voices of lovers hovering in the air into a delectable hum, a gentle song.

"Fleur." A familiar voice tickled Fleur's ears and made her body sing. "Don't stand, you look so serene and comfortable." Hugo planted soft warm kisses on both Fleur's cheeks in the traditional French greeting, then closed in on her lips.

Fleur tried to ignore the butterflies swimming in her stomach.

She felt giddy every time Hugo was near. Dressed in a light grey suit and a pale blue linen shirt that brought out the olive tones in his skin, Hugo looked beyond dreamy. Like a God from a perfume campaign.

"It's nice to see you. I feel like it's been ages."

"It's been a week," Fleur blushed; she didn't want to come across desperate.

"A week too long. You look gorgeous. Have you done something different? Is that a new perfume?" Fleur shook her head from side to side. "The dress? It's divine - you're a sex kitten in red."

Fleur pursed her lips. "It's vintage Lanvin," was all she said.

"What can I say? You have perfect taste, Bluebell."

Fleur swallowed at the mention of her pet name. The name Hugo had called her when they had first met. It wasn't that she disliked it - she'd loved it. Then. But she wanted Hugo to see her now. She didn't want to be his old favourite teddy bear. She wanted to be his new Lamborghini. Hugo was perfect, despite his philandering present.

Despite his kiss with Clemency, all those years ago.

But nobody is perfect. Right? Successful, not jealous, punctual, kind, rich. All the qualities that one needs in a husband.

"I curled my hair."

"It's nice."

"Nice?"

"Yes, if you like that sort of thing."

Hugo tore a seam through Fleur's heart.

"Well, do you? Like that sort of thing?"

"On you?"

Fleur nodded. She felt like a nervous schoolgirl right before taking an exam. Hugo's eyes ran across the menu, before placing it on the side of the white linen tablecloth.

"On you, I like anything. Better yet, nothing at all. Is that why you're pouting? You thought I didn't notice?"

"I was not pouting."

"You were. You still are. Bluebell, I don't care if you dye your hair blue. I love the woman that you are, the woman you've become. You're all grown up and you're magnificent."

"Merci, Hugo."

"You don't believe me?"

A waiter slipped two glasses of wine onto their table, then slipped away as a lean man waved, demanding attention.

"Non."

"You should. I could tell you how stunning you are a million times but it's never true until you believe it yourself."

"So I suppose you perceive yourself as a God?"

"A sex God."

Fleur couldn't help it. She laughed. How did Hugo always manage to do that? To turn a serious conversation light?

Fleur shook herself, trying to release the foreboding sense of insecurity that had been hanging over her head like a rain cloud all evening. Hugo was oblivious to her unease. 'If only you knew,' thought Fleur. Did Hugo even feel guilty? He didn't look it. He looked confident, happy even. Happy he was with her, that was a good sign.

He was answering her questions like a politician. Dreamy, trusting eyes, holding her hand. Fleur had interviewed enough people to know when they wanted to keep something hidden, they buried it.

"Hungry?" A lock of dark hair fell in front of Hugo's eye. He pushed it away and the leather bands that curled around his wrist next to his vintage Rolex slid up his arm.

Fleur didn't have time to wait for Hugo to decide she was the one. At thirty-five, she was beyond Mr. Perfect. If he even existed. She needed Mr. Marriage. Mr. Family. Mr. Right - Now.

Fleur nodded toward a table, where an American family sat devouring bread, slurping soup and cream pasta. Like it was the last supper. A fat man laughed so loud that even the stone walls couldn't mute the sound as the noise cut through the restaurant. His young, teenage daughter, delighted by the attention she was receiving, continued to tell the story of how she had gotten lost in the Louvre earlier in the day. It had, apparently, taken five security guards, three German tourists, and one Scottish terrier to reunite her with her Grandmother, who had wandered into the male toilets and was chatting up an Australian artist.

"Americans, they're always - so American. So loud."

"They look as though they are having fun," Hugo said. "Why are you acting bitter, Fleur? What's wrong?"

"I'm not bitter."

"You're being judgmental."

"So you think I'm bitter and judgmental?"

"I didn't mean it like that. But you were being rude. Are people not allowed to have fun in your presence?"

"How charming."

"Come on, Fleur, let's order some champagne. Relax."

"I can be fun."

"Of course you can." Hugo's grey green eyes flashed like a dragonfly's back, caught in a ray of sunlight.

"You're laughing at me!"

"Am not! Fleur you know that you've always owned a piece of my heart."

"I know."

"Then why are you being so abstract?"

"It's nothing. I had some bad news at Luxe Interiors today."

"Oh, Bluebell."

Fleur was beginning to like the way Hugo said her name. The special name that he reserved for her alone. Her heart soared with pride.

"Tell me all about it. Do you need me to rough and tumble with a deadly foe?" Hugo looked at her with wide, vulnerable eyes. She laughed again. "I may not be very good at inflicting physical violence. I'll do my best."

Could Fleur do this? Suppress her heart. Pretend she didn't know about Hugo's other women. Tabby, Sophia, and who else?

Of course she could. Fleur could do anything she set her mind to. *Plutot mourir que faillir* - Rather dying than failing.

"Am I the one for you?" Fleur asked.

Was Hugo blushing? His eyes fluttered like he was watching flashing images on an internal television screen.

"You're my Bluebell. What's happened? You seem so, insecure."

Hugo's phone rang, pulling Fleur's thoughts from the night sky and back to the restaurant.

"Kitten! How are you? Good? Good. Yes I'm free. Tonight? Ten? I know. I know. I adore you too." He shut the phone. "What?"

"Who was that?"

"My cousin." The lies collided.

A plate of haddock on rocket landed in front of Fleur. Pasta for Hugo. She couldn't even remember ordering. She felt so far away from him. The space between them distant as the Milky Way.

"I thought she was living in London?"

Damn, thought Hugo. Fleur remembered everything. "She's flown into Paris for the weekend. Visiting her boyfriend."

"I thought she was twelve."

"Sixteen," Hugo lied. "Gigi is sixteen."

"Will you introduce us again? She was a toddler the last time I saw her."

"Of course."

"Tonight? Hugo you should have brought Gigi to dinner. I haven't seen her in years."

"Non, she is upset. Her boyfriend broke up with her when they saw each other today." There, that sounded realistic. "The perils of teen love." Hugo was good at this whole lying business. He felt a surge of pride, then admonished himself. "Can you believe some men?"

"No, I can't." Fleur said with all the bitterness she could muster.

"I should head home soon. I hate to think of Gigi, all alone." Hugo glanced at his Rolex. "I didn't bring it up earlier. I didn't want you to worry. Now tell me, what's made you so sad and insecure?"

"Excuse me?"

"At the magazine. You mentioned it a moment ago."

"Oh that, it was nothing." Two could play at this game. "It's just, well, I didn't want to say anything to you. But remember the artist's house you came to visit me at? I did a photo shoot of his home, Diego?"

"How could I forget? The man is one of the best artists of the twenty-first century. Funny you brought him up, I've been thinking of investing in a few new pieces."

"He asked me out to dinner. I can't say it wasn't a surprise, but he's lovely, very handsome. He's been sending me loads of texts and I've been feeling quite overwhelmed." He'd sent one text and Fleur had done her best to ignore it, which was easy when she was busy plotting how to keep Hugo.

"On a date?"

"Yes."

"Smart man, you are incredibly beautiful."

"I said yes."

"You did?"

There, she'd done it. She'd torn something. A heartstring. Hugo looked vulnerable.

"Well, I didn't know if we were exclusive."

"Oh."

"So are we?"

"Well, I really, like you, Fleur. I always have. You're different from other women."

"Excellent. I'll cancel my date then."

"Well, okay." Hugo looked green. He'd committed. His words tasted like acrid poison.

He looks so stressed thought Fleur. Was Hugo attracted to Sophia or Tabby, over her? The thought made Fleur's butterflies scatter and her whole body tense with apprehension.

CHAPTER TWENTY

LUST, LOVERS AND LUXURY

"*I* feel like Hugo doesn't value me." Tabby moaned to Sophia, who in alight of what they'd experienced had become her fallout girl. It all started when Sophia arrived at her apartment the day after the explosive exposure of Hugo with a box of macaroons she'd made herself at Le Chef Delicieux.

Dealing with Hugo's lack of love had created an unexpected bond between the pair. Whereas with Fleur, it felt as though a knife had been sharpened, splitting the women apart. The wound was bloody, festering in resentment and disloyalty.

"What makes you say that? He buys you everything, has bestowed this gorgeous apartment on you, that gorgeous Cartier necklace, and is funding your business venture, leaving me out in the cold."

"Yes, but it's different. He wants to spend time with you. Go to museums, cook together, drive through the countryside. With me, it's all flowers, kissing on park benches and in cemeteries. It's rather morbid."

Tabby didn't add they hadn't slept together despite her

advances. What was wrong with Hugo? When she'd discovered Fleur and Sophia's existence, she'd concluded, perhaps, he liked them better.

"And you resent this because?"

Sophia and Tabby had both dissected their relationship with Hugo. But the one subject they'd avoided was sex. How could you compare?

"Because I'm not just a pretty accessory."

"I don't think Hugo thinks of you as an accessory. He wouldn't have gone into business with you if he did."

"Need I point out, a business producing accessories. I have an actual brain. I have needs as well."

"Needs?"

"I didn't want to mention anything but Hugo and I haven't had sex. Now I'm glad we didn't, but I always wondered if he wasn't attracted to me."

"Wasn't attracted to you?" Sophia couldn't believe her ears. Tabby's beauty was akin to any supermodel. Sometimes, Sophia caught herself staring at Tabby, wondering how it was that one woman could be so genetically blessed and another - namely herself - could be frumpy, fat, and pretty in an old fashioned way. "Tabby, a man would have to be blind not to be attracted to you."

"You don't have to flatter me."

"It always amazes me when someone who is as naturally beautiful as you are can't see it. You radiate youth and innocence. Men love that look. It's sad, but true."

"You've slept with Hugo, haven't you?" Tabby asked. She

didn't want to hear the truth even though she already knew it. Some part of her needed to know.

"I, well." Sophia bit her bottom lip; her cheeks flushed a delightful shade of pink.

"I knew it."

"It wasn't a planned thing."

Images of her night with Hugo pressed down upon Sophia. Hot, sweaty bodies. The way he tore open her dress, his smell, pressed linen, cloves, peaches, and sandalwood. Tongues together, their bodies entwined on the bed.

"He wasn't that good in bed," Sophia lied.

Tabby smiled. She appreciated Sophia trying to make her feel better.

"Did you ever think that maybe you don't value yourself enough?"

Tabby was stunned. "What's that supposed to mean?"

"It doesn't matter what Hugo thinks about you, whether he thinks you're beautiful or not. Whether he takes you to bed or not. If he's not treating you with the respect you deserve, you should forget about him."

"You're the one that slept with him."

"But I'm not in love with him. I don't care what he thinks about me. If Hugo hadn't been a cheater, I never would have met you and we wouldn't be sitting here and gossiping like old friends. I'm happy I met you, Tabby. I'm happy I'm in Paris. I'm on an adventure."

"I don't love Hugo. I never have," Tabby lied. Sophia sighed. She'll make an excellent Mum one day, Tabby thought. She had the ability to know what you were thinking.

"You're a beautiful woman who's smart and funny; you're worthy of true love. You need to forgive Hugo and move on."

Tabby whispered, "but I can't."

* * *

The following morning, Fleur twisted her hair into a tight bun and began to run. It was hard at first; her movements felt stiff and disjointed. The sky split and the heavens opened. A trail of golden sunlight traced her path, warming her pale skin. A church bell chimed in time with the beat of her feet on the cobbled pavement.

What was she doing? Where was she going? The plan had been to take Hugo back; claim her man. Make him her own. But she couldn't do it. Not now. Not now that she knew. Knew that she didn't love him.

A sharp piercing ring broke through the clutter of her mind. Her barefoot splashed into a cold puddle. Fleur pulled her mobile from her pocket and answered. A private number.

"Hello?" Fleur said in the most high-pitched nasal tone she could muster. "Who is this?"

"It's me, Tabby. Fleur, is that you?"

Not Tabby, not now.

"You sound odd. Look I wanted to apologise for the other night. I know it must have been a shock. If you want to talk about anything, you're welcome to stop past the apartment. Sophia's here right now. We're having high tea with cheese sandwiches and macaroons. Are you there? Hello? Fleur?"

Fleur couldn't hear Tabby's voice anymore. She'd seen them. The phone dropped from her palm, and splattered into a puddle. Water splashed up, wetting her tight black jogging pants.

Before her, hand in hand, strolling down the street like it was the most natural thing in the world was Clemency and Hugo. Her body convulsed in pain. Memories of betrayal and disloyalty hurtled towards her, sharp as arrows.

She dodged into an alley, crouched down low behind a bunch of black plastic bags overflowing with rubbish. Had Hugo seen her? She prayed no. Clemency was so perfect looking. Like a reincarnation of Marilyn Monroe.

Cardboard pizza boxes and cans of soft drink, dribbling black goo on the pavement, made her squirm. There were most likely rats living amongst this trash. Trying not to touch anything, Fleur held her breath. The alley stunk of urine.

A white and grey feral cat scrambled amongst the rubbish, knocking over tin cans. It locked eyes with Fleur, its black eyes sharp and sad. Cream and pasta clung in webs in its whiskers.

"Shoo," Fleur said.

The cat didn't budge. It sat down and watched her, intent on reading the dark depths of her soul.

A sharp feminine giggle, resonating like the high notes of an exquisite fruity perfume, floated down the alley.

"Are you still dating all those silly women, Hugo darling? You really must choose one."

"Of course."

They were talking about her, Sophia, and Tabby. She wished she had the strength to confront them. Fleur felt paralysed to the spot. Grief and pain had tied ropes around her wrists and ankles; all she was capable of doing was breathing. She felt raw and broken.

"Well, which one do you like best?"

Fleur pushed herself further into the garbage, slathering herself with the scent of mould and rot. She couldn't be seen here; it was too late to act casual. She couldn't face Hugo like this. Her ears strained, the voices mingled.

Images of Clemency and Hugo, entwined in a magical kiss all those years ago, slapped her in the face.

"Who, Hugo, who?"

The voices drifted away. Fleur was tempted to follow. But she stunk. She felt gross and needed a shower. She needed a new man

* * *

It was late when Fleur arrived at Tabby's apartment. The tea had gone cold. Sophia and Tabby didn't comment on Fleur's presence; it was easier to just accept. She belonged with them.

"I can't date Hugo anymore," Fleur said. "If you spend time with people who are toxic, it's like drinking poison. Over time, you become weak. They drain your life force until, eventually, the poison becomes you." She should have put something dressier on to take part in a dalliance with her boyfriend's mistresses. "I thought I could win, but something happened today, and I realized I never had him. Hugo De La Laville has played me before and I won't allow it to happen again. He's not worth the fight. Clemency won that years ago."

"Who on Earth is Clemency?" Tabby asked, looking ready to faint. Her blue veins pulsed under her pale skin.

"It's not his wife, is it?" Sophia had not yet disclosed to Tabby that she was married. It hadn't come up in conversation, she reasoned.

"Not that I'm aware of. They're old friends, have been for years. She's in love with him. I can seen it in her eyes and Hugo would do anything for her."

"How could he do this to us?" Tabby said through gritted teeth. "I'll kill him."

Tabby's eyes blazing bright as blue tanzanite, made Sophia feel a little nervous. How would Charles react when he found out what she'd been up to? She was still ignoring his calls. Tabby had only been dating Hugo for a couple of months.

"I know, it's sick," Fleur declared. "He makes me ill, my stomach hurts. I can't sleep. I thought this time things would be different."

"This time?" Sophia said, chewing on a loose curl of her auburn hair.

"Hugo and I dated when we were teenagers. He was my first great love."

"Oh, how intriguing! Why'd you break up?" Sophia asked, curious.

"Because he cheated on me with her - Clemency."

"No!" Sophia said.

"We need to teach him a lesson," Tabby said, jumping up. "So he never hurts another woman again."

"Nous allons écraser ses os!" Fleur hissed.

Tabby had no clue what Fleur'd just said. But it sounded dark and exciting. Hugo had no idea what he'd gotten himself into this time. "We'll fight back!"

"We're like the mob," Sophia grinned. "How fun!"

Mr. Bean started to bark with all the excitement. His straight ears pointing heavenwards, sharp and erect.

"The Mafia," Tabby added.

"We're in France," Fleur retorted. "Paris isn't filled with vagabonds. Not like our Italian neighbours."

Sophia smiled coy and bright. "It is now."

"Touché," Tabby said. "Hugo won't be expecting a takedown."

Fleur raised her brow. She fluffed invisible dust from her Stella McCartney jumper dress. "Let's get our ammunition ready, ladies."

"Hugo won't know what hit him," Sophia said.

Tabby walked over to her easel where she'd been sketching jewellery designs. She tore the paper back to reveal a blank sheet. Walking over to the fruit bowl, she found her black marker. The apartment had become a complete mess, and still Tabby knew where everything was.

CHAPTER TWENTY ONE

FLIRTING WITH FIRE

RSENAL. Tabby underlined the word written in bold, capital letters. "I'll be your teacher for today, girls. Now what have we got to bring Hugo De La Laville down?"

"Us," Sophia yelled. "We've got access to his house, his personal property. Every little thing."

"True," Tabby said, jotting down notes. She was impressed. Sophia always seemed so innocent and sweet.

"We need to play it safe. If one of us cracks, they'll blow the whole operation. None of us are sane; we're irrational," Fleur observed in the way that only Fleur can.

"I'm sane," Sophia mumbled, not quite trusting the truth of her words.

"Right, we're like nuclear goods. Come too close, press the wrong button, we'll explode. This tension in our bodies, it's like a weapon of mass destruction. We have to handle ourselves with care." Tabby underlined, HANDLE WITH CARE, on the butcher's paper, and wrote the word YOGA? next to it, with a question mark. "To release the tension," she explained to her invested pupils.

"This is making no sense," Sophia said. "You both need to stop being so esoteric. It's a simple takedown operation and we need a name."

"Paris Mafia Sisterhood," Tabby suggested.

"Non!" Fleur shuddered. "The acronym would be P.M.S."

Everyone burst out laughing.

"I've got it," Sophia declared, "P.M.P. Paris Mafia Princesses!"

"Fabulous," Fleur and Tabby agreed, writing their new name down on the crisp white paper.

"We're taking off!" Fleur said.

"We'll rule the world!" Sophia giggled. "Pump up the princesses!"

"Not before we teach Hugo De La Laville that no man, ever, messes with one of the Paris Mafia Princesses - and comes out alive!" Tabby declared.

Sophia and Fleur nodded in agreement.

* * *

It took three days, five bottles of wine, nine pots of La Fermiere yoghurt, two bars of chocolate, six chocolate croissants and uncountable macaroons, but Tabby, Fleur and Sophia were fast becoming friends. Once they'd spent some quality time together and formed Paris Mafia Princesses, things had started to blossom. As they shared pieces of information about themselves, they began to realise they had more things in common than expected.

"So, what you're saying," Fleur pushed pieces of crème pasta around her bowl. "Is that you would be willing to marry for money?"

They'd been sitting at a low table placed just outside the famous Chez Jannou restaurant for forty-five minutes, drinking wine, gossiping, eyeing couples bathed in moonlight and romance, plotting revenge on Hugo.

"Well, there's no other reason to tie the knot," Tabby said, pulling on the collar of her purple sweatshirt. The top felt like it was trying to strangle her, like a serpent.

"Besides the obvious one, you mean? This soup is divine, carrot and fennel." Sophia smacked her lips together. When Tabby didn't respond, she added, "Love, true love. Like the way I felt when I first locked eyes on a pain au chocolat, then took a bite."

"That's lust," Fleur said.

Tabby snorted. "Love is one of the many ways men repress woman in the twenty-first century. I'm not stupid enough to fall in love. Once you sign on the dotted line, you're sentenced to a lifetime of doting on your beloved husband. Count me out of a lifetime of folding his underpants, washing up after him and cooking for him. It's modern day slavery."

She didn't admit that she already had fallen in love with Hugo. Besides the fact that it was embarrassing it was an equally plausible reason as to why the act of falling in love was so dangerous.

"I'm married and I'm not a slave," Sophia said.

"You're what!" Tabby exclaimed.

"Married."

"No! Fleur, can you believe this?"

Fleur shrugged her shoulders. "It's no big deal."

"But you're the founder of Paris Mafia Princesses, key objective Hugo takedown."

"I didn't found anything," Sophia retorted.

"You came up with the name," Tabby huffed.

"I may have become swept away in the moment. It was all very exciting."

"So," Fleur purred. "Why are you on vacation without your husband?"

"He's dull." Sophia replied. She wasn't in the mood to confess the love disaster waiting for her back home in New York. Talking about Charles always brought up painful memories.

Fleur laughed so light and airy, she sounded akin to an exotic bird.

"Why is it such a big deal, Tabby? I thought you hated the sanctity of marriage?" Sophia asked.

"I do, it's just, don't you miss him? Or did he do something terrible and you're running away?"

"Yes, I miss him. I missed Charles from the day we married. He was never around and I was lonely. We've been married going on seven years. Hugo gave me hope. Maybe there was someone out there for me, besides Charles.

Plus I found an 'A-cup' bra in Charles's suitcase, two months before I came to Paris. I figured if he's taking care of himself, it was about time I did something for me, myself and I."

"That makes sense," Tabby said.

"With marriage, it's much better to take a more French approach. Have an affair, don't get caught. No one gets hurts. That is taking care of yourself," Fleur contributed.

"That's what my friend Ollie's been telling me for years. He'd love it here. You speak his language."

"So you're saying what Hugo did to all of us is right?"

"Right, wrong, it's all so blurry. Take care of yourself, don't hurt others, simple," Fleur responded between bites.

"I found myself always wanting to please Charles. Charles is busy, Charles is tired, Charles is hungry. What happened to the 'I' in Sophia, that's what I'd like to know. Within years, I lost touch. I didn't even know who I was anymore."

"You're both marriage cynics," Fleur deduced. "I want a man who can support me, whilst I support him. We'll be each other's armrest. Besides, Hugo has cooks and cleaners. He'd let you live a life of luxury, if that's what you wanted. But you already knew that Tabby, didn't you?" Her words were sweet, but there was an acid like bite in them.

"That's why we're so different," Tabby shrugged. "You like to serve men. I like to shift the balance of power."

"I always knew you were a putain," Fleur said, delivering her poison of jealousy with the grace of a swan.

"Fleur!" Sophia gasped, spilling hot tea down the front of her Tommy Hilfiger, baby blue denim jacket.

"At least she's looking for love," Fleur nodded towards Sophia.

Tabby, not in the least perplexed, had a guzzle from her wine glass. "There's that word again. Whore. Another guilt trip inflicted on women by the pillars of society. A woman should be free to sleep with whomever she pleases. I know I always have, and I feel good about it. I feel like I'm expressing a part of myself.

Look at you, Fleur, you're a slave to Luxe Magazine when really you want to be decorating manor houses. Being a whore is doing something with, or for, someone that you don't love because you feel it's required of you. Having sex because you enjoy the act is not whoring yourself.

Fleur, you're always trying to stay thin, fighting your every desire to indulge in the delicious plate of pasta in front of you. Because if you get fat, you believe, no one will love you. Everyone is a whore, in some form or another. Anyone who thinks they're anything else is deluded. Love, whores, they're all made up words by men trying to control us and make us feel bad about ourselves."

"I find that offensive," Sophia said.

Fleur sat, digesting Tabby's words. "So you're saying you are not a whore because you have sex with lots of men, but I'm one because I work at a job I don't love?"

"My point exactly."

For a brief second, Tabby let her guard down. Fleur caught site of the real Tabby, hiding behind her white blonde locks, perfect figure, tattoos and piercings. The broken perfection behind her ice blue eyes. The veil of broken glass, blonde and blood that no man would ever see. Underneath it all, Tabby was a cigarette butt, the spark running low, ashen and smouldering, toxic to inhale. She began to feel a little sorry for her. "Why'd you decide to move to Paris?"

"Because I wanted to see what it was like to be a real whore. At least to be called one in public. You know, that has never happened to me before this day. I like to experience the new." Tabby was like a little white mouse, darting about here and there. She was soft and tiny but you never knew what went on inside that mind of hers. "I came because I wanted a new life. I wanted to let go of everything, everyone, and start afresh. To create myself into a whole new persona. Someone happy, successful, abundant - someone more like you, Fleur."

"Like me?"

Tabby nodded; it was the simple truth.

"Well, you must be disappointed. I'm not nice at all. I'm a chienne."

"The opposite, actually. I quite like bitches."

"Well, I love this salad. Beetroot and baby spinach, heaven," Sophia intervened.

"Plus, Hugo invited me. He seemed genuine. The sort of man I should be with. Women spend years conjuring Hugo's, willing them into existence, like Darcy, in *Pride and Prejudice*. I really think Jane Austen must have been a repressed sex kitten. Darcy is Mr. Perfect. I was so ready to pack my bags and run from my life. It felt like Hugo was offering me a second chance."

Sophia flinched. Hugo hadn't offered her so much as a dime since she'd landed in Paris. He had never offered her accommodation. Is this what it came down to? Hugo spent more money on Tabby, so he wanted her more? Was money a real indication of true love?

"Have you ever been in love, like real unconditional earthshaking love?" Sophia asked Tabby.

"Yes."

"And?"

"I don't want to talk about it." Tabby felt oppressed. She did not want to confess that the one man she loved and had given her heart to was Hugo. She wasn't a masochist.

"Well, I don't think I've ever been in love," Fleur said. "Not really."

"What about Hugo?" Tabby asked, before she could stop herself.

Fleur shrugged, impassive. "I love the idea of Hugo. He's my Mr. Darcy. He's like a well marketed perfume. You think that you want to buy it. But you haven't even tried this season's scent."

"Hugo stinks," Sophia interjected and all three woman laughed. "I used to love Charles. When we were together and happy, it felt like nothing else mattered. Everyone deserves love."

"Every woman deserves respect," Fleur said, taking another bite of pasta.

"Charles and I dated since I was eighteen years old. Our parents set us up," Sophia shrugged. "Two good Jewish children. I haven't had the time to be heartbroken, I was always too busy being in love."

"Mon dieu," Fleur said. Her body shivered and she pulled the white fur shawl draped over her shoulders closer. "Hasn't Hugo damaged your heart?"

"The opposite, he opened me to the possibility there is such a thing as real, unconditional love. That relationships can be fun and light hearted."

"She's untarnished," Tabby said, picking at the crumbs of Sophia's bread bowl. "You're like the heroine in those old romance novels. Eyes full of wonder at the world, everyone you see still radiates goodness."

"Naïve and stupid?" Sophia said, a cheeky grin playing at the edge of her lips.

"Free of emotional hardships."

"Because I haven't had a man tear out my heart and stomp on it, you think I'm emotionally immature?"

"I didn't say that."

"It sounded like it,"

Tabby pouted.

"I've been married for seven years - seven long years. I trapped myself in a bubble because I was so scared that if I ever did something wrong, my Mum, or Charles, would disown me. I've been so busy trying to please everyone I love, I've forgotten to live."

"Okay, sister, you're as miserable as the rest of us," Tabby proclaimed. "We get it, no need to wallow."

"I am not wallowing!" Sophia snapped.

A couple walked in. The man, tall in his early twenties, clamped his arm around the shoulder of his young lover. She was a pretty girl, ginger hair, red, frostbitten lips. He kissed her and the chilled breeze that crept into the café after them evaporated in the heat of their embrace.

"Tabby, don't stick your lip out like that; we're in public. I'm shocked Sophia has never had her heart broken. Though it does sound like Charles has been a very naughty boy - and Sophia is handling it all with the grace of a Princess. But I'm more shocked that you would brave the streets of Paris in that..." Her eyes ran over Tabby's outfit. Charcoal grey tracksuit pants. An outdated sweatshirt, Doc Martens and a Tibetan beanie.

"Where did you find those clothes?" Sophia asked Tabby.

Tabby looked down at her purple sweatshirt. "This old thing? I picked it up back home in a vintage store. The tracksuit pants I've had for so long, I don't even know where they came from and the beanie, Zen bought it on eBay."

Fleur scrunched her nose in distaste. The girl - she was hardly a woman - smelt of mothballs and toasted cheese sandwiches.

"What's wrong?" Tabby felt like Fleur's gaze could see right through her clothes to her naked, ice white skin beneath. A single look had never left her feeling so exposed.

"I'm an American, New Yorker," Sophia drawled. "I may not be of the Parisian fashion sect, but New York is a fashion capital. You look like you dressed in the worst clothes at the bottom of your suitcase. Honey, didn't your mother ever tell you, 'It's okay to dress down at home, but in public you should always dress as though you're going to bump into your worst enemy?' It's my personal mantra."

"You'd want to be seen in jeans and that top?" Tabby said, a cat like hiss sizzling from her lips.

Sophia looked down at her own attire. She knew Tabby was trying to get a bite from her to deflect attention.

"Sophia looks like the classic American beauty, chic, understated glamour." Tabby didn't agree with Fleur, but she didn't say anything. "You look like you found your clothes in a dumpster."

"That is not fair," Tabby said. "London is also a fashion capital. I'm sure The Queen would love my outfit."

Sophia burst out laughing. Tabby scowled.

"Don't you think about what other people must feel when they see you?" Fleur asked.

"I don't care what people think. I never have."

"Dressing with elegance brings joy and self-esteem to you, and pleases those around you. Take a rose, its beauty will lift any room."

Tabby rolled her eyes. "I don't need to please everyone I meet, Fleur."

Sophia caught the giggles.

Fleur remained calm. "It is self-respect. I never save my favourite outfit for a party or some fancy occasion on my social calendar. A woman should strive to wear her best outfit every day. When you slip a silk dress over your corset, it makes you feel good. You look like the world has come to an end. Like the man you love has left you for another woman."

"Isn't that how we all feel?" Sophia sung between giggles. As morbid as the situation was, Sophia had always found that laughing at her troubles somehow made them feel less painful.

"It's true," Fleur said.

"I did wake up feeling under the weather. Dealing with Hugo

has been a nightmare," Tabby admitted. "We're supposed to be starting a business together and I want to destroy him. I should never have mixed business with pleasure."

"So claim your power. If we rolled over at the sight of every man who tried to bring us down, we'd all be miserable. Tabby, I know Hugo hurt you. But he isn't the one making you feel the sun isn't shining or you're not in Paris. Like the world doesn't have space for you. This is your life. Wear it. Own it. I like the girl I met in the black Doc Martens, leather pants and comfy loose black silk shirts. She didn't know who she was, but she looked ready to become someone."

"You're actually pretty nice when you want to be, Fleur," Tabby said.

"She didn't sound that nice to me," Sophia retorted.

"Now try some cheese, Tabitha," Fleur purred.

CHAPTER TWENTY TWO

SPARKLY NIGHT

"I've found her, the perfect woman," Hugo said into his mobile.

Joy sung through his voice. The new day smelt sweet and fresh. He strolled down the street fast, feeling the power of his young legs. His muscles crunching and stretching. "I wrote like five thousand words before I ate breakfast."

"That's fantastic. Do you want me to get Yves-Jacques for you? Or I could get him to ring you back; he's on a conference call."

"No, I wanted to talk to you, Poppy. Yves-Jacques and Clemency have been acting a little odd every time I bring up my love life."

"How so?"

"It's nothing, really, just a feeling I've been getting - like they're up to something."

A woman in a red trench coat pushing a bright and bubbly baby along in a stroller caught Hugo's eye. She was beautiful. The baby looked up and smiled at Hugo, warming his once frozen heart. Passing a newsstand, he saw a picture of Arabella on the cover of a magazine, kissing the leading man in her latest movie. He looked a lot like Johnny Depp. Once the photo would have bruised his ego like a frequented punching bag, today he just smiled and kept on moving.

"How bizarre," Poppy squeaked. "That's not like Yves-Jacques."

"Anyway, I wanted to ask if I could bring a date to your wedding?"

"A date or a girlfriend?"

"The latter."

"Is it one of the women you've been dating?"

"Of course! That's what I've been trying to tell you. I am so happy. I'm in love."

"With one woman?"

"Yes! Of course, guess who?!" Hugo wanted to scream Tabby's name from Paris's rooftops. To dance along the Seine chanting the name of his one true love. He'd never felt happier or, if he were honest, more vulnerable. Love had a sneaky way of stripping you bare and exposing your wounds. Hugo realised that deep down the one thing he was most afraid of was being hurt yet again.

"Tell you what, why don't you surprise me? We've all been dying to know who you were going to choose."

"I'll bring her to the wedding. Thanks, Poppy, for being such a wonderful friend. Despite what Clemency says, I know you make Yves-Jacques very happy. He's one lucky man! I am so excited for this wedding; it's going to mark the beginning of the rest of my life."

"Fabulous! Look, I have to go. The florist has arrived and I'm picking flowers."

"Sure, sweetheart, we'll talk soon. Only nine days left!"

"I know - I can't wait!"

* * *

"Is there anything you want to share?" Tabby purred like a kitten having its belly rubbed.

"Like what?" Fleur asked.

"Oh, I don't know, like a secret lover we don't already know about?"

Fleur gulped. Did she still smell like sex? Or was Tabby a mind reader? She hadn't expected anything to happen between her and Diego but after he'd persisted in his txts she'd agreed to have dinner and well, one thing had led to another. She liked him, that was all she knew. "I'm a private person."

"Oooh, how fancy," Tabby cooed.

"Your first kiss," prompted Sophia.

"Your last boyfriend," Tabby said, trying to read Fleur. "Come on, it'll be fun. I feel like I know you, but I don't really know you."

"Anything," Sophia said, taking a bite of one of the chocolate chip cookies she'd baked earlier. The fireplace in Tabby's apartment cackled, the heat of it should have softened Fleur's prim icy demeanour.

"This might help," Tabby poured some whisky into the

champagne flute resting beside her on the antique Chinese blanket chest. She passed the drink to Fleur, taking a gulp from the bottle for herself.

"I'm not English. I don't need a drink to loosen me up."

"Well, you need something," Tabby said. "I've always wondered what a woman like you would be like in bed."

"Excuse me?"

"I'm not hitting on you or anything," Tabby said. "I just wonder if your lovemaking is as stiff as your conversation."

"That's it. I'm leaving. I do not need a personality analysis from a woman who wears tracksuits as evening wear, drinks like a sailor, and has no personal decorum."

"Please stay," Sophia said, trying to retain the balance. "She didn't mean it. Did you, Tabby?"

"No," Tabby replied, grinning. "I always thought you'd be an animal in the sack. A caged beast let loose."

"That's enough," Sophia snapped.

Fleur's whole body felt tight. The truth was, she wanted to fit in. People like Tabby made being cool seem simple. Like sharing intimate bits about your love life was easy and fun. But in truth, Fleur didn't feel like that, she never had. Since she was a little girl, she had guarded herself from the world. Why share secrets when you don't have to?

"My first," Fleur's lips tightened, as though they wanted to keep a lock down on her secrets. They felt like two ripe cherries wedged together, bruising as time went by, revealing nothing. "My first real kiss," she tried again, "was with my Uncle Fredrick. On

Christmas Eve. I was nine, he was forty-two," Fleur swallowed. It felt like she'd just consumed a glass filled to the brim with razor blades. The memory of the night, Uncle Fredrick's tongue, his breath had smelt of chicken and red wine. It gave her chills, and made her body flush with pain and shame.

"I'm sorry," Tabby said. "I had no idea. I'm such an idiot."

"You didn't know. How could you? Can I have that drink - now?"

Sophia pulled the champagne flute from Tabby's, sweaty fingers and handed it to Fleur. "I don't know what to say."

Fleur shrugged. "There's nothing you can say. Don't worry, it's in the past and therefore doesn't need to exist."

Sophia nodded. There was no pity in her eyes, only concern. Fleur liked the way Sophia looked at her. She was like the mother she'd never had. Sure, sensible, caring and solid.

Champagne scorched Fleur's throat, still tasting better than words and secrets kept inside for so long.

"My ex-boyfriend, Gaston is round, jolly and has a sweet moustache. His family owns several wineries and he lives to drink, dance and be merry. He used to sing in the shower," Fleur said, smiling at the memory. "I met him three months after Hugo and I broke up - the first time."

"So why did you leave him?" Sophia asked.

"He was a terrible singer."

Tabby laughed. "That's no reason to leave someone."

"Well, he now lives with my ex-best friend, Jean Marie. They have two delightful children, Gabrielle and Mariette."

"Oh, that's sad," Sophia said.

"Not really. I introduced them. He lifted me and gave me the blessing of realizing that I was beautiful and it was possible for another man to make me smile. Gaston was so happy all the time. I needed someone who could feel pain, feel life."

"You prefer men who are depressed?" Sophia asked.

"I prefer men who are real. Who ride life like a roller coaster. Sometimes I feel like such a stoic, well-balanced person, I need someone who takes me away from myself."

"You're not boring," Tabby said.

"Oh?" Fleur's look was distant, disbelieving.

"Tabby's right," Sophia said. "There's nothing boring about being beautiful, funny and intelligent. You just haven't met the right man yet. And the right man won't take you away from yourself. He'll help you to bloom."

Fleur thought of her relationship with Hugo. Did he make her bloom? He certainly made her laugh, relax and feel comfortable in her own skin. If nothing, they had a wonderful friendship. Then she thought of Diego, her own secret affair. He was her opposite, the relationship was unplanned and exciting. Something special, untarnished, that she wanted to keep to herself for now.

"Sometimes, when I visit Jean Marie and Gaston, I watch their family. I look at the way the light hits the cracks of their old oak table. I notice how Gaston watches Jean Marie when she's doing the dishes. I look at their children. Their pink innocent faces, full of laughter and tears. I wonder what life would be like if I had settled? Once when Jean Marie was out, Gaston and I had sex. I imagined this life, their life, was my life. I'm sick."

"You're not sick," Sophia said.

"I've done worse," Tabby admitted. "I used to think it was a challenge to get a married man to bed. They're always so resistant, loyal even. But when you get them going. Whoa!"

"Okay, Tabby, you're sick," Sophia said. She was thinking of Charles. How many young, beautiful, skinny, blonde women like Tabby had tried to seduce him since she'd been away?

"How come I'm sick, and Fleur isn't?" Sophia couldn't answer that. "Oh, I get it. You're worried about Charles? Who he's sleeping with right now."

"I'm not worried about Charles."

"Good. Because you shouldn't be. I swear men who really love their wives, never play up. And if they do, it breaks them from the inside out."

Sophia didn't know if Charles ever did love her. Could he? She'd just left him for another man. And yet, she felt sick at the thought of him caressing another woman, making love.

"We're all crazy," Fleur declared. "Hunting down Hugo like he's wildebeest. He doesn't love me. He doesn't love us!"

"Maybe he does," Tabby said.

"Now you're the crazy one," Sophia said.

Tabby glared and came to sit on the couch with Fleur, the soft cushions comforting her bony bottom. She wrapped an arm around Fleur's shoulder.

"He has a ring."

"He what!" Sophia said.

"I saw it one day when I was going through his draws."

"You went through his draws?" Sophia pried.

"We're in business together. I thought it wise to do some research on the man I was banking on. Obviously, I didn't do enough. I'd just come over from England. I thought he must have been serious about us, what we had."

"Why didn't you say anything earlier?" Fleur asked.

"What does it look like?" Sophia said.

"Around three carats, rose gold and a marquise diamond. It's exquisite; I tried it on."

"Did it fit?" Fleur said, her heart beating fast. How did Hugo always manage to give her butterflies?

Tabby reminisced the way the diamond had sparkled against her pale finger, the rose gold complementing her skin. It was so big it made her feel like a rich heiress. "It was a tad loose. I don't know why I didn't say anything earlier. If I'm totally honest, I think it's because I didn't want to give up on the dream. I thought what we had felt close to perfect."

It took a while for anyone to speak. To say something, anything. United in the loss of love. It felt like the moment in the Miss Universe contest when all the girls hold their breath, waiting to see the shining star. The most beautiful, intelligent, well-rounded woman.

The winner.

Chapter Twenty Three

ALL THAT GLITTERS

*S*ophia pulled her black sunglasses in close to her eyes. A large black felt hat flopped in front of her face. The air was cold and crisp and smelt like fresh bread and the beginning of winter. It was so cold that Sophia bit her lips and they felt numb. She felt positive the red lipstick she'd applied before leaving, The Ritz, must now be a shade of ice blue.

She passed Mr. B, a piece of chocolate croissant. Her pup adored chocolate, she'd discovered soon after his adoption. With a little grunt of thanks, he guzzled the lot. She picked her pooch up, rubbing the white spot between his ears and popped him into the folds of her jacket. Grateful for the grey duffle coat, and the warmth of Mr. Bean's breath as he snuggled in; Sophia, pulled a pair of binoculars from her pocket.

Paris, Sophia thought, was the easiest city to travel incognito. Glamorous woman, dressed in pashmina shawls and white cashmere dresses, glided along sidewalks followed by fluffy white poodles and men in grey suit jackets and jeans. Old ladies sipped tea, hair in beehives, draped in fur coats that looked like deceased polar bears, pinky fingers pointing skywards. Even the building decorated with hand carved cherubs and intricate mouldings overpowered Sophia with its beauty. She felt lost in the midst of the painting that is Paris.

There he was, Hugo. Sophia raised her binoculars. She'd been so busy people watching she'd almost missed him. But even here in Paris, you couldn't miss Hugo. He was so cool, grey fedora, round black sunglasses, his walk powerful, confident. Sophia drew her binoculars in closer. His hair had fallen loose from its ponytail and hung around his shoulders in thick dark waves.

"Your tea, mademoiselle?" A waiter placed an ornate silver tray in front of Sophia, overflowing with tea, a lemon tart and a chocolate crepe. Unable to choose between the tart or crepe flambé, Sophia had ordered both. Perhaps that was how Hugo felt about this whole business of love. She pushed thoughts of Charles to the dark recesses of her mind. It was becoming near impossible to think of one without the other.

"Thank you," Sophia said. The waiter lingered his dark eyes, resting on her bosom.

Sophia pulled her binoculars in closer. Wait, who was that? Clemency? A woman dressed in a pastel yellow suit kissed Hugo on both cheeks.

"Tart," Sophia muttered.

"Wee. Lemon tart and this is the crepe flambé."

Sophia looked up to see the waiter still hovering above her. "Can I help you?"

"I have the spirits for the pancake flambé, Mademoiselle."

"Oh, you do? Of course. Go ahead," Sophia blushed. The

waiter must think she was crazy. She felt mad; she hadn't even told Tabby or Fleur about her intentions to spy on Hugo.

He poured the liquor over the pancake, and removed a packet of matches from his pocket.

She was skinny, if you liked that sort of thing, Sophia thought, eyeing her competition. Young, if you like that sort of thing. Beautiful, if you like that sort of thing. She looked closer - she should have brought her glasses. She was elegant, regal. She had poise and grace. She looked like a swan. How could she ever compete?

It was funny how she felt that Tabby, Fleur and herself all owned Hugo now. A prize divided. Placing her hand on her warm stomach, she knew he was hers. It was written in the stars, they were destined to be together.

There was a whoosh; the waiter began to speak in fast French. It was hot for such a cold day.

The waiter screamed, "Madame, Madame, Madame," over and over again.

"Very good," Sophia said.

She felt a sting of heat, fire - she was on fire! Her hair was burning.

"Oh no!" She screamed.

Clemency looked across at her; she couldn't let Hugo see her like this. Mr. B squealed as she flung him from her lap. Sophia couldn't stay; she jumped up and ran into the bathroom. She left the café feeling the eyes of all the patrons on her back, wondering what had happened to her incognito plan.

"Come along, Mr. B. Let's go to the park." She swished her hips and breathed a sigh of relief when the café was well behind them.

Looking up at the sky, a loose strand of sweaty hair covering her right eye gave Sophia a pixelated view of the world. A flock of white pigeons flew overhead, making life seem simple. The endless blue, succumbing to a good dose of mundane nothingness was exactly what Sophia needed. She had come on holiday to Paris and now needed a serious dose of rest and relaxation. She definitely looked forward to resting at Mummy's, in Brighton where she would be making a short stopover on the way home.

The world went black. Pitch black. A musty, oak smell tickled Sophia's senses. Baby smooth hands blocked the light.

"Guess who," said a deep and husky voice.

"I'm not from here," Sophia snorted. Her stalker was cutting off her oxygen supply. "I don't know anyone in Paris." Bar my secret lover, his two girlfriends and a depressed and lovable artist.

There was a giggle, then a soft, spongy kiss was planted on both her cheeks. Sophia twisted loose, hands on hips, ready to give her attacker a good dose of 'get lost, pervert, before I grind you to a pulp.'

"Surrr-prise!."

Sophia's eyes rolled back into her head. Birds flying past now revolved around her head, just like in the cartoons. The air became stiff and busy Parisians pushing past in the street became vivid blurs.

"Ollie?"

Wearing a purple suit, paired with green Gucci loafers and a Hermes clutch purse, Ollie gave a twirl.

"Darling, don't look so startled. You look as though you've just had Botox. You haven't, have you? Because I thought we were doing the whole voilà natural beauty thing together."

"Botox? What, no! I haven't had Botox. What are you doing here? How did you find me? I should've guessed it was you. I'd recognise your perfume anywhere."

"With the GPS tracking device we linked to both our phones. Remember that month I lost three phones? It was your idea." Sophia nodded. They'd found Ollie's mobiles in the oddest places: public restrooms, in a lover's underwear draw, even at the back of a bus - and Ollie never took the bus. "You don't look too happy to see me. Being your bestest friend in the world, I was expecting a hug, a pair of glamorous French side kisses, a stroll along the River Thames, and whoops of joy."

"Ollie, you know I'm happy to see you. I love you. I just wasn't expecting this. You would not believe the week I've had. I've been trying to call you." Sophia now realized the reason for the unanswered emergency calls.

"I know all about it, darling."

"You do?"

"It was rather unfair of you, leaving me stranded. I'm supposed to be the outlandish one in our relationship. You're supposed to take care of me when I get myself stuck in love puddles. You know how selfish I am, other people's dramas - ugh. I get jealous when someone steals the limelight. Someone had to do something."

"Do something? Ollie, what did you do?"

"I told your husband if he didn't take the first flight to Paris, there was a good chance he could lose the best thing that'd ever happened to him."

"You told Charles? Everything?"

Ollie blushed. "Well, not everything. As soon as he invited me to lunch, I knew he knew something was up. I mean, hello, you've been married to the man for seven years, and we've never had a lunch date. I felt like a naughty schoolboy!"

"What did he say?"

"He said he had a gut feeling, like something - or someone - was up."

Sophia's heart began to pound. "Someone?"

"Okay, I added that part, but you know Charles. He always makes everything sound so dull. I didn't tell him everything - not at first."

"You explained that I had been cheating on my husband? After you advised me to have an affair because my marriage had destroyed my libido, and I needed an exotic adventure to rediscover my life purpose?"

"Charles was so confused and helpless. I found myself explaining the whole situation to him."

Ollie pulled up the sleeves of his suit, pushed back the Richard Gere inspired haircut he'd been experimenting with, and winked at a gorgeous looking Frenchman dressed in white pants, skin-tight black skivvy and beret.

"De-lic-ious." Ollie licked his lips.

"Ollie," Sophia snapped. "Focus."

"Relax, darling. I told Charles that a gorgeous Frenchman had been *attempting* to sweep you off your feet. And if it were me, I would have been swept away by now. But given that it was you - a woman of high moral standards - there still might be time."

"He booked two first-class tickets then and there. Told me I had to come for moral support. I think he was a little scared of facing you alone, and here I am."

"What about your haberdashery business?"

"It's all under control. I've hired an assistant, Victoria; she's fabulous. I heard the name Victoria, and I thought of Victoria Beckham instantly. It's a match made in heaven. Ollie and Victoria."

As usual, Ollie was doing very well at relaying the events of his past week to Sophia in lightning bolt speed.

Sophia was stunned. "But you hate Charles. Why would you help him?"

"Dislike, darling. He's boring and bland. With all the fun you were having, I couldn't help but feel a little sorry for him. As much as I dislike Charles, I love you, and I know that deep down you love him. I hope you'll forgive me. When I received your voicemail about Hugo dating three other women, I had to do *something*. I was secretly hoping for a fight as well. Charles vs. Mr. Handsome. It would be like watching Bridget Jones's Diary in real life. You know, when Mark Darcy gets it on with - what's the other fellow's name?"

"Daniel Cleaver."

Sophia began to cry.

"Take my handkerchief," Ollie pulled an orange hanky with a pretty O embroidered on the corner from his inner pocket.

Sophia blew her nose. "Thank you."

"It's all yours."

"Have I done the unforgivable?" Ollie swept a hand across his brow. His long fingers wiggled in the wind.

"It's nothing to do with you."

Ollie's face looked disappointed for a moment, before a swift recovery. "Spill."

"It's no big deal."

"What's the scoop?"

"I'm pregnant."

Ollie fainted.

Thirteen minutes later, surrounded by an entourage, including a French doctor (at least according to Sophia's limited French, that's what he was), a clan of dreadlocked German tourists who'd dragged Ollie's limp body to a park bench. Three Australians wearing board shorts and Billabong T-shirts stood clapping and dancing in front of Ollie, trying to rouse him.

Ollie came to, aroused by the pungent scent of liquor, shoved under his nose by one of the Aussies, encased in a silver hip flask. His eyes fluttered; he clasped the doctor's hands - beautiful pianist hands - and winked at one of the Australians in one aroused swoop. Panic left Sophia's aura. Everything was going to be okay.

Her hands wrapped about her belly's barely visible bump. "We're okay," she whispered.

When the party cleared, and Ollie had exchanged digits with the French doctor, Sophia found herself sitting beside Ollie on the bench. He took her hand in his. Not for the first time, Sophia found herself sighing, regretting Ollie's sexuality, purely for selfish reasons, of course. In her eyes, he was the perfect man.

Ollie was the first to speak. "We're going to have a baby."

Sophia smiled; Ollie's bright eyes sparkled as his thick black lashes pressed together. Her cheeks hurt and a tear, not of fear, or sadness, rolled down her cheek.

"Yes, we are."

"You took me by surprise."

"I know."

"You should've told me earlier."

"I know. I'm sorry. I haven't told anyone else."

"You know that you're not alone. I'm here for you." Sophia raised a brow. "Whoever you decide."

"I've already decided that," Sophia said.

"And? Is it Mr. Big Apple or Mr. French?"

"Neither."

Ollie's jaw dropped. "What do you mean?"

"I'm not sure I'm ready for the commitment of a long-term relationship."

"But, but, you're married."

"I know, but I'm not happy with Charles. I haven't been for a long time."

"That's because he's so busy. But he's going to slow down. Take things one step at a time. He's going to make the time for you. He promised me."

"Are you his knight in shining armour? Sworn to protect and serve?"

"I serve no one but the Lord, my love." Ollie flung his hand across his chest. "But I am sworn to protect the innocent, and I think you should give Charles another chance."

"You do?" Sophia couldn't keep the shock from her voice. "Well, before I give anyone another chance, I have a few things to sort out. Do you think you could keep Charles distracted for a couple of days?"

"Definitely not."

"Take him shopping, go to the Eiffel tower together. Just don't tell him where I am. You did bring him here."

"You said you weren't mad about that. I thought the whole thing was in the past. You know how I am with secrets. It's terribly irresponsible of you to tell me private information and then leave! I was lonely in New York. I missed my best friend."

"I'm not mad, Ollie; I just need your help."

"Fine. But if I lose him in Prada, good riddance!"

CHAPTER TWENTY FOUR

GLAMOUR, GLOWING, GROWING

"*I* shouldn't have come," Fleur said.

"You could have rung." There was no denying Diego looked hot. At least he looked far more put together than Fleur did at midnight. Even if he was wearing chequered pyjama pants and a grey worn looking cashmere sweater. "It's not often I have sex with a woman and she ignores my phone calls the following week."

"My life's complicated. I went on a date with you to take my mind off another man. I didn't expect us to sleep together."

"So, I'm a sexual distraction? The manly part of myself is telling me I should be pleased. Deep down, I feel hurt."

"Can I come in?" Fleur said, attempting to peer around Diego's shoulders into his messy, artist dwelling. "I promise not to dissect the décor."

"Last time you were here, you said my place reminded you of a hovel. One that an ungodly creature from *The Lord of The Rings* would dwell in."

"Did I really?" Fleur said, taking off her pale pink Chanel

jacket, and pushing her silver Chanel handbag further up her arm. "I don't remember that at all." Taking Diego's lack of protest as an invitation, she made her way inside, leaving him standing at the door looking out into the cold night and twinkling stars hovering above Paris. "I'd love a cup of coffee."

"I only have scotch."

"Perfect."

After Hugo's lack of commitment, Fleur had done what she did best. She'd escaped into the arms of another man. Love wasn't worth the pain; it never was.

Returning to Diego's apartment was a good choice for her, but it didn't look to be good for him. His face, Fleur noticed, had gone a dull shade of yellowish-green.

"I wanted to call." Diego raised his black bushy brow. "After everything, the way I ran out on you. I thought you'd never want to see or speak to me again."

"That doesn't explain what you're doing here," Diego replied, his voice mellow and smooth, a mixture of French and Spanish accents twisting together.

"Hugo and I, he's been seeing someone else - multiple someones." Fleur couldn't find the words to describe what she felt. Or why she thought running to Diego would solve her problems. The way Diego was looking at her right now, she felt so immature.

"Why would I care about you and Hugo?"

"Because you're my friend."

"I wouldn't call us friends."

Fleur began to cry, hot wet tears. They fell like warm pinpricks, spiking her skin with salty dew. Wet, unstoppable tears. The heavens closed, and the charcoal grey clouds, hovering under the moon's gaze, let go; their tears fell in a great downpour. A loud thunder burst jarred Fleur's ears, she shook with the Earth.

Something about Diego made Fleur crumble. She couldn't hide who she was in front of him. Fleur felt vulnerable, safe. Their chance meeting now felt more like fate.

"I'm sorry." Fleur mumbled. "I'm such a bitch. A mental, crazy lost cause," Fleur said between sobs. "I shouldn't have come. I'll go."

"Fleur," Diego called as she pushed past him, back out the apartment. She was acting irrational, and it felt liberating. "It's freezing. Stop being so melodramatic and come upstairs."

"But you said..."

"Forget what I said. No friend of mine is ever sent out into the cold. Come on, I'll find you a chamomile tea, laced with scotch of course, and you can tell me all about it."

"Serious?"

"Serious."

Despite the tears, despite the huge mess, she felt better already.

$$* * *$$

It had taken five unreturned texts from Hugo, and fifteen long phone calls from Ollie, to convince Sophia to meet with Charles. The man had flown from the other side of the world to see her. Charles was her husband – at least for the time being. If truth be told, Sophia was scared to face him. To face everything she'd run from.

Sophia shook as she approached the park where Charles was waiting for her. How could you explain to someone you weren't in love with them anymore? She shook herself and repeated her new mantra. "I am a confident and courageous woman."

She was aware that it took a lifetime to build a marriage. Yet you could knock it down in a matter of moments. Did she want to see her efforts to find happiness with Charles in a mass of debris and dust at her feet? No. That's why she felt so nervous.

For the first time since arriving in Paris, she ignored the delicious scents wafting from pastry shops. Fashionable mums dressed in this season's couture. Pigeons cooing on the sidewalks and the excited laughs echoing from clusters of tourists. The music of her life was the loudest beat, drumming in her ears.

She pulled a lock of auburn hair out of her eyes and twisted it around her little finger. The park was buzzing. Children raced, picking flowers from their beds, and Parisians and foreigners alike munched on baguettes filled with Camembert cheese and tomato. The air smelt of sweet spring blooms; bees hummed and the vivid green grass was offset with row upon row of tulips.

Sophia had dressed for the occasion. A loose white silk dress, bunches of lavender embroidered all over it, clung to her body, highlighting the curve of her tummy, and swell of her bosoms. A black beret sat perched on the top of Charles's head, covering his balding patch. Sophia gently approached her husband.

"Charles, how are you?"

"Very well, Sophia, and you?"

"I'm good." How was it that two people who had explored

every inch of each other's bodies came to a point when every word - lingering in the air between them - felt like a stranger's touch?

"You look beautiful today. I've never seen you so... radiant. Pregnancy suits you, Sophia. "

"Did Ollie tell you?"

"You know how he is with secrets." Sophia grimaced. "He didn't need to. Sophia; you're glowing."

The way he said her name. Charles looked at Sophia like no other man ever had. Like he could touch her soul with his gaze. She shivered, even under the warmth of the spring sun. "We need to talk, Charles."

"I know. I've so much to tell you, so much to say."

"The bench over there, by the Maple tree. I need to be sitting while we have this conversation."

"Of course. Here, let me take your hand."

Charles's own palm was smooth and soft; he took hold of Sophia, guiding her to the wooden bench. Its wrought iron sides had cherubs holding it up. Sophia's bottom sat snug in the cool arch of the bench.

Composed and sensible, Charles, seemed nervous. Sophia could tell from the delicate twitching of his nostrils. He was breathing heavy as well. His breath felt warm against the edge of her neck as he fussed over her, trying to make her relax.

Deep down, Sophia knew that Charles had been thinking of this moment for a long time. She wasn't the only one who'd felt suffocated and neglected by their marriage. Now she knew it'd been killing Charles, as well.

"I," they both said in unison.

Sophia laughed; Charles's face fell.

"You go first," Sophia said.

"Well, okay," Charles's hands were shaking.

"Go on," Sophia nudged him forwards. "I'm listening."

Life in the park became a distant blur. The shrill cry of birds nesting and sitting on eggs floated into a gentle hum. All Sophia could see was Charles. The soft arch of his bushy red brow. Sprinkles of freckles sitting atop his pale cheeks.

"We've been through a lot, and I want you to know, I still love you. The moment we first met you were wearing that crimson dress, with the spaghetti straps, holding an enormous bunch of hydrangeas and singing down the street as you carried brown bags full of groceries. I was swept away in your beauty. Caught in the magnificence of your sparkling aura. You radiate goodness and kindness and a wholesome happiness that is rare, like a diamond."

He's being very sweet, if not a little cliché, Sophia thought. This wasn't how she expected the speech of her divorce to go down. There was no throwing of plates or violent screams. It was a nice, clean end to the goodness that was once their love. Before it had festered and turned sour - Sophia swatted the thought from her mind. For Charles to speak words of romance, she knew it cost him a lot; he was letting his guard down.

"Charles, you don't have to say such things. I understand. I will always love you."

A rainbow of relief washed over Charles. Colour began seeping back into his face.

"And I you. What I'm trying to say is that from the moment we first met, I wanted you to be my wife. I'm proud of you, of the woman you've become. I've neglected the most important thing in my life for too long. We're going to have a baby. I've always wanted to be a Daddy. I can move to Paris. There'll be adjustments to the Architect firm. You can continue cooking in Paris. I'll set up shop here, learn French. I love this city, and it'll be my first demonstration of how I'm willing to be flexible. We'll make a life that involves us both."

Sophia felt her stomach contract. Was Charles mad?

He was on one knee, his cream pants becoming dirty in the mud. "Sophia, I love you. I always have, always will. Please will you do me the honour of becoming my wife, again."

Words escaped Sophia. What could she say? This was not happening. But it was. Charles flipped open the lid of a velvet navy blue box to reveal a brilliant square cut, pink diamond ring. Tiny white diamonds dotted its edges.

"It's beautiful."

Taking this as a yes, Charles slipped the ring onto Sophia's finger. She'd taken off her wedding ring. He acted as though he didn't notice; knowing Charles, perhaps he hadn't.

"Ollie helped me choose it."

"Charles, come sit next to me."

"Of course, darling." Having been on the edge of his wits, Charles seemed content to sit in silence beside Sophia. Content to feel the gentle breeze as it brushed against their faces.

Taking a deep breath, Sophia began. Her heart felt warm, and an inner strength lit her from inside, giving her the confidence to say what needed to be said. "The first thing you should know is that I'm not sure if the baby is yours."

"I don't care. I love you, Sophia. It's all that matters."

Why was he making this so difficult? He was being so caring, so sweet - or was he? "Charles, this isn't a business deal or a trophy. There is a child to think about. I'm your wife, and I'm telling you I've been unfaithful. I'm sorry. You don't have to pretend to be okay with everything I've done to you. To us."

"Sophia, I will love the child because it's part of you and no matter how busy I've been, or what I've done, I will always love you. You're the one for me."

"What you've done?"

"The bra you found in my suitcase. I'm sorry; I cheated on you, too."

"Whose was it? Your secretary?"

"No, her name is Rosetta. She lives in Dallas, Texas; she's an architect. We're partners on a building development. It was only sex, Sophia. I wanted to tell you, but I was a coward. I didn't think you'd understand, but now I know you do. Believe me, I know I've been a fool."

Sophia breathed deeply. Charles's words felt like a samurai's blade twisting its way through her intestines. "We've both been fools in love. I can't believe you didn't tell me earlier."

"Honey, I love you. We've both made mistakes, but we can get past them. We can create a life together. A new one. I can't lose you."

"I'm not a prize, Charles. I'm coming home to New York. But not to our apartment. I'm getting my own place. If you're the father, I want you to be a part of the child's life as much as you wish. But I can't raise this baby in my old life. I need to heal."

"Are you saying I'm too late? That I don't deserve a second chance? That I'm not good enough to raise your child?"

"Don't be manipulative. You're important to me, and you'll make an excellent father someday."

"How much time?"

The sun slipped behind a cloud and dark shadows spread across the park.

"Right now, I don't know."

"Should we get a divorce?"

Sophia shrugged; here was the tricky part. "I'd like to stay married, if that's okay with you. I just feel like I need some space right now. I need to learn to love myself, before I can dedicate my time to anyone else."

"Of course," Charles said.

"I should give you your ring back," Sophia tried to pull the fabulous diamond from her swollen fingers.

Charles put his hand on hers, covering it. "Keep it. You might be the mother of my child. Take it as a token of my devotion to you, and our baby."

"Charles, you are sweet."

"You fell in love with me once before." Charles leaned forward and kissed Sophia's forehead. "For you. I'll wait as long as it takes."

CHAPTER TWENTY FIVE

ROMANTIC MESS

*T*abby's whole body felt exhausted. How would she ever fill the blank spaces in her heart? She was used to rejection. In a sad, sorry way, she always seemed on the rejected side of life, hovering in the loser zone. When she was feeling this beat, there was one person she could turn to. She found her mobile under a stack of silk embroidered green and white cushions and sunk back into the coffee coloured sofa.

"What's up, hun?" Just her voice was a breath of fresh air. Tabby could imagine Mia, sitting at home in her favourite torn to shreds, pale blue, almost white, Levis, a steaming cup of Mexican chilli hot chocolate in hand.

"You're too good to me," Tabby said.

"Don't say that."

"What?" Tabby shrugged, tucking a loose strand of white blonde hair behind her ear. "You know it's true. I wanted to call and say thank you. I always dump my problems on you. It's selfish. I'm scared that one day you'll get over my dramas and I'll lose you as a friend."

"At least you're aware that you can be selfish." Tabby raised a brow. "You said it first."

"I know, but you don't have to make the wound deeper than it already is."

"The thing is, Tabby, you're an amazing person. You have so much to offer the world. You're smart and funny, and you emit this aura, this glow that lights up a room wherever you are. It's only you that doesn't see it. You're your own worst enemy. Frankly, I'm surprised you even called."

"I can hang up. If you'd prefer."

"That's what you don't get. I don't want you to. I never have."

"I can't stop thinking about Hugo. I miss him." Tabby bit down on her tongue, hard. She didn't want to upset Mia anymore. "I've been ignoring his calls and when he came to the apartment the other day, I pretended to be out. He must think I'm a terrible person and business partner."

"Tabby, I know Hugo betrayed your trust, but you can't deny he's been good for you. Paris has been good to you."

"I'm a romantic mess," Tabby groaned.

"It's the first time you've chased a dream since Zen died." Tabby winced at her dead brother's name. Every time she heard it, it felt like a bullet exploding through her heart.

Tabby knew the truth behind Mia's soft-spoken words was undeniable. She focused on the dabbled light oozing from the ancient Indian lampshade on the side of the room. Specks of dust danced in its warm glow. If she squinted at the light long enough, she was sure she could stop more tears forming.

"I think you're asking for reassurance. I think you rang because you want validation that you've done the right thing moving to Paris."

"And your verdict is?"

"Whether you should stay or go is up to you. Make sure you're not just running away, because you're scared. Love is scary. I know you're in love with Hugo. You've never spoken about one guy so much in your entire life."

"Do you think I only like him because he's off limits? He's so unavailable."

"I think you should give Hugo a chance to explain himself."

"What's to explain? He brought me over to Paris as a business deal and received a bonus."

"It's easy to judge someone, Tabby. It's harder to give someone a second chance. Before you write him off, see what he has to say."

After she'd got off the mobile to Mia, Tabby sent Hugo a quick text, asking him to come over.

b there in 30, came the instant reply.

* * *

Licking her lips and pulling her knees under her chin, Tabby watched Hugo as her poured thick, musty red wine into two oversized kitchen mugs.

"Very posh," she grinned, accepting the offer of a mug with a large Santa Claus smiling at her from its side.

"I do my best." Firelight flickered against the harsh lines of

Hugo's face, making him glow.

Wine sat on the edge of Hugo's plump lips. After relishing a sip of her own vintage red, Tabby felt the urge to suck Hugo's lips and drink the abandoned drop. Its delicious chocolaty flavour, hinted with clove, sent a warm pulse through her body and made her inhibitions dance and fall away.

It was his turn to study Tabby, thin tendrils of white blonde hair trickling down her back, the way she sat, so concave, protecting herself from the world. An animalistic urge made Hugo want to wrap Tabby in his arms and shelter her from the dark things lurking in the shadows that'd drained all the joy out of the beautiful woman before him.

"Have you been trying to avoid me?" Hugo asked.

The air hanging between them, thick and dank, shattered like a pane of glass.

"What gave you that impression?" Tabby lied.

"You've been distant lately. I've barely seen you."

'Because you've been three-timing me!' Tabby wanted to scream, but she didn't.

"I thought something was wrong," Hugo pressed.

She shook herself and replied. "I've been busy. Designing new pieces for the collection. Here, I have some with me." She handed him a brooch with a silver snake twirling around a large onyx.

"It's beautiful. You're beautiful."

"Honestly, Hugo, you don't have to keep pretending. We're business associates, that's all."

"Maybe that's the problem," Hugo said. "Maybe I don't want to be friends with you."

"Wise decision. I'm quite a handful. You wouldn't believe how emotional I can be, and I do tend to talk a lot. Which psychiatrists seem to think is a good thing in a relationship, but some men find it annoying." Tabby bit down on her lip, hard. She was rambling about her insecurities to this man, this cheater. Wine was the culprit; it made her do embarrassing things.

Hugo chuckled. It sounded like a deep low growl. "I like the way you talk just fine. I like a woman who can feel the pulse of life through her veins."

"Then what is it? What don't you like?"

"I think the problem is..."

"Yes?" Tabby said, eager to get to the point of why she wasn't good enough for Hugo. If she could just figure out why, she'd feel much better. Then she could escape back to London and forget this whole ordeal.

"The problem is that my feelings of *like* towards you have changed."

"Oh."

"I am beginning to *love* the little oddities about you. The way you twist your hair around your fingertips when you're nervous. How your dainty nostrils flare when you're mad and the way you bite your lip when you think you've revealed too much about yourself."

Tabby shuffled, unwinding her legs she allowed her bare feet to press into the reindeer pelt lying on the oak floorboards. "Oh."

"Oh, indeed. So, you see, it is not you who has the problem. It is I."

"I think I could solve your problem."

"Do you?" Hugo asked. Each syllable dropped like a cat, purring.

Standing up, Tabby found herself at a precipice. She liked Hugo a lot. Tabby walked over to face Hugo. She took the mug he'd been holding from her fingertips and lifted it to her lips where she drank. Placing it on the chest to the side of the chair, she rested both hands on Hugo's shoulders. Before he could stop her. Before he could utter a word, Tabby bent down and pressed her lips to his. Hugo drank deep, falling under the spell of the enchantress above him, claiming him as her own.

* * *

Hugo rang Yves-Jacques first thing in the morning. He'd escaped from the apartment before Tabby woke, leaving a note.

"I'm in trouble."

"What happened?" Yves-Jacques asked. His voice was groggy, sounding like last night's liquor had caused his tonsils serious damage. "Are you still suffering from writer's block? Your deadline is in three weeks."

"No, nothing like that. I've got enough happening in my life to spark inspiration. I'm surprised how little faith you have in me."

"You're the one ringing me all flustered. Couldn't you wait for a more polite hour to ring on Sunday? Poppy is making pancakes; I keep telling her to make them thinner, crepes, but she insists on thick pancakes."

Hugo rolled his eyes, feeling the heat of Yves-Jacques's impatience. "It's Tabby."

"No wonder you need my advice. Sorry, I can't help; some men are Gods in the bedroom; others aren't. I can teach you, though."

"We're not having any problems in the romance department. That's the issue."

"So you've bedded the woman?" Yves-Jacques voice perked up and all at once he sounded more awake.

"That's not what I rang to talk about Yves-Jacques."

"Then you've got no reason to ring me so early. I want details, juicy snippets I can replay in my mind after I'm married. I bet she was an animal."

"You're disgusting, Yves Jacques; the details of my sex life are personal. I respect Tabby. I don't know why I thought it was a good idea to ring you for advice."

"Me neither. I'll speak to you later."

The mobile rang dead. Hugo pulled it from his ear and rang Yves-Jacques straight back.

"Some friend you are. I said I have a major dilemma on my hands, and you hang up the phone on me?"

"You called me disgusting and didn't even tell me details. I don't have time to deal with your dramas. Poppy's parents arrived last night, I need my beauty sleep before we tour Paris; sur pied - on foot."

"Shouldn't you be getting out of bed?"

"Of course not. They won't be here until midday. Until that time, I'm free to sleep in till my little heart is content. Goodbye."

"Wait! Don't hang up. You're the only one I can talk to right now."

"Because?"

"I know you won't judge me. No matter what."

"I'd prefer: because you're smart, funny, handsome and a loyal friend and business partner. But I'll take it. You've got five minutes."

"Okay, let's say I broke the pact."

"What pact?"

"Thy shall not sleep with any one woman, whilst dating three. The pact that takes me from being a nice guy to a sleaze."

"So you did have sex with Tabby? I knew it. Now I'm awake! No man in his right man could ignore that woman. Je suis tellement fier de vous."

"I'm planning on inviting her to your wedding."

"Where is she now?"

"Asleep, in the apartment."

"If you don't mind me saying, maybe you shouldn't invite her to our wedding."

"Why not?" The line was quiet. Hugo waited for a response.

"Because it would make things between the two of you official if you're planning on introducing her as your girlfriend. And it pains me more that you can imagine to admit, that maybe she's not the right girl for you. She's so damaged and, from what you've said, the woman's more than a little unstable."

"Tabby's not damaged. She's been through a lot in her life."

"I threw her in the running so you'd have some entertainment. You're making me lose. Poppy is going to be so mad at me for talking you out of seeing Tabby."

"Lose what?"

"It's not important."

"I didn't think you'd fall in love with Tabby. She's not the sort of woman you take home to meet your family and friends. She's the sort of woman who makes you forget."

"Tabby's not the sort of woman you take home?!"

There was a light tap on Hugo's shoulder. He turned round to face Tabby. Her face was ashen white, like the dead. She'd overheard; how much? Hugo had no idea. Too much, by the expression of hurt masked by the daggers her piercing blue eyes sent his way. She must have left the apartment and come looking for him.

"I've got to go, Yves-Jacques."

"Fine, come past the apartment. Clemency is stopping by so you may as well join us before the to-be-in-laws arrive."

"Fantastic."

This time it was Hugo's turn to hang up on his friend. Hugo turned to face the music. His grey green eyes searched Tabby's. She was dressed in his white business shirt, and a pair of black leggings. Hugo had to stop himself from flipping her hair behind her shoulders and reaching down to her waist and drawing her to him. Now was not the time. They were in public for heaven's sake.

"What are you doing here? You must be freezing."

"I came to look for you. I missed you when I woke. Clearly you didn't miss me. Planning an early morning escape?"

"Tabby, I can explain."

"Explain how I'm not the sort of woman you take home? It's okay. That's what I am to most men, a joy ride. I've been so stupid! We had a professional relationship; I crossed that barrier. I should've known better."

"Tabby, don't be like this. What you heard earlier, I didn't mean it like that, not at all. I was talking to a friend. In fact, I meant to ask if you'd like to attend a very special event with me as my girlfriend?"

"No, Hugo, I have no intention of going anywhere with you. All I want is to forget this whole thing ever happened. To forget that I'm in love with you. I'm going to go home, to England. I miss my Mum; I miss Mia. Paris, France, this is your world, and I don't belong in it. I thought, stupidly, for a moment that maybe I did, but I can see now I was wrong. You've got enough on your plate as it is. I'm sure taking me off the menu won't even dent your ego. You got what you wanted."

"Listen to me. I've never been certain about anything in my life before, but I know this, you're the woman I've been searching for. I want to wake up next to you everyday for the rest of my life. Tabby, I think you're wonderful."

"Wonderful? A couple of months ago this whole situation wouldn't have bothered me. I know how men think. But I want something better for myself now. I want a man who loves me, only me, and treats me right. If I can't have that, then I think I'll be happier with nothing at all."

"Tabby, you're not listening to what I'm trying to tell you. I'm in love with you."

The anger in Tabby's eyes had faded. The scent of fresh croissants drifted through the air, and the crisp morning breeze wrapped the pair in a shower of icy particles. Through her Tiffany blue gaze, Hugo saw two hollow shells.

"I wish I could offer you the same in return. But I can't."

"So you don't think you could ever fully love me, surrender yourself to me?"

"I know I couldn't." Tabby walked away.

A cab pulled in alongside the curb. It tore away, splashing great goblets of water onto Hugo's Prada suit. He was stunned. It'd happened again. Flat-out rejection.

Hugo didn't blink as he watched Tabby walk away. He wanted to chase after her. Drag her back and into his arms, back into his bed. He wanted her, needed her. Who was he kidding? Hugo knew deep down he was a coward. He wasn't a fictional character from one of his novels. He was flesh and blood, a middle-aged man who lacked the self-esteem to fight for what he wanted. Besides, you couldn't make someone love you - could you?

The thrum of his Blackberry pulled Hugo out of his self-loathing stupor and back into the present day.

"Hello?"

"Hugo?"

"The one and only."

Tabby was drifting further and further from sight. Too late now, thought Hugo, turning his back. Hugo needed something real, someone who he could sink his teeth into and not get hurt.

"It's me."

"Who?"

"Fleur, silly."

"Oh Fleur," Hugo knew he sounded disappointed; he'd have to amp it up a notch if he was to avoid hurting Fleur.

"I've been trying to call you all morning. Do you know how annoying it is when you're ringing and ringing someone, and they never pick up?" She snorted a nasal, high-pitched laugh and went on before Hugo could even blink, let alone reply. "I've got tickets."

"Tickets?"

"Only the most fabulous front row tickets in town, to the Chanel Haute Couture show. Would you like to join me? I mean if you're busy or something, I'll call one of the girls." She didn't intend on sounding too eager.

How on Earth had Fleur managed to score tickets? Maybe life without Tabby wouldn't be so bad after all. I mean, Fleur did have some amazing connections, no he was being ridiculous. Fleur was simply a safe bet.

Fleur purred. "So what do you say?"

"I'd love to come with you. There are some things we need to talk about." Over a dry martini, thought Hugo. The time had come to call it quits with Fleur. True, she was a diamond in the rough, but she wasn't Hugo's diamond. Tabby was, and he needed to set things right, before it was too late.

"Fabulous. We've got so much to discuss."

It was time, Fleur thought, time for them to break up officially. She'd no desire to play Tabby and Sophia's revenge on all men game anymore. Not when she was falling in love - with Diego. "I've missed you." The sound of your voice. Words left unspoken that now would never evolve. "I'll pick you up at eight."

"Tonight?" Hugo gulped; this was going to be rough.

"Yes tonight, sweetheart." Hugo was so disciplined, thought Fleur. Not at all like Diego - rough, wild. Poor Hugo, he must be having a dreadful time juggling so many women, Fleur thought, her anger dissolving. How could you stay mad at someone, when there was so much good in the world?

"I thought the show would be later in the week?"

"I'm going to ask you one more time. Can you or can you not make it to the show tonight? Before I sell your ticket to the highest bidder," Fleur teased.

"I'll be there."

"Fabuleux! See you soon. Kisses mwah, mwah, mwah."

"Mwah," Hugo replied. He couldn't click exit on the receiver quick enough. Looking up, Tabby was nowhere in sight.

* * *

An emergency meeting was called pronto to Tabby's departure.

"So you've fallen madly in love, and now you've lost the girl of your dreams, and you've got a date with the girl of lover's past?

Where does Sophia fit?" Clemency asked, taking a bite of her Florentine.

"I don't know, and that's not entirely what I said," Hugo retorted.

They were crammed into Poppy and Yves-Jacques's apartment. The place was strewn with flowers, streamers for the wedding and almond bonbonnieres.

Yves-Jacques was taking a shower, door open and his baritone voice echoed throughout the apartment as he sung, "Here Comes the Bride."

Poppy pulled her lilac shrug tight across her shoulders as she dipped a shortbread biscuit into her café latte before taking a bite. "So you've sex with Tabby, let go of your barriers, and turned into a melting mess."

"He told you already? Yves-Jacques, I am going to kill you." Hugo shouted down to the bathroom.

Clemency's baby blue eyes opened wide. "You had sex with Tabby? You've turned into the player, from being played."

Poppy covered her face with her hands, pulling them down, making her perfect features morph into the charisma of a ghoulish monster.

"Be my guest." Yves-Jacques said, walking into the living room with naught but a towel wrapped around his waist. "That way I won't have to go flower shopping with my mother-in-law to be, on Friday. I told her that's why we hired a wedding planner. And do you know what she said to me? She said, 'it would make *me* appreciate the day more.' You know I have terrible hay fever; just the thought of all those flowers makes me sneeze."

"What happened to secret guy stuff? Bro code," Hugo said.

"Poppy's off limits; she's my fiancée and I swore the day that I asked for her hand there would be no secrets between us. Till the day I'm in my grave."

Poppy beamed as Yves-Jacques bent down to give her a sloppy wet kiss.

"Guys, can we get back to the problem at hand; Tabby." Hugo's body felt tight with frustration.

"Don't forget Fleur and Sophia. You are going to break up with them, aren't you?" Poppy said.

"I'm going to break up with Fleur tonight, and Sophia, it explodes my mind just trying to think of how I'll deal with her. I don't want to hurt anybody."

"I think it's a little late for that," Clemency reprimanded Hugo, who grimaced, feeling the heat and truth of her words sink deep into his bones.

CHAPTER TWENTY SIX

OH BABY! MAMMA MIA!

Walking through the streets of Paris, Sophia felt light, even though her belly had grown, and her breasts had swollen to the size of two ripe melons. Speaking with Charles had given her hope. They'd breakfasted on multiple occasions and were exploring Paris, together and separately. Sophia attending cooking school, brunching with Diego on occasion, who was fast becoming a wonderful friend, and exploring the Louvre with Ollie. Could Paris get any better?

"Darling," Ollie waved at her, leaving a gorgeous, German tourist looking forlorn as he abandoned his latest squeeze to cuddle her. "Can you believe I have but one night left in Paris? I've been talking to Victoria, and she thinks I should set up shop over here. Apparently the New York store doesn't miss me at all."

"That's fabulous. You're going global."

"I know! Think of the variety of men I'll meet. I can have boyfriends all over the world. I'll be just like you."

"I don't have boyfriends all over the world!"

"Well, you are beginning to verge on the promiscuous side of life. You and Charles aren't getting a divorce. Non? – see I sound French already, *and* you haven't found the time to leave Hugo."

"Well, not exactly. I am planning on breaking up with Hugo."

"He is a delicious specimen. Men like that can be hard to find. For the moment keep your options open. He may very well be the father of your baby."

"Thank you for being so supportive, Ollie. You're a darling; I don't know what I'd do without you."

They'd just past a newsstand loaded with newspapers and interior design magazines when Ollie screamed.

"What is it?" Sophia asked, spinning around, flicking an imaginary spider away.

"Nothing, darling. Let's walk the other way. This side of the street smells funny."

"Ollie, whatever's the matter? You're a terrible liar. Your flaring nostrils give you away every time."

His bottom lip quivered, and his white angora cardigan shook like a frightened rabbit. "The newsstand."

"What?"

Sophia turned to examine the messy rows of magazines, crowded with tourist souvenirs, Parisian themed coasters, key rings and beer mugs. Then she saw it: Hugo on the front cover of several magazines kissing Arabella Sparks. Hugo had mentioned to Sophia about his famous ex, but what were they doing plastered all over every magazine newsstand, *together*? They were kissing in some images, holding hands in others; they looked very much in love.

Searching for a magazine written in English, Sophia found one and began to read aloud.

"Movie star and beauty goddess, **Arabella Sparks,** *is set to marry,* Hugo De La Laville, *real estate heir, author and playboy, this weekend in a secret ceremony in Monaco. After splitting in public three months ago, the couple is believed to have rendezvoused, deceiving the public they were no longer involved to avoid media hype that will now surround their upcoming nuptials.*

The ceremony will be intimate with only a few hundred guests invited. We will do our best to photograph the couple on their big day, but in the meantime, you can catch Arabella Sparks on the big screen in her new romantic comedy, Love tastes like Chocolat. How could he!" Sophia screeched in outrage.

"Madame, are you going to buy the magazine or just read it?" The newsstand owner, a thin and hairy man, asked Sophia.

"No," Ollie said, returning the magazine to the attendant. "We would never purchase such filth!"

"Les tourists," he muttered, returning the magazine to its shelf. "Shoo!" he demanded.

Ollie dragged Sophia from the site, where after her initial burst of outrage she stood stone still, and sat her down on a bench. "Relax, you're in shock. You have the baby to think about. Breathe."

"How can I breathe when that bastard's sucked the air from my life?"

"You don't know if it's true. Call him, find out. Magazines lie to sell stuff. The whole thing could be a publicity stunt." Ollie didn't sound hopeful.

"What if it's not? What if the possible father of my baby is getting married?" Sophia cried. "I'll look like one of those crazy women trying to claim fame through my connections to a celebrity."

"Call him."

Shaking, Sophia picked up her phone and dialled Hugo. "He didn't answer. He hasn't answered any of my calls all week."

"Oh my Goddess! What if it's true?"

"He did have a ring. Tabby found our numbers on his phone. But he could have had a second mobile, one for her, Arabella Sparks."

"The magazine did call him a playboy."

"I have to tell him about the baby. Before he ties the knot."

"I wish I didn't have to leave tomorrow. Shall I cancel my flight?"

"No. This is a quest for the Paris Mafia Princesses." Ollie looked baffled. "Fleur and Tabby will be by my side."

CHAPTER TWENTY SEVEN

SOUL SOOTHING

One train ride later, Tabby, found herself staring at a black door. Three slash marks, looking as if a vampire had crashed the joint, shocked Tabby into the reality of how far she'd come. Scrounging for courage, she raised her petite fist - lotus flower and crystal bracelets floated down her arm, making delicate chiming sounds as they fell - and knocked. No reply. She knocked again.

Leaning forward, Tabby pressed her ear to the door. All was quiet; maybe nobody was home. Not unusual for a Saturday. London had been a mistake. Then again, so had Paris. She may as well call it a day and head back to her Mum and Ravii's house. Twisting away from the door, Tabby was drawn back as she heard a loud smash - a vase breaking, a cat meow, the longest list of profanity she'd ever heard boom though the post slot.

Flung open wide, Tabby was greeted by the stench of pickles and hot chips. Richard, in his superman underwear with floppy red hair and a thin splattering of hair on his chest, stood taking her in.

"Tabby," he said in his distinct Scottish accent.

Tabby stuck her Doc Marten in the door. "I'm looking for Mia."

A grumpy looking Mia walked into the living room. She was wearing her favourite Venice Universitia jumper, a dodgy pair of grey boxers, and knee-high, blue, red and white socks.

"You look like a time bomb!" Mia said grinning, grabbing her friend and giving her a huge hug. "What are you doing here?"

"I needed to come home, and you said if things got any worse I'd be welcome," Tabby relaxed. Mia wasn't mad; she was - as usual - irrevocably unshakable. "I caught the train this morning and left all my stuff in Paris." Breathing deep, Tabby took in Mia's familiar scent - old books, wood smoke and something new, citrus, like exotic tangerines - as her friend wrapped her in a warm cuddle. "You smell amazing."

"And you smell like you haven't showered," Mia laughed. "Come on," Mia pulled away first. Tabby wanted to cling to her, to breathe in her safety. For Tabby, Mia was like the stuff of comfort food, carbs and sugar; she was all Tabby ever craved. "I'll run you a bath."

"And I'll warm some milk on the stove. I've got cinnamon; I can sprinkle it on top," Richard offered.

He wasn't the most confident man in the world, but Tabby knew he was trying to make her feel comfortable.

"Sounds perfect." Tabby reached towards Mia. She wanted to clasp their hands together, but Mia had turned away, heading towards the bathroom.

After Tabby had bathed, and come to sit on Mia's comfy couch, in a borrowed pair of soft, peach coloured flannelette pyjamas. She found herself spilling the whole sex saga to Mia and Richard. It was a bit embarrassing talking about sex with Hugo in front of Richard, especially when Mia asked what it had been like. Richard hummed and hahhed in all the right places, nodding in consolation when Tabby explained how hurt she was to find out that Hugo didn't consider her the sort of woman you'd take home to your family.

"Are you sure he meant it like that?" Richard asked. "You only heard one side of the conversation."

"That bastard," Mia said. "Of course he meant it, Richard. You don't have to defend him because you're members of the same sex. He used Tabby, it's deplorable."

Richard shrugged. "Sometimes we make mistakes. I find it hard to believe someone would treat a woman like that; it's so ungentlemanly."

Tabby felt a glow of warmth spark her heart. Richard was nice; she was happy Mia had fallen in love with him.

"I'm afraid he definitely meant it," Tabby said to Richard. There was just no shaking the hardness in Hugo's tone. She knew he'd been speaking the truth. "It sounded like he was outraged at himself for even taking me to bed."

At that very moment, her mobile buzzed. It wasn't Hugo's sixth unanswered call. It was Sophia. She answered and listened intently.

"No way!" Tabby gasped. "That slimeball!"

"What's going on?" Mia asked.

"One minute, I'm putting you on speaker phone, Sophia. I'm

in London with my friends, Mia and Richard. I know, it's a long story, I'll explain later. Firstly, tell us everything you know."

Hanging up the phone, ten minutes later after promising Sophia she'd take the first train possible back to Paris, and Sophia had said she was going to ring Fleur, Tabby looked at Mia. She could see the worry lines etched all over her friend's face. Hugo was getting married to Arabella Sparks! But for some odd reason, she felt calm. Like this whole thing wasn't happening to her. Like her heart hadn't just shattered.

She needed to clean out her Paris apartment, and although gate crashing her ex's wedding wasn't as appealing an idea as Sophia made it out to be, she did need to talk to Hugo. It seemed as though this might be the last opportunity she'd have to do so.

"What should I do? What am I going to say to Hugo?" Tabby said to Richard and Mia as soon as she'd gotten off the phone with Sophia.

"Well, one thing is clear, you're in love with the man," Richard surmised.

"I know! It's terrible; I'm perpetually the other woman. Without even trying to be! This time I'm swearing off men on a permanent basis."

"Don't be so hard on yourself, Tabby. You didn't know Hugo was engaged or that he was dating three, no four, women simultaneously. How could you? You didn't know Francis was married, either," Mia comforted her friend.

"What do you think I should do?"

Richard shrugged. "I don't know."

"I'd love to stay, but the wedding's on the weekend and I need closure."

"Monaco is a long way for closure," Mia said. "We'll take you to the station tomorrow. Tonight, we're drinking hot chocolate and watching *Breakfast at Tiffany's*. It's Richard's favourite movie."

"Is it really?" Tabby asked Richard, who nodded shyly.

"It's true, I came home and found him curled up on the couch watching it one evening. That's when I knew I wanted to spend the rest of my life with this gorgeous man."

"How romantic," Tabby sighed.

CHAPTER TWENTY EIGHT

LOVERS: LOST AND FOUND

"*I* love this place," Clemency purred. "It's so sexy. I love the silver drapes. Dita Von Teese is performing this evening."

"What's it called again?" Hugo asked as he took in the plush red velvet interior, and slid into the booth next to Clemency, soaking in the elaborate surrounds. It was a beautiful club, but where was the beauty in life when the woman you loved had left your apartment and didn't return your calls? Why did every woman he meet, run away?

Fleur had txted to tell Hugo she couldn't make the Chanel fashion show. He knew he was being stood up, but had been so overcome with Tabby's sudden departure from his life he hadn't found the energy to feel rejected.

He'd been so selfish over the last couple of nights, ignoring several phone calls from Sophia and Fleur. Why was it that everyone you didn't want to speak to called all the time, yet the one you did want to explain everything to, Tabby, ignored every single one of your calls?

He wasn't looking forward to breaking either Fleur or Sophia's heart. It was arrogant to think that one of them would feel as shattered as he had by Tabby's rejection. But on the off chance that they did, right now that he was experiencing the very depths of heartbreak, he couldn't wish the pain on another soul. Especially not two people as nice, kind and caring as Sophia and Fleur. As a result, he'd been avoiding them.

Right now, he didn't feel like being around people, let alone breaking someone's heart. He knew it was a cowardly move, but he felt so shaken after everything that had happened between him and Tabby.

"Le Crazy Horse. It's the hottest Burlesque club in Paris, baby."

Hugo would recognise that voice anywhere. He turned to face Arabella; it was enough to snap him out of his love forlorn daydreams.

Her rich red hair was pinned up into a messy bun; contrasting blonde loose curls twisted forward and kissed her cheeks. Her lips stained red, made Hugo blush, as he thought of hours spent in tender embrace.

"You're like a schoolboy with a crush. I love the way you look at me. Isn't he so funny?" Arabella said as she turned to Frederick, her new director fiancée.

"I'm not in love with you anymore, Arabella," Hugo said through gritted teeth. What the devil was she doing here?

"Hugo, old boy. How are you?" Frederick said, extending a hand, which Hugo shook, whilst awkwardly leaning across the booth. Frederick's hand squeezed his tight, and he felt the bones of his fingers crunch together.

"I'm fine, thanks," Hugo said. 'After you broke my heart by stealing the woman I loved.' He wanted to add.

"I hear you've missed me." Arabella slipped in next to Hugo before he could escape. The club felt hot and stuffy. Arabella's warm breath, smelling of fine champagne and cherries, tickled his neck. Hugo needed to feel the cold whip of fresh air against his skin.

"I didn't realise she was invited," Hugo said, turning to face Clemency who'd just returned with a fresh round of champagne.

"Arabella, wanted to wish Yves-Jacques well, but can't attend the wedding as she and Frederick are flying to Thailand tomorrow to begin filming her latest movie."

"Oh, don't be like that," Arabella purred.

"So," Frederick said, setting his beady black eyes on Hugo. "What is it you do exactly?"

"I'm a writer," Hugo said between gritted teeth.

"He writes romances," Arabella smiled at Frederick as though she was looking at the most adorable man on the planet. It made Hugo's gut clench.

"I write about finding love. Not romances."

"Sounds about the same," Frederick grunted and turned away. "I think I'll go to the bar."

"So have you chosen a winner?" Arabella asked Hugo.

"I don't know what you're talking about."

"Between Sophia, Tabby and Fleur."

"Excuse me?"

"Clemency told me all about the little bet she had with Poppy and Yves-Jacques."

"What bet?" Hugo turned to Clemency, whose eyes were wide and innocent.

"Who could choose the woman who'd mend your heart after I broke it."

"Is this true?" Hugo asked Clemency. The swirl of people filling the club blurred in the background as he tried to read her face. He could see the fine veins under the skin of her neck pulsing; her nostrils flared. "I don't believe it. How could you."

He turned, ready to escape. Arabella grabbed his face between his hands and kissed him on the lips.

"What are you doing?"

Arabella shrugged. "Frederick is getting boring. I've missed you."

"I have of get out of here," Hugo headed for the door.

He ran into Yves-Jacques, who'd just arrived, on the way out. "Hey, where do you think you're going?"

"You had a bet over my love life?"

"It was just a silly little thing. We were trying to help you out."

"By playing with my heart and three innocent women? I have to get out of here." He pushed his way through the club until he found the closest exit. The outside air was gentle, cool and calming. The full moon lit, dancing shadows across the cobblestone street.

"Hugo! Wait!" It was Clemency. He turned to see his friend,

her black velvet vintage Laura Ashley gown blending with the night sky, chasing him onto the lamp-lit street.

"Where are you going?"

"I have to sort this mess out."

"I'll come with you."

"Non."

"I'm sorry. Je suis désolée. We were only trying to help you. It was Poppy's idea."

"It's no one's fault. I'm so angry at myself for juggling three women. There's something wrong with me."

"Don't be mad; you're a great guy, Hugo. Any woman would be lucky to have you."

Clemency stepped forward and pushed her icy cold lips to his. Hugo didn't move; he was too shocked. Two sudden kisses in one night? She stepped back and smiled. A bunch of tourists, late to the show, cheered and whistled as they walked past them on the street.

"What was that for?"

"Over these last weeks, Hugo, I realised something. I'm in love with you. I always have been. I just didn't know it."

Hugo ran his hand across his forehead. "Clemency."

"You needn't say anything."

"Clemency, I'm in love with Tabby. And you're not in love with me, you're scared of losing me. But I'm not going anywhere. You'll always be my best friend."

"Non, I don't believe it. You just don't realise how much you're in love with me. Neither of us could see it, but it is the truth. Besides I always get what I want. I know deep down you know it."

"I'm sorry, Clemency, but I don't. I don't believe that you're in love with me, either. I think you're just afraid of losing us, our friendship, because you can see how much I'm in love with Tabby. You've never seen me like this before, and you're afraid. Plus you believe your brothers abandoned you for another woman, now you think I'm doing the same. I'm not going to play your game, Clemency. I'm in love with Tabby; I think she's wonderful and I hope you can respect that. I'm sorry I can't give you what you want."

A tear dripped down Clemency's cheek. Hugo stepped forward to wipe it away, but she pushed him in the chest.

"Can we forget this ever happened?" Clemency asked.

"Of course," Hugo promised before turning his back and heading home.

CHAPTER TWENTY NINE

WEDDING BLISS

"You look like a shooting star," Tabby said. Her eyes glided over the silver dress hugging Fleur's curves. Beautiful long, semi-see-through sleeves of sheer pastel blue silk kissed her arms, Venetian glass bangles clinked on Fleur's wrist. She held the grace and sense of style that French women all over the world are reputed for possessing.

"Thank you. The dress is Valentino."

"Who?"

Fleur rolled her eyes. "You remind me of myself in high school. It's like you've never grown out of the, *I'm a rebellious teenager who wears horrid clothes to rebel against my parents phase.*"

Tabby scowled. "This is cool."

"You can't wear that," Fleur said, glaring at Tabby's outfit.

"What's the big deal? It's vintage." Tabby grinned. Secretly she was proud of her eclectic taste. The best thing about wearing recycled clothes was that you never looked like everybody else. In Tabby's eyes, she had swagger.

"The problem is that sweat jumpers, pleather leggings and Doc Martens are not suitable celebrity wedding attire. We are going to Monaco, darling, and you won't even get past the front gates."

"Who knew Monaco had gates? Is it surrounded by guard dogs as well?"

"You should have reminded me of your *complete incompetence* to dress like a civilized human being. You've left me with next to no time to improve your looks. But I'm sure we can rustle up something."

"I'm glad you have faith in my ability to morph into Cinderella." Tabby knew she could *never* be Cinderella.

"I have faith in my ability to make things beautiful: a house, a person, anything. Fresh clothes, a lick paint, and you might just pass for charming."

"That'll be a first," Tabby muttered as Fleur grabbed her wrist, dragging her towards the bedroom. "Your apartment smells nice," Tabby said. "Like old books, rose geranium and oil paint." Tabby's eyes lingered over the ice white walls and imposing paintings of men and women tangled together in knots staring at her from the walls. Piles of books were stacked on a glass coffee table, and pink shelves housed glass jars filled with gold wrapped chocolates.

The bedroom was minimalist. So perfect, Tabby, found it hard to relax. The walls were white, matching the running theme of Fleur's home. The ensemble bed pressed up against a giant, framed embroidered tapestry of gold silk that had been woven with brilliant reds and greens to create an Oriental ethereal scene.

On one side of the bed was a wooden chest stacked with Vogue magazines and on the other was a rickety old rocking chair; a plush teddy bear sat in the centre. Tabby wondered if it had been a gift from Hugo. She pushed the thought out of her mind.

"Now, where to start," Fleur said, studying Tabby's face. "I'll be right back."

She disappeared from the bedroom; leaving Tabby feeling alone and vulnerable. Truth be told; Tabby hadn't even registered that she was going to a wedding. A celebrity occasion. Where most normal people competed in the style stakes.

Last night, she'd felt glued to the sheets. She hadn't wanted to face Paris. How could Hugo do this to her? To us? She'd been so stupid to believe that he loved her. She was nothing more than a number in his long list of conquests.

Everything he'd said, about wanting her, only her... it had felt so real. Like she could reach out and touch his emotions. She shook her head. How could you trust a man that had been dating three - no make that four - women at once? Tabby swallowed, hard; she would not start crying in front of Fleur.

Fleur slipped back into the room.

"Do you always wear high heels at home?"

"No. We were supposed to leave soon as you got here. Mon dieu!"

"What about Sophia?"

"She sent a txt message, we need to pick her up on the way."

"What's this?" Tabby pulled back from the white washcloth Fleur was thrusting under her nose.

"You need to wash your face. Did you sleep in your makeup last night?"

"I was on a train from London at five a.m."

"Dépêchez-vous de."

Tabby didn't have to speak French to know Fleur wanted her to speed up. She began wiping the washcloth over her skin. She hadn't bothered to shower. Black eyeliner came off under her eyes in great clumps. The towel was soft and soothing, cooling her skin and refreshing her energy.

"Okay, now let me take a look at you," Fleur said, hauling a big black makeup box into the room, her arms sagged as though she was holding a ton of bricks. She dropped it onto the floorboards with a loud bang, popped open the silver latches and, like opening a treasure chest, revealed sparkling rows of designer makeup.

Silver topped Dior lip gloss glittered in the early morning sunshine rays. Chanel eye shadow in signature black cases with the twin Cs sat stacked in rows. Gold Yves Saint Lauren highlighters shimmered, as Tabby, like a goldfish, lost herself in the case.

"Wow. That box must be worth like ten grand."

"It pays for itself," Fleur shrugged as she pulled out a bottle of Sensei Foundation.

"What do you mean?"

"I mean," Fleur replied, drizzling some foundation on the palm of her hand before sprinkling some Estee Lauder shimmer powder into the mix to lighten the colour, "appearance is everything. You walk around with your Doc Martens and piercings and don't care what people think of you. But people do think. It's easier to get what you want when you dress the part. Look at me, my hair, my clothes - conservative yet sexy, understated elegance. Not enough to make other woman compete with me and feel threatened by my presence, just enough to make everyone admire my style. Don't you think I haven't thought about my appearance? I do every day. It's calculated to read: empowered women who will someday be the Editor in Chief of Luxe Décor, Paris, France."

"Okay," Tabby said. "Who's the real you then?"

"What?"

"The one hiding under your façade."

"The real me is a nerdy girl who wears oversized T-shirts, black skinny-legged jeans, wears glasses and reads like a tyrant. Never goes anywhere, except when food is needed and overindulges daily on flambé pancakes."

"She sounds cool," Tabby said. Thinking no wonder Fleur is always so uptight, it's like she's wearing a prim and proper jumpsuit. An alien inhabiting another person's body.

"She's a depressed, sick looking thing, who's been dumped by every man she ever dated. Cool maybe. Inspiring non."

Tabby shrugged. "Well then, Fairy Godmother, if you promise you can wash away a broken heart - be my guest." Tabby bit her tongue and sat for what seemed like an hour as Fleur remade her face. "I feel like the doll you never had as a child."

"Oh, I had plenty of dolls." Fleur purred. "You just look like a real life Barbie."

"Great, my life's mission is complete."

"Most girls would kill for your looks."

"Well, not me. In general, I look like a drowned rat; dead straight hair that I never wash. I never brush my teeth. I rot my insides with junk food. I thought Paris was going to change me, change my outlook on life. I don't know what to think anymore."

"So meeting me and Sophia has left you in a depressed slump? Interesting. I'll be sure to write that in my diary."

Tabby snorted. "I liked Sophia instantly, but you took a bit of warming up to. You can add that in as well. Meeting you and Sophia has been both a blessing and a curse. I feel like I've known you both forever, and I had hoped before coming here that maybe I would know Hugo, forever."

"Nothings forever. Shattered dreams are like falling stars, beautiful as they disappear into the abyss representing the breath of life's offerings."

"Poetic."

Fleur ignored the sarcasm in Tabby's tone. "You took a leap of faith, Tabby. I've never said it before, but I admire you. What you did, giving up your old life for love and belief in a dream of creating beautiful jewellery - that's brave."

"Not when you consider how bland my life was before."

"You left your family and friends for a foreign country on the drifts of a dream, daring to hope for more. You just haven't uncovered your own magnificence yet. Don't give up because one guy breaks your heart. You are *magnifique*. Hugo doesn't know what he's missing out on."

Tabby breathed in a great gulp of air. She felt the white walls pressing in around her. She was horrible at suppressing her feelings, especially when people were nice to her, and she had no right to upset Fleur. She should be comforting her. A fat tear rolled down her cheek. She stuck her tongue out and licked the cold salty bead.

Fleur had left her side and was rummaging through her wardrobe. It was painted pastel blue and looked like something you'd see on Antiques Roadshow. "I've found it; put this on."

Fleur emerged triumphantly, holding up a silk summer dress. She twisted the silver and velvet hanger in her hand. The dress was backless, and canary yellow. Turquoise beaded straps hung low over the back where the silk floated down into a neat v.

"Now this is vintage, to die for, it's Versace," Fleur said.

"I'm not wearing that."

Fleur's mouth hung open like a codfish. "Stand up," she said tight-lipped. "Take your clothes off and put this on."

"I can see why Sophia was intimidated by your sexual prowess. If you wanted to see me naked you just had to ask."

"I'm not asking."

"And I hate being told what to do. It's lovely of you to offer me this dress. But, it's so *yellow*. I just can't do it."

Fleur lowered the dress. Her expression of steel determination faltered. "Please, for me, just try it on. If you still think non, once you're in the dress, I'll let you choose anything you want to wear from my wardrobe."

"Anything?"

Fleur nodded.

The dress smelt like the ocean, seaweed and sand, summer

holidays and ice cream cones topped in peanuts and chocolate chips. Fleur gasped when Tabby popped her head through the top of the cool silk fabric.

"I told you. I don't do yellow." Tabby said. "It makes me look cheap."

"It's not that. Tabby, take a look in the mirror."

Tabby's feet rubbed against notches in the hardwood floor as she made her way to the gold gilt mirror resting on the sidewall of Fleur's bedroom. The reflection staring at her didn't look anything like her usual self. She looked glamorous, wistful and almost angelic.

Tabby spun, and the dress floated around her like feathers caught in a light breeze. Her makeup was simple, bringing out the angles and shadows of her face like a young woman posing on for cover of Vogue magazine. "Wow. I look..."

"Stunning," Fleur answered for her.

"I look beautiful."

Fleur's thin lips snapped into a gorgeous smile. "So, you'll wear the dress?"

"I think you'll have to pry it off me."

"Good. Now let's get going. We're already late. Sophia texted me ten minutes ago asking what's taking us so long."

The two women abandoned the apartment and headed into the streets. Tabby felt her spirits lift. She felt lighter. Not like they were going to resurrect the hurt that came with dating a four-timing philanderer, who had snapped her heart in two. More like she was going to a party. The way she'd felt when she was a little girl and her Dad had made her choose friends to invite over, and they'd wrapped a giant present for pass the parcel. She felt good. Like the weight of the past five years had lifted and she could breathe.

Paris was deserted so early in the morning, except for a lonely fruit cart wheeling its way down Fleur's street. The old man pulling the cart along nodded his beret in their direction. Tabby could have sworn he winked at her, before she jumped into Fleur's Mini Cooper.

Fleur drove - wild, free and completely bonkers. As the pale blue Mini Cooper pulled in tight alongside the curb, Tabby, took in a deep gulp of air. Her lungs felt ready to burst; she'd been holding her breath the entire drive.

"When's the last time you drove?" Tabby asked, jumping out of the car. Its engine purred like a content kitten.

"Three months ago," Fleur replied with a flick of her wrist. "I went to visit my parents in Normandy."

"Right, I'm driving the rest of the way."

"You can't wear that." Fleur said as she took in Sophia standing on the pavement.

It had begun to drizzle, the air's bitter chill sunk into their bones. Protected by an oversized black umbrella, Sophia pouted as she looked down at the white lace dress she'd squeezed into this morning. Granted she was all tits and bum, but she felt good. Sexy. Fleur's shrill tone and Tabby's gapping expression did nothing to boost her confidence.

"Don't worry she said the same thing to me this morning." Tabby consoled Sophia.

"Does it make me look fat?"

"You look like Sophia Loren," Tabby said.

Sophia beamed, turning to Fleur.

"Sophia Loren - about to walk down the aisle. What are you planning on doing? Kidnapping the groom?" Fleur asked, perplexed.

Tabby burst out laughing. Sophia had obviously spent hours choosing her outfit, and it was true, she did indeed look ready to walk down the aisle.

"I need to get his attention," Sophia snapped.

"Ma cherie," Fleur's expression softened. "He's hurt all of us. I didn't say anything earlier, but I've been starting to think this whole trip is a waste of time. What are we going to achieve? Ruin Hugo's wedding? Make him look like a fool in the media?"

"Exactly," Tabby replied. "And let Arabella Spark's know what she is getting herself into."

"But what do *we* get out of it? We're so focused on bringing Hugo down that we've forgotten about bringing ourselves up. I've had enough. I'm out. I'm going to go and get a croissant, put my glasses on and read a good book. We could share a champagne breakfast? There is a gorgeous café round the corner."

Tabby sighed. She hated to admit it, but Fleur did have a point. Crushing Hugo was crushing her just as much. Is this what Zen would've wanted? The thought blasted through her brain like a loudspeaker.

"You're right," Tabby said to Fleur. "I need a cup of tea and a holiday."

"You're on holiday," Sophia replied.

"I think I'm going to book a trip to India. Want to come? I might find some inspiration for my new jewellery collection. The one I'm going to start myself."

Fleur shook her head, then grinned. "Sounds like a plan. They have some amazing palaces. I could organize some fantastic photoshoots for the magazine. I could do a piece on Niels Schoenfelder, he's designed some fabuleux mansions there. I'll combine business *and* pleasure." She thought of inviting Diego along, after all, everything between them had been going so well.

"Well, as long as the pleasure doesn't involve a man, you'll be fine," Tabby grinned, and Fleur's face flushed pink.

The two women felt a surge of pride and relief. They'd claimed part of themselves back.

"You two are missing the whole point," Sophia blurted out.

"You can come with us," Fleur suggested.

"Yeah," Tabby chimed. "It's something we can do for ourselves as independent women of the world. You could learn to cook Indian, my favourite." Tabby added, thinking the allure of amazing food and exotic spices would convince Sophia.

"Think of what Hugo's done to us. The betrayal. The hurt. The lies," Sophia pleaded.

She was beginning to sound desperate, Tabby thought.

"Ma cherie, you need to let go," Fleur said. "I know it's hard. Hugo hurt us all, but there are always people out there in the world who can cause us pain. We need to rise above things. Learn to take care of ourselves. Not be brought down into puddles of negativity."

"I can't let go." Silent tears dripped down Sophia's rosy cheeks. They felt like icy particles against the warmth of her skin.

"Oh, sweetheart." Tripping in the nine-inch Louboutins Fleur had lent her, Tabby swung her arms around her friend. "Don't cry; everything's going to be okay. You don't have to forgive Hugo right now, but in time you will. As much as I dislike the man, Hugo showed me how to have fun and be myself. Ruining his wedding, it would be like I've morphed into all of the things I hated so much about him. I know it doesn't make sense right now, but it will. I promise."

Sophia pried herself free of Tabby's grasp. "Maybe for you. But not for me. Not now, not ever."

Cut, Tabby pulled back. Fleur caught something deep in Sophia's distant gaze.

"What is it?" Fleur asked. "What are you not telling us?"

Tabby looked at her friend. Trying to catch a glimpse of the secret Fleur had seen. She could see only empty dark pools of sadness.

"I'm…"

"You're what?" Tabby asked, breathless with anticipation. The suspense was killing her.

"Pregnant."

"You're what?" Tabby spat, her mind locked in repeat.

Fleur gasped. "I should have guessed. Not drinking wine. Turning green at the sight of my escargots. It all makes sense."

"No, this makes absolutely no sense. Zilch," Tabby huffed. "You could have told us! We're supposed to be friends."

"That's why I'm telling you now," Sophia retorted. "I haven't even told Hugo."

"How could you do this?" Tabby snapped. "How long have you known? A couple of days?" Sophia looked blank, like she was biting back tears. "A week. A month?"

"Three weeks. I tried to tell him. Honestly. But I could never find the right moment, and now he isn't answering my calls. And there's another complication."

Tabby felt as though another complication from Sophia would flatten her. Was it possible for a person to spontaneously combust from heartbreak, combined with shock?

"Spill," Fleur purred.

Tabby glared at Fleur. She was so composed, drifting through the day as though nothing could hurt her. At one point, Tabby felt like Fleur found the whole thing a game. Maybe it was the mask of perfection that most women paraded around with on the streets of Paris. Or maybe it was that she didn't care about Hugo.

"Whatever it is we'll sort it out. Together." It was Fleur's turn to return Tabby's glare.

"The reason I didn't tell Hugo," Sophia stopped short.

"Oui," Fleur said, her French accent curling over the word.

"Yes," Tabby snapped.

"I'm not sure who the father is."

Sophia felt the heat rushing to her face. She knew that she looked as red as one of the beetroots sitting on the shelf of the farmers market.

"What?" Fleur choked.

"Yeah, who else have you been sleeping with?" Tabby said.

"Tabby, that is not helping." Fleur said. "You're so crude."

"Me? I'm crude. If anyone's crude, it's Sophia. She doesn't even know who the father of her own baby is."

At that, both women looked up to see Sophia storming down the street, looking somewhat between a runaway bride and Bridget Jones.

"Now look what you've done," Fleur said. Her tone was cold as the icy air, kissing their cheeks. "You fix this."

"Why should I?"

"Go," Fleur pushed Tabby in the back. Her hands slid off the tight yellow, silk dress, clinging to her hands. "It's time you did something to help someone else rather than wallow in your own misery all day."

"I do help people out."

"No, you don't. You're constantly replaying the traumas of your own life. You need to change your mindset and get out there and live."

In sky high Louboutin heels, Tabby began to hobble down the street. French women gliding down the pavement beside her, also in heels, seemed to float, making her feel inferior. She found if she lifted one-foot high enough and clomped it down with a boom on the pavement, she could reinvent the moonwalk - no lack of gravity necessary - and run.

When Tabby caught up to Sophia, it felt like her lungs had split into dozens of tiny razor blades. She grabbed Sophia's white dress and gasped. "Slow down."

Sophia's mascara was smudged down the edges of her face. She looked crumpled, tiny and small. Nothing like the strong, funny American that Tabby had met in her apartment for the first time all those weeks ago. They were standing at the front of a crepe stand where a fat woman spooned gooey mix onto a flat pan. The smell of burnt sugar cut through the air.

"I'm sorry. I shouldn't have reacted the way I did. You took me by surprise. If I'm honest, I was jealous."

"Jealous?" Sophia's voice was tinged with disbelief.

"Yes. I want to get over Hugo. But I never wanted to believe that it was possible that you or Fleur or his elusive bride could have been closer to him than I was. You have to understand. I'm not just giving Hugo up. I fought for him; I was in love with the man. I am in love with him. It's just, I know when it's time to stand down."

"Oh."

"Can you forgive me? I promise no snide remarks, nothing. I'll do whatever you want. I'll help you get Hugo back or Charles. He is the other man, isn't he?"

"Yes," Sophia giggled.

Tabby looked up; there was nothing funny about her handing over the man of her dreams to his bride to be, or to Sophia. It was like offering someone the last golden Lindt chocolate.

"I don't want Hugo back," Sophia said.

"You don't?"

"No. I did at first, but this baby," she ran her hand over her stomach. Tabby detected a soft motherly glow that illuminated Sophia, a golden aura. Why hadn't she noticed earlier? "It's changed everything. At first all I could think about was myself. But there's two of us now. I've just been too much of a coward to tell Hugo the truth. I didn't want to look like a bad person."

"You're not a bad person."

Sophia shrugged. "That's not important. Hugo needs to know the truth. He needs to know that we know, and he needs to know that very soon, he might be a Daddy." It was the first time Sophia had said the word *Daddy* out loud.

"It's why I have to get to the wedding. Hugo has a right to know what he's getting into and so does Arabella Sparks."

"More like what he's gotten himself into." Tabby felt her heart shatter. It felt like a thousand tiny pieces of broken glass; a jigsaw that could never be fixed. Deep down she'd been hoping that, by some miracle, Hugo would change his mind about the whole thing and come back for her. She knew now she'd never been so wrong. That could never happen.

Fleur was walking towards the Mini Cooper.

"Where are you going?" Sophia called. Her voice was hoarse and rough.

"Come on, ladies. We've got a wedding to crash."

CHAPTER THIRTY

MONACO'S DARLINGS

*T*abby sat silent for most of the trip. Sophia gave her a few furtive glances. Fleur pointed out tiny cottages and discussed the history of St. Tropez's rocky peninsula and the views across the sea to the Maures mountains, as they whizzed past.

"Are you mad at me?" Sophia asked Tabby when she could take the other woman's lofty silence no more.

"Why would I be mad?"

"Because I'm pregnant and because I didn't tell you."

"I wouldn't have told anyone if I was pregnant with Hugo's baby," Fleur drawled. "It's no one's business but the mother's, the father's and the baby's."

Sophia wanted to snap that she had tried to tell Hugo, multiple times. It was a difficult task when you didn't know who the father was.

"What was he like?" Tabby asked, breaking her silent spell. The question had been burning the inside of her stomach. It felt like fireworks had exploded in her chest. So this was the feeling when your heart shattered, she thought. It was interesting when you looked at the pain through a sort of out-of-body vantage point.

"What was who like?" Fleur asked. Her French accent seemed to thicken the closer they got to St. Tropez. Her eyes were sparkling, bouncing against the rays of light the diamond and opal rings she wore all over her fingers let off.

"Hugo," Tabby said.

"Hugo?" Sophia replied, not comprehending Tabby's meaning.

"In bed. When you had sex. What was it like, what was he like?"

"Isn't that an odd question to ask the mistress of your lover?" Fleur purred.

"Sophia asked what I was thinking."

Fleur shrugged in resignation.

Sophia stammered. "I don't remember."

"You don't remember?" Tabby said. She could summon images of Hugo on top of her in an instant, the soft smell of his sweat, the hardness of his chest, his firm muscles pressing against her own cool skin. "I don't believe you."

"It's true. I do remember his lips pressed hard against mine, his breath was warm, and it was like no other kiss I've ever experienced. I remember wanting him so much it hurt. I ripped his shirt off and ran my hands over his smooth naked chest and then next thing I knew, I woke up in Hugo's apartment. He was lying next to me in his bed, shirt off, boxers on. We'd been out drinking.

I'd been riddled with guilt - leaving Charles at home all alone.

But then I thought, how many times has he done this to me? How many times has Charles had this opportunity? An opportunity to escape from one life and into another. Even if it's only for a night. I remember kissing him; he tasted like honey and red wine. I remember dragging him into his bedroom. I didn't even know where it was; I navigated my way around his apartment, guiding him into a linen closet first."

"Hugo does have stunning linens," Fleur chimed.

"So what happened?"

"I took my top off, swung it onto the gorgeous Murano glass chandelier hanging from his bedroom ceiling, started laughing... and that's all I remember."

"That's all?" Tabby couldn't believe Sophia. How could she have forgotten sleeping with Hugo? And manage to wind up pregnant?

"If you had slept with Hugo, you'd remember, Sophia. I can assure you. He was my first," Fleur said, obviously doubtful.

Sophia shrugged; it didn't matter what she remembered. Whatever had happened, it'd been enough. The look on Hugo's face the morning after, that look of lush relaxation had confirmed what Sophia thought she knew about what happened that fateful night.

"First what?" Tabby said.

"Lover, of course. Sweet, muscular, gentle and rough," Fleur replied. Her lips kinked upwards at the corners in memory.

"Too much information," Sophia said. She could feel her baby's ears burning.

"How often do you and Hugo have sex?" Tabby asked Fleur in all seriousness.

"I don't think that's any of your business," Fleur said.

"I need to know."

"Why?" Sophia asked.

"Well, he slept with me only once. Maybe he wasn't attracted to me." Tabby felt stupid saying it out loud. "He never really loved me."

"Hugo never loved any of us." Sophia said.

"He used us," Fleur replied.

"I guess," Tabby said. "Fleur, you don't seem very upset. I feel like you're acting as though we're going on a summer holiday."

"We're out of Paris. The country air is refreshing and revitalising. Birds are singing to their loved ones. The sky is climbing out from behind the clouds. Why wouldn't I be happy? I'm not going to spend my life moping over one man."

"Fair enough," Sophia said. "Though you do seem happier than normal. More relaxed."

"If you're not going to spend your life moping over one man, then who is the other one?" Tabby asked.

"You make no sense, darling," Fleur said, her features sinking into rigid composure. "I'm relaxed and I'm happy. I know a darling little bakery we can pop into along the way. Who's in the mood for croissants?"

* * *

The wedding crowd was bustling. An excited cluster of

glamorous rich people. Women with oversized hats blocked Sophia's view and left her feeling as though she were attending a rock concert - not a wedding. Women held champagne flutes, waving them about as though they were red bull flags and would make men charge at them as they lured them in with long silk bustier style dresses, littered with Swarovski crystals, ostrich feathers and sequins.

"Everyone looks like they are trying to compete with the bride," Tabby whispered to Fleur. "I don't know why you were so worried about Sophia's dress."

"This is Monaco, darling, if you're not someone, you're no one," Fleur smiled, taking a flute of Moet from a passing waiter dressed in a white tux. She turned and took a breath of fresh ocean air; she could almost taste sea salt on her tongue. The glamorous gardens and super yachts lining Monaco's bay always made her feel like she'd arrived in a fairy tale land that she never wanted to leave.

"He's cute," Tabby said, eyeing the waiter. Despite the tragedy of the situation, her heart felt lighter. Maybe things would get better. They had with Zen's death. She thought about him a lot, but not in the morbid, depressed way she used to. More like a guardian angel. Hugo, however, wasn't dead, nor was he an angel.

"I think we should split up," Fleur said. "Sophia and I will look for Hugo and you can find the bride."

"Find the bride?" Tabby hissed, hoping no one was listening in on their conversation.

"Well someone has to warn Arabella Sparks. The media will have a field day, and I expect the poor girl is going to be devastated when she finds our her fiancé has been dating three other women simultaneously. We're going to drop a bomb, and she shouldn't be a fall out victim."

"I don't think that can be helped."

"Is that Kate Moss?" Sophia asked, eyes wandering over the swelling crowd.

"We're on a mission," Fleur snapped. "Don't lose focus Sophia, nor you Tabby." Tabby was now searching for a glimpse of Kate. Was she just as beautiful and skinny in real life as in Vogue magazine?

"I think I should go with Sophia," Tabby said. "It's not fair that I have to be the other woman - again. I don't like breaking hearts."

"Would you rather hunt Hugo down?" Fleur asked.

Tabby shuddered involuntarily at the thought of Hugo. What could she say to him? That he'd torn her heart in two, and the sky would never be a vibrant blue for her again? That since he'd rejected her she'd never felt more lost - or more in love?

"I'm gone." She began to back away, leaving her two friends.

"Tabby, we'll meet back here in thirty-five minutes," Fleur called into the thrum of the crowd.

Tabby waved her hand in response and disappeared into a mess of flapping hands, women squawking, posing and preening, and men boasting about the size of their Ferraris and the colour of their new Lamborghini.

How, Tabby thought, was she supposed to find the bride? Wasn't she, Hugo's fiancée, supposed to arrive an hour later than all the guests? She could be in Timbuktu, for all Tabby knew. Plus, Arabella Sparks, was a movie star; she'd likely have body guards.

"I need a sign, something pointing me in the right direction," she said out loud. A handful of balding, middle-aged men stared at her, trying to decipher whether or not she was a mad woman. No one had the opportunity to ask, as their wives, in swirls of black velvet, gloves and silk, pulled them far away from the albino haired girl. "I'm not mad, truly." Tabby said to no one in particular.

Seeing an arrow pointing towards the lady's restrooms, Tabby shrugged; it was as good a sign as any. Fleur's feet were a size smaller than Tabby's, and the heels of the borrowed Louboutins cut into her. She lifted her legs like a stalk wading over lily pads, trying to prevent blisters.

Tabby pushed her way through the black door covered in gold gilded flowers, emerging into the most beautiful toilets she'd ever laid eyes upon. A huge gold mirror, framed with cherubs and carved vine leaves, bounced her reflection into several other mirrors on the opposing wall, which were filled with the faces of three women, fluffing their cheeks with blush, one smoking a cigarette and another licking red lipstick from her teeth. At first, Tabby didn't recognise her own reflection she looked so refined in Fleur's, Versace dress.

Yellow silk, a colour she'd never even thought of wearing before, complemented her ice white hair. And Fleur's magic with the makeup brush meant the black moon circles that hung under her eyes were now invisible. Blush ran along her cheeks, elongating the sharp curves and plains of her face. If she didn't know how wretched and heartbroken she felt deep down, she would have almost thought she looked elegant. As though she belonged in a glamorous place like this. She didn't have to laugh at the gastronomic poshness of everyone and everything around her; she almost looked as though she fit right in.

"You look like sunshine," a woman wearing a black hat, black netted veil, and a bright red lipstick smiled at Tabby's reflection. She looked like a redback spider, her eyes as black as her hat.

"Thank you," Tabby replied. "So, how do you know the groom?"

"I'm Valerie, his mother. You must be a friend of the bride. I'm sure I'd remember if we'd met before. You have such an unusual complexion."

Tabby blushed, her cheeks glowing like two bruised plums in the mirror. "But of course," Tabby stumbled. So this was Hugo's mother? She had his dark hair; other than that they didn't look alike. She was round with sharp features and pointy, vicious eyes.

"Weddings are the most trivial occasions. After several of your own, you tend to grow tired of the silly affairs. I only came to this one as you can imagine how it would look if I stayed on the yacht in Venice. I was having such a nice time too," she pouted. "Hugo insisted I come watch my son marry a foreigner. Humph, you're not a fool, are you?"

"Tabitha."

"Tabitha?" Her named rolled off Valerie's tongue, sounding like a viper's kiss.

Tabby met Valerie's eyes in the bathroom mirror. The chatter of women in the background had grown to a dull blur. It felt as though no one existed in the world but Tabby and Valerie.

Frightful and fascinating, it was easy, thought Tabby, to see how this stylish woman had lured so many men into her web. In that regard, she and Hugo were identical. Fighting the urge to run as quickly from the restroom as possible, Tabby held her ground. She had a mission to complete. This was mafia business, and she had run head first into the godfather or, in this case, the godmother.

"Aren't we all fools?"

"In love we are. That's why I've avoided the whole silly business of loving a man my entire life. All we have is ourselves to care for, no one else matters. Take my advice. You're young enough not to be broken. Never give your heart to a man. He'll trample it and use you. Love is for fools. My son is a fool and yet you, this pretty reflection in the glass, have the opportunity to be something great. Don't waste it on a man."

Tabby was dumbfounded. Could Valerie see her soul - read her heartbreak? Was she that much of a broken, open book? The woman spoke in riddles.

Tabby's brain felt fuzzy. "I'm having an affair with your son. You have to cancel the wedding. It's a terrible mistake," she blurted out before she could stop herself.

"Valerie, darling!" A shrill voice interrupted their conversation. "I've been looking all over for you." A large buxom lady dressed in a bright orange gown that clung to her broad waist beamed at Valerie. "What are you doing in here talking with this stick insect?"

A ripple of pain shot through Tabby. Stick insect? She was

talking about her. It felt like she was back in pre-primary again.

"Are you trying to insult me?" Tabby asked.

"Of course not," the woman squealed. "You're just so thin, I almost saw through you."

Tabby didn't feel beautiful anymore. She felt like a squashed ant.

"Stop acting so jealous, Pearl. This is Tabitha, my son's mistress."

Pearl rolled her eyes and went on, ignoring Tabby. "Everyone is looking for you. The Prince of Monaco is here. You have to come and meet him. He has potential, darling; I'm thinking number 8?"

"Number 8?" Tabby blurted.

"She's talking husbands, dear," Valerie said.

"Oh," Tabby felt uncomfortable, as though everyone could see right through her. She didn't belong here. "I have to go," Tabby said. "Valerie, could you tell me where I can find the bride?"

"Whatever for? Haven't you heard a word I've been saying? It doesn't do to dwell on love."

"I know you're the last person who wants to deal with this right now. But the bride has a right to know. Aren't you going to do something? Don't you want to help me fix this?"

"How? It's none of my business. Thank goodness my son isn't as loyal as I thought. I want him to experience life."

"But what about me?"

"What about you? Would you like an award? A certificate for

your efforts."

"We could crown you, Miss Promiscuity!" Pearl enthused, and both women cackled.

"The bride, shouldn't we help her? She needs to know what she's getting herself into!" Tabby pleaded.

"Well, now Pearl knows, you've just told every guest at the wedding."

"It's true," Pearl cooed. "I love gossip. But I never intentionally hurt anyone."

Tabby knew that was a lie. "I have to find the bride. It's important. Hugo has a message for her," Tabby added as an afterthought. Damn, she wished she were better at lying on the spot.

"A message from Hugo? How intriguing. She's staying at The Hotel Hermitage Monte-Carlo, room 117. You can send my son a message as well."

"Okay."

"Tell him I always knew he was an idiot and now the rest of the world can see just how foolish he is. Congratulations on your special day, Mummykins."

"Mummykins?" Tabby said with raised brows.

"Yes, dear. Now, Pearl, where is this Prince?" Valerie looped her bony arm into Pearl's and together the two women left Tabby alone in the bathroom. "This wedding is turning out to be rather a laugh!"

Tabby stared at her reflection. These women had managed to kick, slap and beat her without lifting a finger. She felt more bruised than when Hugo had stolen her heart. She wanted to fit in with this elite crowd. Tabby knew that now. But she needed a thick skin, and muscle, if she were ever going to compete. Feeling small and insignificant, Tabby carried her red, blistering, stinging feet from the bathroom.

Poor Arabella, she kept thinking. Despite wanting to resist her growing swell of sympathy for the woman, Tabby realised that she wasn't that cold. Hugo hadn't destroyed her. If she could feel empathy for the woman that had stolen her lover's heart, she could learn to love another again.

I thought my mother was a nightmare, Tabby mused. She thought back to all the times when she had felt envious of girls who'd grown up in the lap of luxury. At the time, she believed they had everything that she didn't possess: beautiful frocks, presents wrapped in ribbon, new puppies, clothes made of silk, velvet and couture dresses. All along she had never known that love was not something that was freely given. When it came, in any form, it was a gift and needed to be treasured, like a rare and precious diamond.

Tabby stumbled out of the restroom. She needed air, and she needed to get to Arabella before she found out about Hugo through a bunch of gossiping woman. Or worse still, before she walked down the aisle, a thousand eyes upon her, whispering behind her back. How horrid!

"Tabby, there you are!" Sophia appeared from behind a giant bouquet of roses clustered together in a rust coloured French urn.

"We've been looking all over for you," Fleur snapped.

"I've been trying to locate the bride."

"In the toilets?" Sophia said, biting the tips of her nails before Fleur slapped her hand down in disgust.

"She's staying at the Hermitage," Tabby replied.

"You didn't say anything about why we're here did you?" Fleur asked.

"Tabby?" Sophia's voice was like a coaxing headmistress. She wanted to confess everything at once and at the same time knew it would be safer if she kept her dalliance with Valerie to herself.

"It's written all over your face. Who did you tell?" Fleur said.

"Is it that obvious?" Tabby groaned. "What's the big deal anyway? I was supposed to locate the bride, and I have. She was going to find out what a grease-ball her fiancée is at some point. I just need to let her know before that gossip, Pearl, spills the beans and she finds out through the grapevine."

"Pearl?" Fleur said, eyes growing wider by the minute. "You told Pearl Vandertrump?"

"I don't know her last name. We have to find Arabella and outline the facts," Tabby said, triumphant that her levelheadedness had returned.

"Pearl Vandertrump is the biggest gossip in the South of France!" Fleur closed her eyes and took a deep breath. "Find Sophia a chair, she's pregnant and will need some air to deal with the shock."

Tabby glanced at Sophia. Where Fleur looked pale and rigid, like plaster ready to crack, Sophia looked strong and determined, as though she had a baby soldier growing inside her.

"Let's get outside, find the first car we can and take it to the Hermitage. If we get there quickly enough, there won't be too much fall out damage. The wedding must go on," Sophia said.

"Must go on?" Tabby scrunched her petite features into a tight knot. "You've gone mad, Sophia! The whole purpose of this trip was to expose Hugo. I'm sorry if you feel a sudden wave of empathy for the bride, but she needs to know the truth. She has a right to know about the man she's going to marry. As soon as she finds out about Hugo, I don't think she'll go through with the whole white wedding."

"That's just it," Fleur groaned. It was such an inelegant sound escaping Fleur's lips that Tabby was shocked into silence. "This has nothing to do with Hugo."

"Hugo *was* engaged to Arabella," Sophia explained. "Six months ago. The tabloids lied, although they were spotted together at a nightclub earlier this week. It's not Hugo's wedding. It's his best friend's, Yves-Jacques.

He's marrying the Australian woman who helped me book my flights and hotel. Poppy, she seemed nice. It's no wonder she didn't have time to catch up with me, she's been busy organising her wedding. We found out moments ago and came to tell you.

The whole thing is a terrible mistake. It's the reason so many paparazzi are hanging around this place; everyone thought this was Hugo and Arabella's wedding, but it isn't. She's on holiday in Thailand with her new lover. Tabloids lie; it's what they do."

"And we made up chapters that never existed in the first place," Tabby whispered.

"We have to fix this," Fleur said, determination adding some much needed colour to the whites of her cheeks.

"Right," Tabby said. "Poor Poppy. I thought I was speaking to Hugo's mother when Valerie must be Yves-Jacques' mum!" Tabby slapped her forehead. "I practically implied that Yves-Jacques and I had an affair, that I'd slept with the groom. They thought I was talking about Yves-Jacques! What a mess! To think she was delighted when I told her!"

"Well, at least we've pleased someone," Sophia replied as the three women pushed through the crowd until they were standing at the car park lobby, where row upon row of limousines were delivering V.I.P. guests.

"How are we going to find my car? I gave the keys to the valet when we arrived. It's probably held up behind all of these chauffeur driven rides."

"We'll take that one," Sophia said, pointing to the limousine at the front of the queue.

Fleur flung open the passenger door just as Hugo, Yves-Jacques, and two other groomsmen stepped out. Yves-Jacques looked pale and nervous. Hugo laughed in good nature, his smile falling as he lay eyes on Fleur, Sophia, and then he turned white seeing Tabby.

"Well, are you going to hurry up and get out or not?" Fleur snapped.

Climbing out of the limousine, Hugo looked abashed, like a cowering puppy dog. "Ladies, I can explain." His face turned green. The smell of rich perfume and cloves stung the air.

"No need," Tabby said. The driver, who'd jumped out to pop the trunk, looked bemused as she took his seat. "We already know everything. To think I loved you." She pushed past Hugo and climbed into the limousine, almost falling over Yves-Jacques as he exited the vehicle. "Sorry about your mother." He turned to her, bemused. "Hold tight, I promise, we'll do our best to fix everything. Hugo's the cheating brute, not you."

"Fleur!" Hugo spluttered as he turned to face her.

"I really don't have time for your excuses, Hugo. Let's forget the whole thing ever happened." She climbed aboard the limo.

Sophia turned to see her husband, red as a beetroot, running like a bull towards Hugo. Charles's pink shirt whipped through the air as he went to punch Hugo in the face. "Charles! What on Earth are you doing here?"

"Ollie told me where I'd find you and him!" He glared at Hugo. "I've been searching all over this wedding for the groom!"

Ducking, Charles wrapped his lanky arms around Hugo's waist and the two men began to roll across the cobbled ground in front of Sophia.

"How could you cheat on her and then marry a celebrity? You're vile," Charles growled at Hugo.

"Marry? I'm not getting married. Besides, we were never an official couple. I need to talk to Tabby to explain."

"So you're going to deny you ever cheated on my wife?"

"I think this is between the two of you."

"This is between us!"

"You're acting like madmen," Sophia yelled. Softening her tone, she added, "Get up before someone gets hurt. Please. This is ridiculous; you're grown men. Stop fighting, over me."

Over me! Two men were fighting over her! Ollie would have a field day with this one! Finding it hard to believe that men would fight for her, let alone over her, made her flush with new rose coloured confidence. This was fantastic.

Charles, who made a fuss to clean under his fingernails every night before bed, was allowing filth to wash over his entire body, rolling in the gutters for her. He was fighting for her. He'd found the strength. There was still hope.

Coming to her senses as she caught site of the guests, shoppers and passersby standing in the street staring at Hugo and Charles, Sophia yelled, "Hugo, stop, you're hurting him!"

"Why, what right does this man have to you?" Hugo asked.

"He's my husband, for heaven's sake!"

"Your husband?" Hugo looked down at Charles, who he had strapped in a headlock. "Why didn't you tell me?"

"Most likely the same reason that you didn't tell me you'd been three timing me!"

"Tell this brute to let go of me, Sophia!" Charles demanded.

Sophia blushed a bright shade of rose. "You're not exactly innocent, Charles; don't think I haven't forgotten all those nights you left me home on your own whilst you stayed out at the *office*."

Charles blanched. Hugo surrendered his grip on the man's neck.

"I'm a fool. A terrible husband." Charles's wasn't looking at Hugo anymore. "I'm sorry, Sophia. Darling, I wish there were some way for you to forgive me, truly I do. I wish that I could turn back the clock and make things right between us. You have to believe that I love you. Everything I have always done has been for you."

Sophia felt her emotions soar like a thousand butterflies had burst from her heart.

"I love you," she whispered before following Tabby and Fleur and jumping into the limo.

"Sophia..." Hugo mumbled. "Fleur... Tabby... I can explain everything."

"I'm pregnant," Sophia snapped. "Just thought you should know." Before Hugo could reply, she climbed into the back of the limousine, and slammed the door shut. "Put your foot on it," Sophia said to Tabby.

The limousine's wheels grinded against the eighteenth-century stone pavers as they pulled out of the hotel's lobby, leaving Hugo, Charles and a string of wedding guests staring after it in consternation.

Hugo raised his right hand to his forehead. He had a splitting headache. Cameras flashed at the entrance to the wedding - greedy paparazzi waiting for a bridal scoop. If they weren't here to witness the nuptials of the infamous Arabella Sparks they could at least grab a story on the sordid affairs of her playboy ex-lover.

Clemency, blonde curls bobbing, wearing a pastel pink bandage dress that dusted her petite ankles, pushed her way to the front of the crowd. Yves-Jacques, dressed in a black and white tuxedo, busied himself, pouring a glass of champagne down Hugo's throat.

"What's going on?" Clemency demanded.

"He's suffered a blow to the head," Yves-Jacques announced.

"Hugo, are you all right darling? The paparazzi are having a field day! This is Yves-Jacques's wedding. They are supposed to be photographing him. Not you!"

"That's what you get for having a best friend who dated a movie star," Yves-Jacques said. Shaking his head, his crisp cut light brown hair clung to his scalp in a slather of extra gel. Looking more put together than normal, he looked a combination of a nervous schoolboy and a character from, F. Scott Fitzgerald's, *The Great Gatsby*.

"He's in shock. Hugo, can you hear me?" Clemency cooed. "How many fingers am I holding up? Are you hurt? Who did this to you?"

Hugo shook his head. If the champagne hadn't roused his sense of belonging, Clemency's Chanel No. 5 perfume awakened him to his senses.

"Sophia."

"Sophia? She was here?"

Hugo nodded lamely. "And Tabby and Fleur," Hugo groaned. The words to describe Sophia's blow were lost on him. It felt as though a bullet had ripped through his heart.

"Yves-Jacques, help me lift him up. Hugo needs to freshen up in the bathroom; a clean. You there," Clemency called to a photographer, skulking in the shadows. "Bring me a clean towel and some ice."

"He hasn't told you the whole story yet," Yves-Jacques muttered.

"What more is there to tell? The women are obviously lunatics. Look at the state of him, Yves-Jacques. I haven't seen Hugo zis pale since, since ever! They have come here, on the day of your wedding, and attacked him. It's disgusting."

"No one attacked me," Hugo spluttered. "Besides Charles; Sophia's husband," he added by way of explanation. His curly brown hair sat in a tangled, sweaty heap in front of his grey-green eyes. Clemency pushed it back from his face. "Everything has fallen apart."

"Sweetheart, you don't have to defend *them*," Clemency said. Pulling at Hugo's tie, she loosened it and unbuttoned the first three notches of his white silk shirt. "They're all mad. There's no excuse."

"Sophia's husband did, Charles, he's over there." He nodded towards Charles, who was escaping through the crowd.

"Oh, darling, what a monster. That man had no right coming here and attacking you! How could you have known the woman was married?"

"Sophia is pregnant."

Clemency clasped her hands in front of her perfect pout as though in prayer.

"Told you he hadn't completed the story," Yves-Jacques said. "The secret is most obviously out. Now, if you'll excuse me, I have my wedding to attend. Guests to greet. Congratulations, Hugo, you'll make an excellent father. It may come as a shock now, but everything will be okay in the end, I'm sure of it. That's what everyone's been telling me about this whole wedding thing anyway." Yves-Jacques chuckled to himself, ruffled his friend's head and allowed the swallow of guests to devour him.

Clemency's eyes blazed. She was staring straight at Hugo. He wasn't sure if she was mad at him, or worried. The second her cold hard slap caressed his face he knew the answer.

"How could you do such a thing?"

"Ouch! Clemency, you don't understand. I didn't do anything. Sophia and I never had sex! I don't know why she's saying we did. I mean, we did spend one drunken night together, but nothing happened, I swear. What's Tabby going to think? She'll never have me now that she thinks I've been cheating on her! This is so messed up."

Most of the camera wielding men had escaped into the throngs of the crowd, hunting for heiresses, movie stars and a glimpse of Kate Moss. The paparazzi guy, who with generous ambition, had returned with a bucket of ice and a cool towel, dropped his wares and took a photo.

"Did you get the slap?" Hugo asked, not caring what the general public of Paris would think of him from now on. The cameraman nodded with enthusiasm.

"You're a selfish fool," Clemency snapped him out of his reverie.

"Didn't you hear what I said? I didn't do anything!"

"Didn't do anything? The woman thinks she's pregnant with your child! A woman who has a husband." Standing tall, Clemency brushed invisible dirt from her dress.

"Clemency, you're acting crazy, and you're not listening to me. You don't believe me, do you? I swear to you; Sophia and I never had sex. How could I be with another woman when all this time I've been blindly falling in love with Tabby."

Hugo was beginning to feel desperate. He needed Clemency, needed her to understand the mechanics of his heart right now.

"Please, just stay with me. I need a drink, and I'll explain everything. I've always wanted to be a father. Clemency, you must know that if the child belonged to me, I would do everything in my power to be there for it. To love it, to protect it. But I swear to you, it's not my baby!"

"I know," Clemency spat, "that you are a fool. You're a fool in love. You never know who you want, or what you want. You're always surrounded by people who love you, even though you're not worth an ounce of their love. You'd make a terrible father, Hugo; you are, without a doubt, the most irresponsible man I know."

"Is that how you really feel?" Hugo asked. "Or is this about the other night."

"It is," Clemency said. She couldn't bear to tell Hugo what she felt deep down. A sickening feeling began to swell in her stomach.

"Clemency, where are you going?"

"To find a bathroom, or a pot plant, anything tucked out of the way where I can be sick."

"You're being ridiculous," Hugo called. The words bounced off the swinging curves of Clemency's hips and retreated back. Like poison darts, they shot at Hugo, filling his body with venomous dread.

CHAPTER THIRTY ONE

LOVERS LAST WORDS

"You couldn't find the right way to tell Hugo you've been pregnant for a month, and this is the way you drop the bomb? Mon dieu!" Fleur said.

"Well, I had gone over various scenarios in my mind," Sophia explained. "I imagined the two of us sitting in a park at sunset, the sun peeking through gentle clouds, pigeons pecking at my feet, whilst I told him, I might be pregnant with his child. Every time we sat down to eat, or walked through a park, I could never find the right words. It's much easier to do a difficult thing sporadically, like tearing off a Band-Aid."

"But you don't even know if he is the father," Tabby said from the front. Flicking switches, she brought the glass divider between passenger and driver down.

"I will explain it to him," Sophia snapped. She was not in the mood to be reprimanded. "Besides, I'm quite sure he is the father. The baby feels French."

"How can a baby feel French?" Tabby asked.

Sophia shrugged. "She just does. Besides, since I found out

I'm pregnant, all I can think about is chocolate croissants. An American baby would want Pop-Tarts."

"She?" Fleur said, sounding amused.

"Wasn't Charles magnificent?" Sophia mused.

"He seemed kind of old and crazy," Tabby said.

"He is, older and gorgeous."

"Tabby, do you even know which way we are headed?" Fleur squealed as Tabby swerved on a crosswalk, just missing a white poodle, led by an aristocratic looking old woman, a white beehive topping her head.

"No idea," Tabby said. "Can you believe this dude doesn't even have a GPS device."

"Open the roof. I'll navigate you," Fleur said.

Tabby pushed several more buttons. A champagne bottle appeared from a hidden compartment, the temperature skyrocketed to beyond boiling. There was a creak of rubber on glass, and the roof slid back, revealing flashes of blue sky.

Fleur stuck her head out into the fresh air. "Take a left here. Watch the woman with the seven Chihuahuas, Tabby darling. Well done."

Sophia was beginning to feel squeamish. Tabby's driving was nothing short of erratic and jumpy. It was as though she lacked the ability to remove her foot from the peddle; she slowed for nothing and no one.

"This place is, wow," Tabby said as the limousine pulled into the Hermitages entrance, and three porters dressed in white suits ran to open the cars back doors. "I think I'm in love."

Sophia and Fleur slid across the cream leather seats in the back and climbed out the side doors.

"Imagine if this were your house," Sophia squealed.

"It was built in the Belle Époque era. Everything is gilded and glamorous," Fleur said.

"If we don't find Poppy, our bride won't be building a lifetime of happy memories. If she thinks that Yves-Jacques has been cheating on her, I don't like to think what will happen."

The women strolled into the lobby. Tabby had slipped off her heels and was gliding barefoot alongside Fleur. They looked like a shot from a high school movie, where the popular girls take center stage and stroll the corridor in slow motion; they owned the place.

"You can't take the elevator without a key. We'll have to go to the front desk," Fleur said.

Approaching the lobby counter, Fleur, speaking in fluent French, took charge. Tabby and Sophia glanced at one another. Fleur swung her hands in rapid, argumentative strikes at the concierge. A woman, with hair pulled into a bun so tight that it looked ready to peel a layer of her scalp off, stood shaking her head. She was calm and collected.

"What's she saying?" Sophia whispered to Fleur.

"I am saying," the woman's English accent was sharp and pointy, with a distinct American lilt. "That we are under strict instruction to allow no one into the Hathaway suite."

"But we have an important message for the bride," Sophia exclaimed in protest.

"Non, that means nothing to me."

Sophia slapped her hands on the counter. Black swirls of hair had come loose from her side pony and swirled in a mess around her face. "Listen, I'm pregnant. My hormones are running wild. I need to speak to Poppy, now. If I don't, there is no telling what I might do. This is a matter or bride and death!"

The concierge looked at Sophia and Fleur as though they were ants she'd like to squish.

"She does not look pregnant, fat maybe." The woman smirked.

Fleur gulped, and Sophia looked as though hot steam was beginning to pour from the sides of her ears.

"How rude!" Sophia exclaimed.

"Look, woman to woman," Fleur said recovering, "we think that Poppy, your guest, might be about to make the biggest mistake of her life."

"You see," Sophia said, "by now Poppy probably thinks I'm pregnant with her, fiancé's child. The wedding is today, and she has to marry Yves-Jacques; he loves her."

"It's Hugo; we've been dating, not Yves-Jacques."

The concierge no longer looked angry. She looked baffled. "I'm sorry. There is nothing I can do. You're story sounds convincing, but I am under instructions from on high. Mademoiselle Poppy told me she did not wish to see anyone the day of her wedding. I'm going to have to ask you to leave."

"I give up," Sophia groaned. Where was her American optimism when she needed it most?

"You'd ask a guest to leave?" Tabby said. Her tone was as soft as a kittens purr.

"You're not a guest."

"I am; I'm staying with the late James Liam Preston. I'm his plus one." Tabby battered her fair lashes. She flashed a key card. The concierge raised a brow. "Welcome then, Miss?"

"Tabitha Brown. You can call me Tabby."

"I see that your leading man has arrived."

Tabby turned to see a stout middle-aged man with a white beard and soft white hair kissing the edges of his earlobes. She gulped. He was gliding through the lobby.

"James," Tabby called. "You hoo," Tabby waved. "James, darling, is that you? Where are you going, you sneaky sausage. I left my handbag in our room, we need to get to the lifts."

Sophia and Fleur exchanged a subtle glance and shrug that wasn't lost on the concierge.

"Thank you for your help," Fleur said.

"You've been divinely rude and conceited," Sophia said.

They strolled across to the lobby where Tabby was kissing James on both cheeks. He had her arm linked through his and had slipped his jacket over her shoulders. James led them back through the lobby. His movements were stiff with age.

Once they were inside the lift, Tabby slunk against the gold railing. The elevator was dressed with mirrors and looked like a crazy fun house.

"Now," James said. Speaking in a low husky voice. "You're a charming young lady. I'm flattered by your attention. But why are you allying yourself with me to sneak into The Hermitage? I love charades, but I am old and weary. I'd like an explanation." His grey, green eyes were so much younger than the creases folding into his soft skin thought Tabby. In an odd way, James looked familiar, like a grandfather she'd known her whole life.

Tabby gulped and introduced herself then Sophia and Fleur. She gushed what they were up to and waited.

James listened, silent in thought. Finally, he said, "pregnant?" to Sophia.

She nodded, bemused.

"Well then. I can't have a great-grandchild of mine destroying Poppy and Yves-Jacques' wedding."

"Great-grandchild of yours?" Fleur said, her face contorting.

"Why yes! Hugo is my grandchild."

"No!" Tabby stammered. No wonder he looked familiar. "It's such a small world."

"Yes indeed. There are no accidents my dear. This must be a divine intervention. The angels are on our side. Hugo's told me so much about you three. I've been begging him to bring you all around for tea. But, well, when a man has one thing on his mind, he'll avoid disrupting his plans with an old interfering grandparent. How wonderful we're all together at last."

"His plans?" Fleur said.

"Why yes! Our Hugo is trying to find the love of his life."

"This is ridiculous," Fleur said.

"You've been saying that a lot," Sophia said.

"Now, I hate to be the bearer of bad news," James said, "But, Poppy, has already left. She's on her way to the church."

"Oh no," Tabby said.

"We'll take my Porsche. Come on, my darlings. There's no time to waste."

"Why did you come back to the hotel?" Tabby asked.

"I forgot something."

"Which was?" Fleur intoned.

"No idea." James grinned.

And for some reason, all three women found themselves grinning right back.

CHAPTER THIRTY TWO

I DO

*H*ugo took his place at the altar. An excited hum filled the church, as more and more guests took their places. Stepping forward, Hugo winked at Yves-Jacques: his best friend's face had turned the colour of soggy oatmeal.

There were so many eyes upon them. Hugo knew that Yves-Jacques hated being the centre of attention. An elderly lady dressed in a rose-pink suit licked her lips, blue eyes glued to Hugo. He tried to look away, but the monstrous hat on her head, vivid blue and covered in fresh yellow and red roses, was such a clash of colour that he couldn't. She winked at him and blew a kiss.

"Did you hear me?" Yves-Jacques whispered.

"What?" Hugo said. "Sorry, I was distracted."

Yves-Jacques, gripped Hugo's right arm. His breath smelt of whisky.

"Agh, how much have you drunk this afternoon?"

"If you are implying, that I would allow myself to become, intoxi-ci-c-c-cated on the day of my wedding, you'd be mistaken."

"You're drunk! Poppy is going to kill me. I was supposed to take care of you."

"That's not the point."

"Well, what is?"

"I don't think I can do it," Yves-Jacques said, his whispering inhibitions forgotten. "Marriage - it's not for me."

"Keep your voice down," Hugo said. "Someone might hear you."

"Good. I say what I mean, and I mean what I say."

"You're acting crazy," Hugo said. "Come on. We'll go out back to get you some fresh air and water. This place stinks like a perfumery, crossed with a brewery. You can forget this whole crazy last minute notion."

Yves-Jacques nodded reassured by the soothing tone of his best friend's voice He was petrified but he knew that he had never been more in love. He was simply scared, of new beginnings, that he might somehow not match up to being everything Poppy hoped for in a man. All he could offer was his love and an open heart.

* * *

"The wedding was supposed to start at one," Fleur said. Her hands were shaking, and her palms felt clammy. Weddings always made her nervous. Her view of marriage, had become a hazy blur, like a magical prophecy you read about in books - knowing it may never transcend into the reality of your own life.

"I'm never getting married," Tabby said. "The whole mushy concept makes me sick. It's another way to push women into

enslavement. We get stuck with a husband who we have to serve."
James chuckled in the driver's seat of his black Porsche. Tabby
shot the back of his head a fierce glare. "Marriage is a boring,
outdated concept. No offence, Sophia," Tabby said.

"No offence because I'm married? Or because you think I'm
a slave to my husband?"

"You have a husband?" James tuned around, and the car
swerved jumping across a wide curb. Fleur reached over and
grabbed the wheel. The brakes slammed, and the car jolted to a
holt beside the hotel chapel.

"Yes, James, I have a husband. I have for the past seven years.
He's a good man, but he's so work obsessed that I feel like he
doesn't even know I exist. I came to Paris because I wanted to
experience life. I wanted to shake up my world and live. I wanted
to get to know the old Sophia, the girl I used to be."

"And did Hugo help?" James asked Sophia.

Not knowing why, Sophia wanted to explain to this old man
in his crisp grey wool suit and white linen shirt how she felt. His
paper white crumpled skin looked as though it had weathered
life's storms.

"He showed me a different way to live. He encouraged me to
cook; he listened to me, really listened. He made me feel like the
most important woman on the planet when we were together,
and he showed me that it wasn't just attention from a man that I
was lacking. For so long, I blamed Charles, for all my problems.
All the while, I'd been neglecting myself. I didn't need to find the
old Sophia, rather discover the new me."

James nodded. "When we learn to love ourselves, love flows

into our life from every angle. Sometimes we sacrifice things that are important to us because we believe we aren't worthy of goodness. We choose to believe others will be disappointed if we follow the path of our hearts. True happiness comes from within. It can never be taken from us or given to us. The key is to find the strength to shine and live from the heart."

"I'm in love with another man," Fleur blurted out before slapping her hand over her mouth.

"You are?" Sophia said. Her own worries forgotten over this gossipy confession.

"It happened a couple of weeks ago."

"Sound's promising," Tabby's tone was sarcastic. She pulled at the collar of Fleur's canary yellow dress. It was digging into her skin.

"Go on," Sophia said. "I'm listening." She pinched Tabby's thigh and before Tabby squealed in protest shook her head.

"His name is Diego Puicci Poloma." A whimsical smile enhanced Fleur's fine-boned cheeks. "He's an artist."

"Diego!" Sophia shrieked. The car suddenly felt hot and muggy. Despite the cool chill seeping in from the air outside.

"Who's Diego?" Tabby asked.

"He's a successful artist, the most relaxed man I've ever met - the complete opposite of Fleur. He understands how to go with the flow of life."

"How do you know him?" Fleur said turning to face Sophia. "You're not together are you?"

"We attend La Chef Delicieux together. He is incredibly

gorgeous."

"You can't have every man, Sophia," Fleur snapped, her silver dress sparkling in the afternoon sun.

"So, you're really in love with him?" Sophia asked Fleur.

"What's that supposed to mean?" Fleur asked.

"I just always thought of you as the woman who goes for the serious man. Someone a little more uptight - the man version of yourself."

Fleur's nostrils flared. "He's my opposite, but that's what makes this romance magical. Are you or are you not dating, Diego?" Fleur turned to Sophia. She didn't think she could handle another major disappointment in the man department.

"What?"

"And I thought my love life was confusing," Tabby said.

"I am not in love with Diego," Sophia answered. "How could you think such a thing?"

"Well, you did fall for Hugo," Tabby said. "Maybe we all have identical taste in men."

"Paris is beginning to feel like a very small town," Fleur said through gritted teeth.

"You don't have to worry," Sophia said. "We're friends; that's all. I've grown fond of him. But love, how could I love another man when all this time I've been missing my husband like crazy? Diego and I are friends. We've never been more."

"It's not just Sophia that you don't trust," James interrupted, directing his observation at Fleur.

"You think I shouldn't trust Diego?"

"How should I know? I've never met the man. I think that you should trust yourself. Sophia could tell you a thousand times that she wasn't in love with Diego. But from the look on your face, I doubt you'd believe her. You need to trust your own instincts. Good things come to people that trust themselves. You're relationship with Hugo, has it gifted you with the opportunity to put the past behind you?"

"What do you mean?"

"It's my understanding that sometime ago, you and Hugo were girlfriend and boyfriend. Ma petite amie et ami. Hugo broke your heart, correct?"

"He smashed it." A single tear floated down Fleur's cheeks smudging a thick layer of foundation and blush.

"And how did you feel when he came back to you?"

"At first, it felt good. I claimed my power. All those nights I'd spent crying and lamenting over him, they felt worth it. Hugo was still beautiful and smart and funny, but I had changed. I'd lifted myself. It wasn't just that I felt prettier, smarter, or more accomplished. I felt I had moved on from the *Hugo's* of the world. I felt invincible. A part of me still buries the sadness of the way he hurt me."

"What you need to understand, Fleur - and I think deep down you do - is that no man can ever take something from you."

"I think I understand," Tabby said. "You're saying that Fleur should forgive Hugo to heal her own heart?"

"That's the ticket! If we dwell in pain, we close ourselves to the joy that life offers. Our lives are on borrowed time; there's no point in putting our head in dumpsters, cursing those who hurt us. We have to learn we are already embodiments of unconditional love. We deserve love in all its forms. When we radiate true inner joy; we attract goodness, love, and new beginnings."

"I don't understand," Sophia began. "Are you saying that Fleur should trust Diego, or forgive Hugo?"

"Both - they're one and the same. Fleur, my dear, if you can forgive Hugo, you'll be free to move on to new experiences. In forgiving Hugo, you forgive yourself. Your heart will guide you in the right direction, be it to Diego or another great adventure."

"You're being very quiet," Sophia said to Tabby.

Tabby felt her heart constrict. All this talk of Hugo was beginning to make her feel claustrophobic. "Look, there's the bride!" Tabby called. Saved by the bride!

"That one will need some serious therapy before we're through with her," Fleur said.

Tabby didn't hear a word. She'd already flung herself out of the car and was running barefoot across the hot asphalt, feet stinging in the heat, towards the bride.

"Come on, girls, we've got a wedding to save."

Hugo waved at his granddad who slipped into the aisle third from the front. There was a bright gleam in the old man's eye. "What mischief has he been up to?" Hugo thought.

CHAPTER THIRTY THREE

WEDDING

One year later. A quaint wedding in Paris...

"Who invited you?" Tabby hissed.

The church had a serene quietness. It was a sacred sanctuary. Saints and angels painted on the roof seemed to come alive, watching Tabby as she turned to face the gentleman dressed in a brown tweed suit who'd come to stand beside her.

"Fleur did."

"Oh, I doubt that. This is a wedding; it's supposed to be a joyous, momentous occasion."

"Well, here's my copy of the invite. Go on; read it if you don't believe me."

Tabby eyed the piece of paper flapping in Hugo's hands. It was emerald green and dove grey. It was as the colour of Hugo's eyes before a thunderstorm.

"Did you ever stop to think that Fleur may have invited you out of politeness? She likely didn't expect you'd come."

"She rang me on Tuesday of last week."

Tabby rolled her eyes. "Well, in my opinion, you've sucked the festivity from the occasion. Standing next to you, I feel like I'm at a funeral."

"That's because something died."

"Who died?"

"We died."

"You killed us Hugo."

"I wrote you. You never replied to my emails, letters, texts, or phone calls."

"Shhh!" The organ began to play, and Tabby stared at the bald head of the priest who'd walked down the aisle, his feet making small shuffling steps.

Her knee high black leather studded boots felt sweaty and hot. Her charcoal jeans gripped her thighs, and the light blue silk button shirt she was wearing clung to her skin. Was it hot in here, or was Hugo still so gorgeous he made her break out in a nervous sweat every time they locked eyes?

"Where's Sophia?" Hugo whispered. His warm breath tickling her ear and sending shivers up her spine.

There was a loud crack as the church door was thrust open, creaking on its old hinges. "Hold everything; we're here," Sophia said. She was dressed in a red silk maxi dress. Swirls of feathers clung to her bust, and a gorgeous, redheaded child clung to her hips. Ollie, dressed in a flamingo pink suit, had his arm linked though hers, and Tabby could see Charles pulling a bow tie down over his head as they bounded into the church.

"Thank God! It hasn't begun," Ollie began.

Sophia spied Tabby and bounded over. She kissed Hugo on both cheeks and pulled Tabby into a bear hug. "Darling, I've missed you so much. How's London? I hear Harrods is interested in your jewellery line?"

"Yeah. I had a meeting with them last week."

"Harrods? That's amazing, Tabby! Why didn't you say something?" Hugo interrupted.

"Because we're not on speaking terms."

"Darling," Ollie kissed Tabby smack on the lips and slapped Hugo's bottom. "Who's on the dating roster this week, sweetheart?" He purred. "I could help you shake things up a little!"

"Err, thanks," Hugo said. "I've been single for a while now - a year actually," he said, still staring at Tabby. He couldn't bare to take his gaze from her, lest she disappear.

"Don't mention it."

"Hello, Charles," Tabby said. "Congratulations on little Paris." She ran her hair over the little girl's head, soft red curls twisting through the light touch of her fingers. "She's beautiful and looks just like you."

"Thank goodness for that!" Ollie grinned.

Charles waved, pursed his lips, and took a seat in the back row. His grey suit hung snug to his shoulders. The stiffness that held his spine rigid and straight had loosened from his body Tabby thought. Paris was doing wonders to plump up his skinny form.

She'd spoken to Sophia a lot since leaving Paris. Sophia had stayed to become a pastry chef, and Charles had extended his holiday to stay with her. They weren't an official couple or anything yet. But Paris, Sophia had declared, "Was the best form of marriage counselling she had ever experienced."

"Charles looks healthy," Hugo whispered to Tabby conspiratorially as Sophia twirled around and left Tabby stranded with Hugo.

"Why don't you go and sit with him?" Tabby suggested.

"Look Tabitha."

"Don't call me that."

"Tabby."

"Don't call me that either. I think it best if we didn't talk at all."

"This is ridiculous." Hugo lifted his right hand to tap his third eye. "You're impossible."

"Me? You're the one who led three intelligent woman on a wild-goose chase through Paris."

"Tabby, you of all people know that's not true."

"Do I? I know how you made me feel - like a fool. Like I loved a man who never loved me. I unlocked a piece of myself, a part of my heart I'd never shared with anyone, and you broke it."

Tabby bit down hard on her tongue; she could taste blood. The church felt very small and hot, as though filled with people, not just five guests and a priest who was staring at Hugo and Tabby as though they were interrupting his sermon.

The *last* thing Tabby wanted was to admit how much she'd loved Hugo or how much she *still* loved him, how having him standing next to her in the church made her feel nervous, excited, and made her heart pound into her chest. It beat so loud she was positive Sophia could hear it in the back row.

"Tabby, I'm sorry. I didn't mean to hurt you. If you would give me a minute I can explain."

Tabby turned away and began walking back down the aisle, as the organ began to play Pachelbel's Canon. "How could anyone get married?" Tabby thought with bitterness so sharp that it stung her heart. As she pushed through the church's exit, she collided with Fleur dressed in a vintage silk and lace, pale blue Chanel suit.

"Tabby, where are you going?" Diego asked. He wore a black suit; a paisley print in shiny black thread had been embroidered all over.

"You invited Hugo?"

Fleur looked Tabby straight in the eyes. "I forgave him long ago, Tabby. When you find true love, it's easy to forget the past."

"Well, that's just fabulous," Tabby's voice was husky and sarcastic. She was trying to hold back tears. It felt as though her best friends had betrayed her.

"He wanted to speak to you, and since you aren't returning any of his calls, I thought I would do my best to help you out."

"Help me out?"

"Well, since you won't talk to him - but all you ever do is talk *about* him - I figured I could bring him to you."

"You're insane."

"I do my best."

"My darling," Diego said, "the priest is waiting."

"Tabby stay," Sophia called. "I never thought I'd see this day."

Diego smiled. "Love can make us do funny things. One of the most fortuitous and healing is that it guides us to forgive the past."

Sophia beamed. "I'm so happy for you both."

"Thank you darling," Diego and Fleur replied in unison.

"I can't stay. I'm so sorry." Gentle tears caressed Tabby's cheeks.

Fleur kissed Tabby's forehead. "I understand."

Pushing past her friend, escaping the chapel to be embraced by fresh Parisian air, Tabby grabbed the closest thing to her resting against the chapel's stone walls - a blue bicycle with a cane basket filled with fresh flowers. She jumped on and pushed her legs as fast as they would go.

As Fleur and Diego walked down the aisle, Diego, threw the keys to his Austin Windsor, that was parked out front, to Hugo. Hugo left calling after Tabby, but she was already gone.

Petals scattered across the hood of the car, Hugo jumped in and slammed his foot on the accelerator. Cool air stung his face through the window, stealing his tears. He found Tabby peddling like a demon down the French boulevard on a bright blue bicycle.

"Tabby, will you slow down?"

"Go away, Hugo."

"Not until you hear me out. If you don't like what I have to say, I promise, I'll never bother you again."

Tabby peddled faster and faster. "Leave me alone."

"Please don't make me beg. All right. Tabby, I'm begging you. I love you. Please, just hear me out."

Tabby stopped peddling. The crack in Hugo's voice had made her halt, it sounded like she'd stolen a piece of his soul and refused to return it.

Hugo climbed from the wedding car. Tabby locked her legs tight against the bike, in case she needed a quick escape. The smell of flowers wafted through the air. Hugo was so handsome in his white linen shirt and cream pants. The look of broken sadness in his eyes made Tabby want to leap from the bike and hold him to her, to taste his soft, plump lips and feel his hands run through her hair. She couldn't. She wouldn't.

"Look, I'm leaving Paris tomorrow," Hugo said.

"You are?"

"Yes. I've wanted to talk to you for so long. I messed everything up."

"Where are you going?" Hugo couldn't leave Paris. He was Paris. He was Tabby's Paris.

"India. This girl I once knew, she told me I needed to get out, to see the world. She made me want to experience life to the fullest."

"What happened to her?"

"I hurt her."

Tabby was looking deep into Hugo's grey, green eyes. She wanted to push the sweet, messy lock of black curly hair that had fallen into them away from his forehead, but she could do nothing. She was paralysed as his words floated over her, cutting through her heart like Mozart's Requiem.

"She left. My world shattered."

"Oh."

"I've been a fool. If she could ever find it in her heart to forgive me?" Tabby still couldn't find the words. "My veins would begin to pump blood; my heart would start to beat; my life would be complete."

Hugo leaned forward. Tabby closed her eyes. In that moment, the world opened to her; she saw stars, galaxies spinning faster and faster around her, like the Sun and Moon orbiting Earth. When Tabby and Hugo came together, worlds were formed; great tides pulled them together. This wasn't sense; it wasn't smart; it was love - pure, unconditional love.

Hugo's breath was warm; his kiss tasted like summer, winter, spring, and autumn. He was Tabby's world. Her everything. And as she opened her heart to him, like a flower, she came into bloom.

His kisses tender and gentle caressed her neck, her lips, the soft skin of her eyelids. Tabby groaned, and their kiss grew deeper, more insistent, and urgent. Tabby pulled away. Hugo's eyes were shining, glazed as though he too had woken from a deep, all-consuming sleep.

"When do we leave for India?" she asked.

Hugo smiled, so bright and warm it lit Tabby's heart. "Tonight."

AUTHORS NOTE

*T*abby and Hugo are still travelling through India. Tabby has had heaps of inspiration for her jewellery line, which launches in Harrods next month. Hugo has taken time off from writing. He's discovering other interests and is perfecting his bend back and headstand technique at a yoga retreat in Calcutta.

Sophia is single and living in New York. Charles, has a new girlfriend, Morticia. They visit baby Paris, and brunch together every weekend.

Fleur and Diego are living happily ever after. They divide their time between Spain, Mexico, and Paris. Fleur is learning to paint, and Diego has learned to do the dishes as well as cook. Fleur has started an online interior decorating business, giving people advice on their interiors and renovations. Last year, it made a seven-figure profit.

On Christmas Day, they are all going on vacation to Goa, India to discuss the good, lovely, ugly, and yummy times.

This is a story of transformation and love. When you love yourself, goodness can find you. Each character battled with his or her own truth of existence; finding love and harmony within, is the greatest gift. It takes time, but once you've begun to walk the path of self-transformation, the right people at the right time will come to guide you.

Love is the answer.

Nerissa Marie, loves sharing light and love throughout the universe. She sends blessings and smiles to all who surround her. Nerissa Marie is an author, naturopath, and mystic. Travelling the world to experience a myriad of spiritual teachers has given her the opportunity to grow and unfold, opening herself to the light of life. Her goal is to serve universal spirit, and realise eternal love.

A few of her favourite things are crystals, meditation, fairies and cherry smoothies. She has an immense amount of gratitude, to be living on planet earth and for the intertwining of her reader's spirits, on the dance of life, as she shares her heart through the written word.

Namaste.

NerissaMarie.com

INSPIRATIONAL BOOKS BY NERISSA MARIE

Available on Amazon and most other retailers in Hardcover, Paperback, Kindle and Epub format.

Peace, Love and You is a self-help, new age, spiritual guidebook that empowers you to look at the true nature of your being; divine love, compassion, and bliss. You are perfect, whole and complete simply because you exist. You are a divine expression of love. Peace, Love and You is an inspirational book that aims to empower your soul with inner wisdom.

Abyss of Bliss, is a poetry collection exploring the purpose of life. Pain, guilt, regret, shame and lack often haunt our life. This spellbinding poetry book, goes beyond emotion, beyond form, beyond belief and explores the resounding truth of peace, love and wellbeing hidden in the heart. A beautiful collection of soul healing love poems that reach into the depths of the soul. We are nothing more than beams of light floating through consciousness. Projecting desires in the abyss. All the while forgetting we are pure, simple, humble manifestations of bliss.

Princess Kate, loves to meditate. One day deep in bliss, she levitates high into the sky, leaving behind her friends and family. Prince Ravi Yogi arrives at the kingdom, offering to help bring Princess Kate back down to Earth. Will they listen to his advice? Or will Princess Kate, forever float above the palace, just out of reach?

This books intention is to build your child's self-esteem through the use of mindfulness meditation.

FREE GIFTS! Future releases, free book promotions, and more! Available at NerissaMarie.com